Shattered remnants

JO MCCALL

Jo McCall

Shattered Pieces: Shattered World Bk. 1

Copyright Jo McCall 2021
All Rights Reserved
First Published 2021
No part of this book may be reproduced, stores in a retrieval system or transmitted in any form by any means, without prior authorization in writing of the publisher *Wicked Romance Publication*, nor can it be otherwise circulated in any form of binding or cover other than that which it is published and without a similar condition, including this condition, being imposed on the subsequent purchaser. All characters and places in this publication other than those clearly in the public domain are fictitious, and any resemblance of actual persons, living or dead, is purely coincidental.

Edition: 3456789

Cover design: Kate Farlow @ Ya'll That Graphic
Editing: Beth @VBProofreads
Formatted by: WickedGypsyDesigns

PlayList

THE ONE TO SURVIVE: HIDDEN CITIZEN

UNBROKEN: REALLY SLOW MOTION

DOPAMINE: ELLE VEE

HARD TO KILL: BETH CROWLEY

BROTHERHOOD: MIZA

ME AND MINE: THE BROTHERS BRIGHT

WARPATH: TIM HALPERIN

HOW VILLIANS ARE MADE: MADELINE DUKE

QUEEN OF THE CASTLE: VICTORIA CARBOL

*"Never, ever, let anyone tell you what you can and can't do.
Prove the cynics wrong wrong.
Pity them for they have no imagination.
The sky is the limit.
Your sky.
Your limit."*

-Tom Hiddleston

WARNING

The content within this book is DARK and may be triggering to some.
For a full list of triggers for this particular book go to jomccallauthor.com

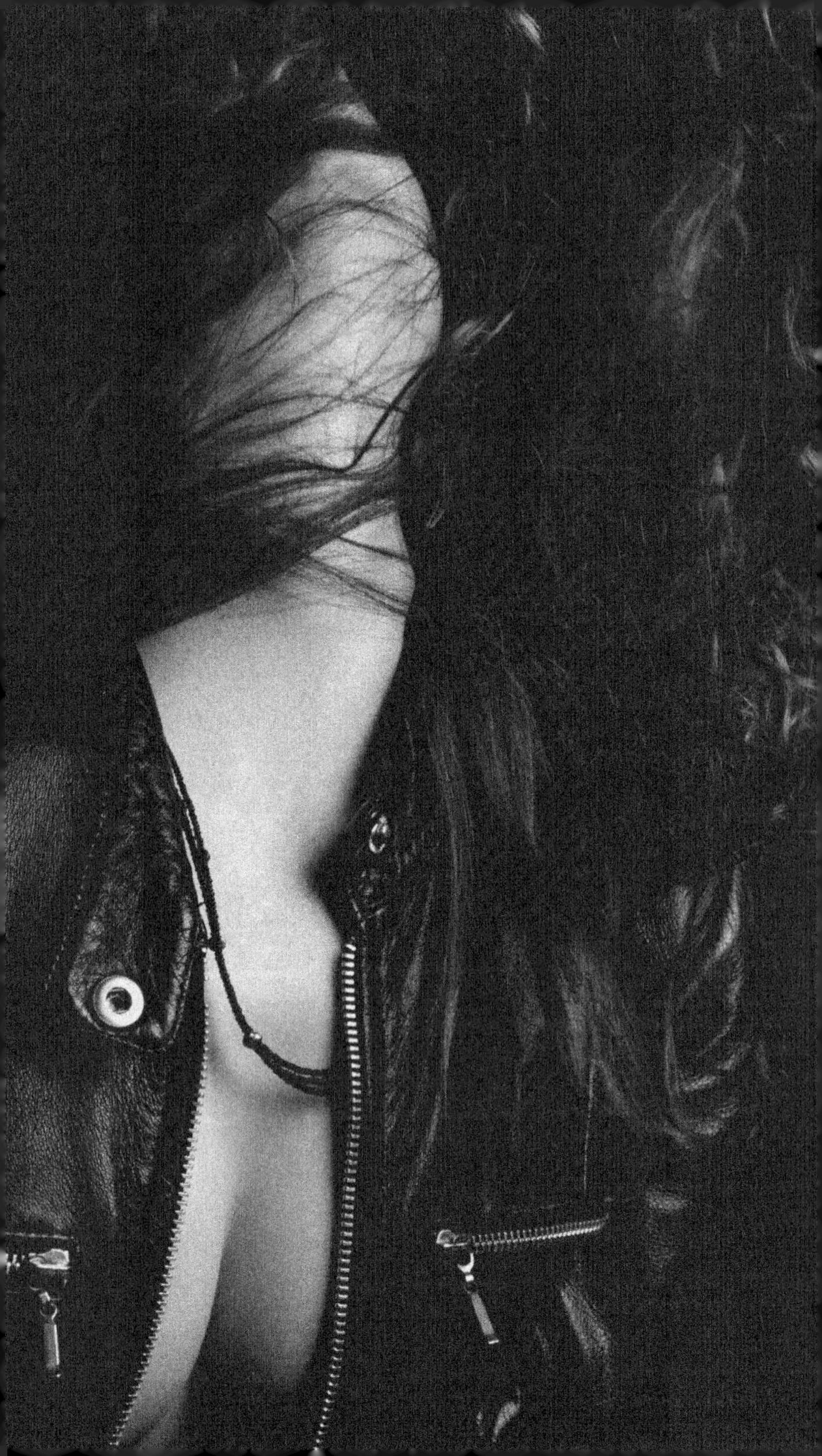

PROLOGUE

Ava

A sharp sting of pain radiated through my chest as I came to.

My eyes fluttered furiously, like butterflies trapped in a glass cage, fighting against an invisible weight. I coughed and sputtered, the pain increasing as I struggled to take a breath. My chest felt like it was caught in the grasp of a boa constrictor. The cracks in my lips split even wider, blood pooling in my mouth as a hoarse cry rose in my throat.

Fuck.

It was like someone had pressed the mute button on the controller. The only sound I could hear was the ear-piercing ringing that tore through my head, sounding like one of those ungodly mosquito tones. Slowly, I managed to open my eyes, the invisible weight pressing against them slightly dampened by my fierce determination to live.

Dust and debris had settled over my unprotected face. I lifted my equally dusty hand to wipe at it, being mindful of my injuries, but it was like trying to wipe away mud with more mud. It just became worse.

A low keening whine spilled from my lips unbidden as I struggled to move the weight of my own body. My chest heaved in ragged sobs, tears spilling down my dirt-marred face as I crawled through several feet of debris toward the still body of Kristian, my guard. He was half-buried in the building's wreckage, his dark face covered in a heavy layer of white dust.

I reached out with a shaky hand to check his pulse.

Nothing.

He was dead. Just like the rest of them—and now I was truly alone.

The old me would have become numb. Would have curled up in a ball and let fate take over.

The old me was tired of war. Matthias was gone. The King. The Ruler. What else was there to do but give in to fate?

Except, this wasn't a game of chess where the fall of the king meant the end of the game.

No. This was war. And the war wasn't over until the queen was dead.

And I was the fucking Queen.

CHAPTER ONE

Ava

"Fuck," I nearly screamed as he pistoned his hips savagely, rotating them at just the right angle that had me seeing stars. "Matthias, please."

There I was. Begging again. Screaming his name into the wee hours of the morning like a debauched whore. And I don't think I would have had it any other way.

"Come for me, Krasnyy," he growled in my ear, the sound emanating low in his chest, causing my pussy to clench around his thick length. A hand fisted my curls, roughly pulling my head back. My neck was now completely exposed to his roving lips that nipped and sucked at my skin. There was no doubt in my mind that he was leaving marks behind; bold statements that told the world who I belonged to.

Him.

Possessive bastard that he was.

It should have bothered me. That primal possessiveness. I wasn't his property. But at that moment, I couldn't bring myself to care about anything other than the sheer pleasure he was wringing from my body.

I felt his hand come down between us, pinching my clit roughly, and I had no choice but to do exactly as he commanded.

"Matthias!"

His name was a screamed prayer as the world around me shifted and lights danced across my vision like fireworks against an inky-black sky. My body writhed beneath his, and I was only partly aware of his completion as he cursed lowly in Russian, pumping into my soaked, convulsing heat a few more times before collapsing on top of me.

Matthias braced himself on his elbows, chest heaving, his tattooed skin slick with sweat. He was careful to keep his full weight off me as he buried his face in my neck, struggling to compose himself.

The only time I'd ever seen the cold, calculating mafia boss fall apart was in our bed. Or on his desk. In the shower… there was a sense of power knowing I could cause a man like Matthias to come undone with just the touch of my hand. My mouth.

"Fuck, Red," he whispered before collapsing on his back next to me, dragging my body against his. We fit perfectly. Like two broken halves of the same tarnished coin. I'd come to relish these tender moments that took place when it was simply the two of us.

My husband had grown less cold with me around the men of his inner circle, but out there, in the harsh reality of his world, there was still a distance he was forced to maintain. Out there, among the wolves, he held on to the hard-ass mafia *Pahkan* persona. It was a part of him I knew he would never be able to let go of.

That didn't mean he hadn't softened behind closed doors and started to remove the stick up his ass. I wasn't naïve enough to believe I could ever truly change him. Just like he couldn't change me. We were both products of our upbringing, and there was no reconciling that. I was well aware that the cold exterior would never truly melt away. It couldn't. Not if he wanted to maintain control. We lived in a world that sought out vulnerabilities and preyed on them like vultures circling a carcass in the desert.

In this house, Matthias could be affectionate. Well, as affectionate as he could be since I was still betting good money that he was, in fact, part cyborg.

Out there, however, he emitted a measure of control that often had me wondering if it times like these were the actual ruse.

Who was the real Matthias?

The man who held me in his arms each night after sexing me within an inch of my life?

Or the tin man he played out there in the real world.

It didn't escape my notice that Matthias winced as he moved to get more comfortable. The shootout last week still had a lingering effect. The harsh colors of the bruises on his left side had begun to fade into a garish yellow, and despite his protests, I knew his ribs were still giving him trouble. He wasn't used to being hindered, and the attack on his motorcade hadn't been something he'd predicted.

There was regret in his eyes each time he took in my own bruised and battered body. The marks on my chest from the seatbelt were nearly faded, and my eye was almost healed. My cheek still pained me when I chewed, but none of these things bothered me.

Not really.

I'd suffered pain before.

The nightmares were the real problem. Which was why Matthias had me chanting his name in near reverence at two in the morning. The nightmares plaguing me now were different. Because the universe seemed to think that piling up even more therapy-inducing incidents in my life was a great fucking idea.

Karma's a bitch, and I'm not even sure what I did in a previous life to deserve this shit.

The only difference was that I was no longer alone to deal with the overwhelming darkness of the past. Now, he was there alongside me, like a steady beacon thrumming in the murky blackness that threatened to devour me whole.

Some might have called him a knight in shining armor.

He was anything but.

Matthias was right when he said he was a monster.

My monster.

The one who kept all the other monsters at bay.

"You're quiet, Krasnyy." Two large, ink-covered, calloused fingers found purchase beneath my chin. He was giving me no choice but to look him in the face. The man was devastatingly handsome. Outrageously so. His stormy eyes peered into mine, eyebrow raised in curiosity as he stared at me, drawing out the deepest secrets that lingered within the depths of my soul.

All without having to say a word.

"These last few days, I could hardly get you to keep quiet, especially with your sister around," he teased. "Did I finally fuck it out of you?"

A rather unladylike snort escaped my lips at his bluntness. A trait I found common among most of his Russian comrades. "You wish."

Then I sighed. "It's nothing." I tried my best to dismiss it, but he wasn't letting it go. His eyes turned hard, his grip on my chin tightening at my lie.

"Ava." The warning in his voice was clear as day. I'd be a fool to ignore it. A small part of me wanted to though. To challenge that tone, but I was far too exhausted. Instead, I let out another dramatic sigh, which caused his deliciously kissable lips to upturn slightly at the corners.

"I just keep...dreaming," I whispered, mostly to the dark because talking to him was kind of hard. Not going to lie. Matthias was a man who wanted to fix everything. It was in the way he was built. The need to protect and slay was woven into the fabric of his DNA.

Or programmed into his software if I kept up with my cyborg theory.

His idea of protection was making the problem disappear, and sometimes—well, sometimes that wasn't possible.

Like now.

"Nightmares?" he whispered as the hand tucked around me gently caressed my naked side.

"That and—" God, this was difficult. Matthias was accustomed to death. He'd grown up with it. To take a life, to see a life snuffed out—it was nothing to him. Just another day at the office. How do I tell a man who'd grown up knowing nothing but violence that the deaths of the men who attacked us haunted me?

That even though they would have killed him and taken me, it still felt...wrong. "I don't deal with death like you do. I don't enjoy it. I'm not used to it."

There. I said it.

Matthias released my chin, settling back into the mountain of pillows behind him, the arm now stretched behind his head comfortably. I felt oddly bereft at the loss of his touch on my chin. His hand around my waist still circled casually, but there had been something more intimate about being made to face him.

His silence now, when I wanted nothing more than to hear the deep timber of his voice, unnerved me. The only sound in the ridiculously large room was the sound of our breathing. Mine still panting, my body thrummed like a live wire, always anticipating.

He had that effect on me. His touch on my skin constantly leaving a trail of electricity in its wake that never seemed to wear off. I thought maybe I had offended him. That at any moment, he would get up and leave. Or maybe even ask me to. Then again, in the little time I'd known my new husband, I hadn't once seen him become offended.

Livid?

Fuck yeah.

But offended?

Never.

My Uncle Dante had once said only weak men get offended. Powerful men let it pass. And Matthias was undoubtedly strong.

"I wasn't always like this, *malyshka.*" He let out a long, heavy breath, his gaze never wavering from the ornate ceiling. Something told me it made it easier for him to speak. "I was never really innocent. Not growing up with a man like my father, but there was a time when violence wasn't who I was or who I wanted to be."

"What happened?" My voice was small. I was afraid that if I spoke too loudly, I would snap the thin thread of openness he was displaying to me, and he would once again shut me out. I didn't want that. I wanted him to be open with me. He knew everything about me, whether I liked it or not, and I knew practically nothing about him.

"You have to understand something, Red," he whispered to me. "I was eleven when my father chucked me onto the cold streets of St. Petersburg with nothing but the clothes on my back. Every day I fought for food, clothing, shelter. The streets could be violent, but no one had ever tried to actively kill me. I'd been in my fair share of scrapes, but for the most part, kids were off limits. Even to the desperate people on the streets.

"I was thirteen when I was first attacked by a kid not much older than me. Maybe fifteen or sixteen. At the time, I was taking shelter beneath a bridge with a few other kids my age, runaways mostly. Foster kids forgotten by the system. I had no warning. No time to think about what was happening. No training. He just came at me. A large knife in his hand, hacking and slicing. When I look back at it now, his moves, like mine, were sloppy. Untrained. But to a thirteen-year-old boy, he looked like an assassin."

"Why would he do that?" I questioned, bolstering myself up on my elbow so I could see him better. "Did you know him?"

Matthias shook his head. "No." He sighed with a small shake of his head. "I'd never seen him before. I managed to catch him off guard. Barely. The knife went skittering. Somehow, I'd managed to pick it up, and the next thing I knew, he'd impaled himself on it. He'd run right at it. No stopping. I remember standing there, knife in my hand, blood drenching the handle, and the last thing he did was cup my face and say, 'I didn't want this *brat*. I'm sorry.'"

Brat.

I knew that word.

Matthias's men used it all the time with one another. It meant brother.

"I didn't know what to think," Matthias admitted as he continued. "He'd called me brother, but I'd never seen him before. Never knew of him, but I knew instantly what he said was the truth. We were blood brothers."

My brow furrowed, perplexed by his words. He must have sensed it because he pulled down the arm he had resting behind his head as he turned himself slightly toward me so I had a better view.

"My father was a bastard," he hissed venomously. "A mean son of a bitch who used and abused my mother until she couldn't take it anymore and overdosed on the drugs he supplied her with."

Matthias showed me his right wrist. There was just enough light for me to make out the dark hue of a birthmark that laid beneath the Dashkov crest tattoo I had absently stroked so many times in the past few weeks.

I'd thought it was a vanity tattoo.

A reminder of his power.

Now, I could see that it wasn't that at all. He was ashamed of that birthmark. Of what it represented. Ashamed of the name he had borne before and its connection to a man who spat him out without a second thought.

Dashkov was who he *chose* to be.

It was a name he built for himself from the ground up.

"Everyone born into the Kasyanov family has this birthmark," he sneered, contempt biting at every word. "The boy I killed had the same one. Our father had sent him to kill me. He sent a fifteen-year-old boy. And he wasn't the last."

"I'm sorry."

There was nothing else I could think to say. No child

SHATTRED REMNANTS

should have to worry about their father sending assassins after them. No brother should have had to kill the other.

It was barbaric.

We both had mothers who'd died too soon and fathers, well, supposed father on my side, who were nothing more than bastards. Our childhoods weren't perfect, and while mine had been lived in a gilded cage, I was no stranger to pain.

Neither was he.

"There is nothing to be sorry for, Red," Matthias assured me with a grim smile.

"What was his name?" I asked curiously. "Do you know?"

"Antony Kasyanov."

Antony Kasyanov. I'd seen that name scrolled across his back in a dusty navy ink. Now I knew who he was and why it was there. A reminder of what he'd lost.

Innocence and a brother he'd never known.

Letting out another long, deep sigh, Matthias stood from the bed, his hand outstretched for mine.

I didn't bother to ask where we were going. He knew I wasn't going to be able to fall back to sleep, so he was going to do the one thing he normally did to get me to relax.

Run me a bath.

I suspected Mia had told him about my love and fascination for the egg-shaped tub and the city view. I'd spent so long locked up that I longed for this view.

This perceived freedom.

Even with Matthias, I wasn't free. Not in the way I wanted to be. Part of me was hoping that once my father and Christian were no longer a threat, he would give me the freedom I craved, but I knew better than to press the issue.

At least for now.

Slowly, I followed obediently behind him, a slight blush

creeping up my neck when his head turned, those stormy eyes taking in every inch of my naked body. You'd think by now that nudity wouldn't bother me, but Matthias's heated gaze constantly made my skin tingle with warmth, causing desire to pool between my legs.

We stepped into the opulent bathroom, the overhead lights slipping on to a warm yellow glow. My eyes narrowed at the sound of running water.

That made little sense.

Matthias hadn't left my sight; how would he have started the bath already?

Unease grew in my stomach as he pulled me toward the tub. No steam rose from the water, and the view outside the window was dimmed and slightly out of focus. Almost hazy, like the images outside weren't really there.

What the hell was going on?

"What's wrong, my love?"

I whipped my head up to look at him, confusion etched across my face. My love? He'd never called me that before. Matthias motioned for me to step closer. I shook my head, adamantly refusing to trust what I was seeing.

What I thought I was seeing.

Had he drugged me?

The features of the man before me darkened at my refusal, his hand whipping out to ensnare the back of my neck, pulling a small, pained cry from me. Roughly, he shoved me forward.

"You don't say no to me, Little Lamb."

A scream tore its way up my throat as his eyes flashed amber. The hand on the back of my neck squeezed harder before thrusting me down into the dark murky water of the tub. I kicked and clawed with everything I had, exhausting myself.

It was no use.

He was stronger than me. I was no match for the iron grip that kept my head submerged below the surface of the water.

Soon, darkness crept along the edges of my vision, and the gates of unconsciousness opened.

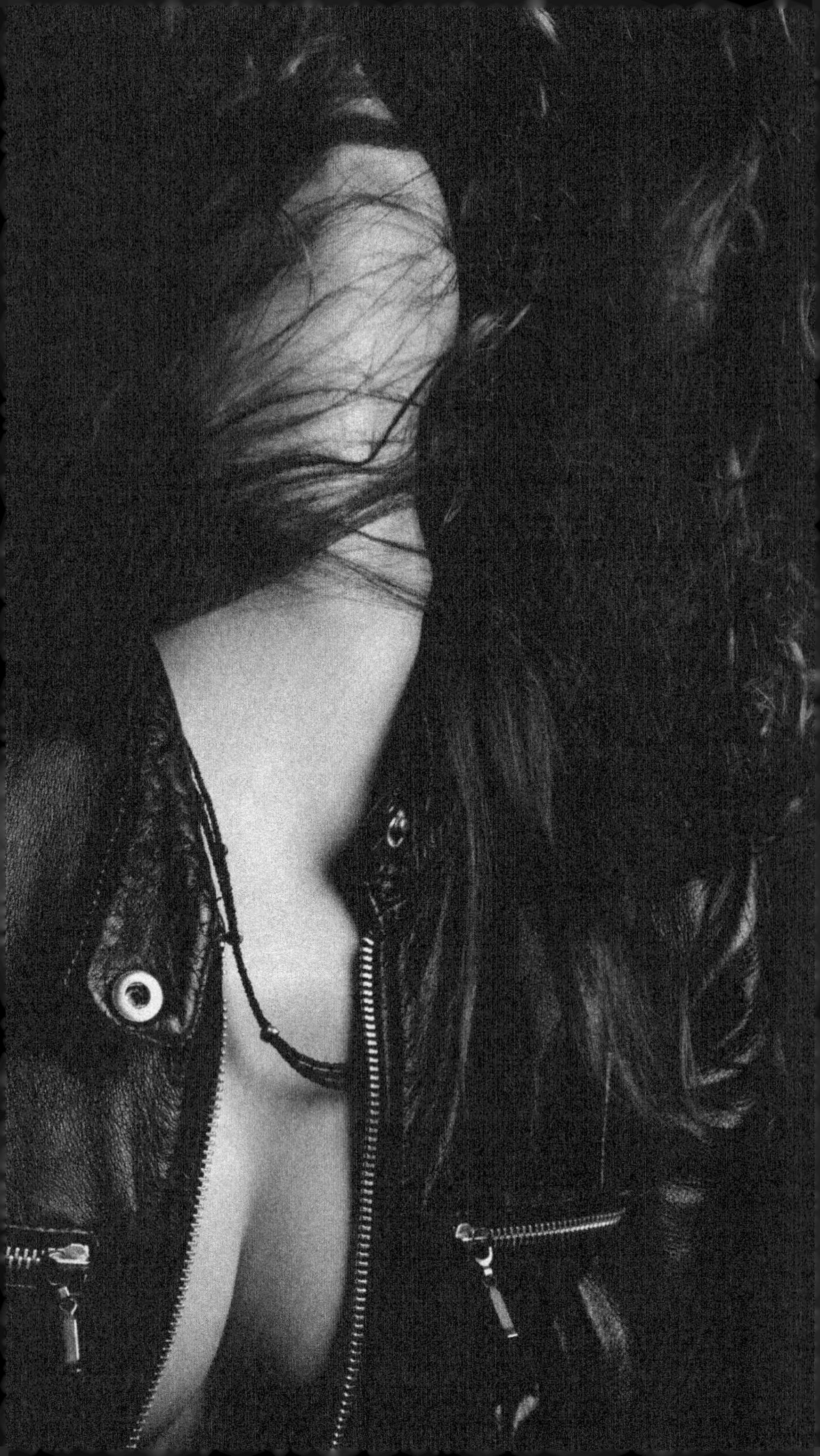

CHAPTER TWO

Ava

Panic.

Pure, unadulterated panic.

I would have screamed if I could, but I was frozen, too afraid to open my mouth or eyes.

Ice-cold water surrounded me on all sides, and in my moment of panic, I thrashed and kicked against the metal tub, to no avail. My lungs were beginning to burn, and I could only thank my lucky stars that I hadn't taken a breath when I came to.

That would have been the end of me.

The hand in my hair wrenched me back, tossing me to the floor like a rag doll. A small whimper left my cold, trembling lips as the cement floor bit harshly into my cooled skin. I coughed and choked, struggling to remember how to breathe.

Waterboarded.

The motherfucker had waterboarded me awake. Guess he got bored with waking me up with the cattle prod. Or the stun gun. Or nearly choking me to death. Honestly, I'd rather be waterboarded than suffer the way his hands had roamed my body, tugging, pulling, caressing, each morning to wake me up. I'd slapped him and spit in his face several times.

That's when he got creative.

"Look who's finally awake." Christian's oily voice dominated the small space. I could hear the sneer in his tone, like it bothered him that I'd woken up. *Maybe he'd meant to drown me?*

"Good morning, Little Lamb."

I didn't bother to respond. What was the point? He wasn't talking to me. Not really. Christian liked to hear himself talk. The man loved the sound of his own voice. There was no doubt about that.

"Get her up."

My brows pulled together as I looked up from the floor to find Archer standing over me, his eyes slightly narrowed as he took in my nearly naked state. He didn't say anything though. *Bastard.* Simply took my arm and heaved me from the floor with a rough pull. His touch, however, was deceptively gentle.

There was no stopping the flash of pain that crossed my face or the heat that suffused my cheeks at my state of near undress.

Christian, the perve that he was, had left me in nothing more than my bra and panties for days now. *Or was it weeks?* Time was pointless down here. There were no windows. No clocks. Just me and the oily motherfucker whom I once thought was my brother.

Thank god I wasn't related to that psychotic mess.

My gaze lingered over Archer, the traitorous FBI agent.

He was dressed in clean, pressed black pants and a long-sleeved white linen shirt. Stubble was growing along his jaw, highlighting the gray in his hair.

I couldn't believe I'd trusted him.

Helped him.

Now I was exactly where he promised I would never end up again.

Under my father's thumb.

"Are you ready to tell me what you know, my darling sister?"

Disgust painted my blue-tinged lips at his seductive use of the word *sister*. Is that how he still saw me? The sick fuck. If so, Christian was more fucked in the head than I originally thought. His eyes narrowed at my unwillingness to answer. The same unwillingness I'd displayed day after day since I'd woken up in this hellhole.

He was like a broken record of "It's A Small World," playing on repeat ever since the doctor signed off that my body could handle the abuse after the accident.

It didn't matter what he did to me though. What he threatened me with. I'd never betray Matthias. *Never*.

"Tell me what you know!"

My body flinched unconsciously at his nearness. Spit from his mouth hit my face, making bile rise in my throat as he continued to scream his useless threats in my face. If he killed me, he wouldn't have any leverage.

Archer shifted beside me, his grip tightening a bit, almost protectively. I shook those silly thoughts from my head. I couldn't live in a fantasy. Not anymore.

"The sky is blue. Your shirt looks like something out of a bad Miami Vice movie, and you desperately need to rediscover a toothbrush."

There.

I told him something.

Next to me, I heard Archer swear, too low for Christian to hear. I braced myself for the pain I knew would follow my little outburst.

Christian was nothing if not predictable. He raged, his face turning a disfiguring shade of purple as he snatched a handful of my hair in his fist, hauling me back to the metal tub set up in the corner.

I sucked in a large breath as he plunged my head beneath the icy surface. This time I was prepared, managing to will my body not to respond with panic. It wasn't until its need for oxygen took over that I reacted. My body jerked involuntarily. The edge of the metal tub dug painfully into my stomach, making it harder to control my ability to release small amounts of air at a time. Still, I refused to thrash around in fear.

Refused to fight against him.

Dots of unconsciousness shifted behind my closed lids as I fought to keep myself from passing out.

Someone was yelling. It wasn't Archer. The voice was laden with rage as it argued with Christian. I couldn't make out what the person was saying. Not completely. Their voices were muffled, muted by the water. One sentence, however, did penetrate through the numbness surrounding me.

You need her.

That was all it took. That once sentence had Christian flinging my nearly unconscious body from the tub. A scream tore through me as the rough cement beneath me tore at my gelid skin. Waves of pain spiraled through me, gnawing at what little resolve I had left as I coughed and sputtered.

"I'm not going to be patient forever, Avaleigh," Christian snarled, crouching down in front of me, tenderly moving a few wet strands of hair from my face. His touch caused my stomach to roll. "You are going to tell me what you know sooner or later, or I will get more...personal with how I get them. And trust me, Little Lamb, you won't get nearly as much enjoyment out of it as I will. Maleah sure as hell didn't. You remember that, right?"

"Where is she, you fucking bastard?" I spat at him. Christian's hand whipped out faster than I could blink, his fingers closing tightly around the back of my neck as he dragged my face toward his, a sneer pulling at his lips. "What did you do with Maleah?"

"Be careful, sister," he growled, his sickly sweet breath assaulting my senses. Bile rose in my throat, and I tried my hardest to keep from gagging. "My patience is wearing thin."

"I. Am. Not. Your. Sister." I punctuated each word with as much venom as I could muster. It wasn't easy since it felt like I was breathing out of a paper straw, but I managed it. "You sick, psychotic fuck."

Christian's sneer dissolved, morphing into a wide Cheshire grin. His cognac eyes danced with a level of excitement that had me more terrified than his snarl.

"Looks like the cat is out of the bag." Letting go of my neck, he stood, brushing the dirt from the floor from his black trousers. "As for Maleah, my father was the only person who knew where she was, and well—he's dead."

"What?"

Was it true?

Had he just said our father—no, *his* father—was dead? That couldn't be right. If Elias was dead, then why was I here? What could Christian possibly want with me besides the minimal information I could offer him on Matthias's compound?

"You didn't tell her?" A low voice spoke from the doorway, his form bathed in the glaring fluorescent light of the hall. It was the third voice I'd heard. The one yelling at Christian while he nearly drowned me.

Neil.

Neil was here.

Why was Neil here? He hated Christian. Why didn't he leave? What was he doing here now? Did he despise me that much? *Fuck.*

My mind was a spinning top. Round and round I spun. Faster and faster. But I could feel it starting to stutter with the loss of momentum. It wouldn't be long before everything went crashing down on me. I could feel it in my bones.

"Didn't really seem important." Christian gave his cousin a nonchalant shrug, as if his father dying didn't matter. Damn, he really was a psychopath. "Now's as good a time as any, I suppose. Yes, Avaleigh, he's dead. I made sure of that."

"You killed him?" That was fairly obvious from the smug look on the bastard's face. Had he done it himself? Or, like my father, was he too much of a coward to get his hands dirty?

It still didn't add up though. I felt like I was putting together two and two and getting five instead of four.

Elias had given Christian everything. Played into his every whim. Supported his darkest desires. He'd given him power, authority, freedom. Limitless supplies of blow and whores. You name it and he'd received it. No matter how large or abhorrent.

He was also the only person who'd ever managed to keep a hold of Christian's leash. Without him, Christian was a rabid dog.

"Why? Why would you commit patricide? What could you have...? He gave you everything. What psychotic..."

"Because he gave you away!" The smirk was gone, replaced by a sharp, bitter resentment that had my skin crawling. His eyes narrowed, chest heaving in anger as he stared down at me as if I was nothing more than dirt beneath his feet. "He promised you to me. Promised you would be mine. Virginity and all, and he fucking sold you to that motherfucking Russian to save his own skin because he got in too deep."

Psychotic *and* delusional.

Great. Just what every world needs.

What the fuck was everyone's interest in my fucking virginity? It wasn't like it made me special. Jesus. It was like reading one of those mafia books where the main male character salivated over having a tight virgin pussy. How he savored breaking through that tiny piece of cartilage that I'm pretty sure was non-existent by the time Matthias fucked me for the first time.

It struck me as funny that Matthias hadn't seemed to care one way or the other if I was a virgin. He'd been more worried about how it would feel for me than for him. In fact, he'd never mentioned me being a virgin. I'd been the one to bring it up. He'd only confirmed that he knew.

And here Christian was, maddened as a bull that I wasn't a sprite little virgin anymore.

I knew enough about sexual education to know that fucking a virgin wasn't all that big of a deal. It was the act of taking something no one else would have that drove men like Christian toward such symbolism.

I mean, what did he think he was going to do?

Wave my bloody bedsheets out the window of our house for everyone to stare at? Maybe fold it up and display it on the mantel?

Then again, Matthias had taken the bedsheet when he'd taken my virginity. I hadn't thought about that until now. If the look on Christian's face was anything to go by, my guess would be that my lovely husband had handed proof of our consummation to him as a large *fuck you* to my father.

At least it wasn't displayed anywhere.

I hoped.

"Fuck you, Christian," I screamed at him, my voice hoarse and weak. "I am not yours."

Christian gave a mirthless laugh. "You think that because Dashkov relieved you of that cherry between your legs, you're not mine?" he snarled. "Don't be fucking ridiculous, Little Lamb. Popping that cherry would have been sweet as hell, but you begging and screaming while I take your ass and every other hole I choose will more than suffice. I assure you. You're the heiress to two major Irish undergrounds, and once we're married, I'll wipe them from the fucking board and take what I'm owed."

Like hell he would.

"I am not marrying you, you fucking pig," I snarled, getting sick of this conversation. The room was cold, and I was dripping wet in nothing more than my bra and panties. My body was beginning to tremble uncontrollably from the lack of heat, and hypothermia was fast approaching. Not even my anger could keep me warm. "I'm not yours. You can't marry me. Matthias is..."

Neil let out a small cough, barely noticeable to anyone but me. Out of the corner of my eye, I could see him shaking his head, eyes widening in a silent warning. *Don't mention the marriage* is what they seemed to scream, but how would he even know we were married? And if he did, why would he keep it from Christian?

Was he still trying to protect me like he did before?

"Matthias will come for me."

"You think so?" Christian snorted, tilting his head to the side as he studied me. "Right now, he's sitting pretty behind federal prison bars. I doubt he's in the position to make a rescue attempt. Let's not forget, the man is under the assumption you betrayed him, so..."

He let the rest of the sentence hang in the air between us.

So why would he come for you?

The only problem was, I never betrayed him. Well, not really. Not knowingly and not maliciously.

"I did no such thing," I refuted, turning my cold gaze to Archer. "You want betrayal? Your buddy *Anderson* over here is FBI."

Suck on that, you Poligrip douchebag. I didn't feel the least bit sorry for outing him to Christian. If anyone hated betrayal as much as Matthias, it was the man I'd once called brother. Archer had lied to me. He never knew where Maleah was.

He used me.

Used Mark.

He could suffer the consequences, the asshat.

Not that fate had ever been on my side.

It took my brain a minute to realize that they were all smirking down at me. Even Neil.

"Well, he plays one on TV, anyway." Christian chuckled, unconcerned with the viper he had in the henhouse.

"I'm serious," I told him. "He works for the FBI, his name is—"

"Jonathon Archer?" Christian interrupted, his smirk deepening. "Came to your door. Offered you an ultimatum... yada, yada, yada...I'm well aware, Little Lamb. That was the plan all along. We needed someone to get the SD card from Mark so we could set Matthias up for killing my father. And you did it so beautifully."

Abject horror settled over me as reality crashed around me. I was the one who set Matthias up to fall. They'd played me. Set me up. "No. That's not..."

"How desperately naïve, Avaleigh," Christian tsked. "Dad knew all along who Anderson was and that he was playing you. What he hadn't realized was that the ultimate plan was to end him and make that filthy Russian pay. There are bigger things at work here. My father was a small fish in a big pond trying to play at being a shark. And he failed. So, I took his place. Made a better deal. I get you and an entirely new empire for helping take down the Dashkov and Ivankov Bratvas."

My stomach churned, bilious and sour. His words dug at me like a chisel against rock. One small hit at a time, but sooner or later it would crack. *I* would crack. But that wasn't going to be now, and I would die before I ever let it get that far. There were parts of myself I was still discovering. Still being molded. There was one thing I knew for damn sure...

Ava Dashkov was not weak.

"You will never have me, Christian." I left my tone flat, calm. The resolve that had been fading away had begun to weave into something stronger, more concrete. I didn't need Matthias to save me. Not this time.

I'd do what I'd have to in order to survive.

To get the hell out of here.

Because no one, especially Christian, would ever own me.

"And I will never submit to you." A small gasp caught in my throat as pain racked my head. Christian pulled sharply on my wet curls, pulling my head back, leaving me no choice but to look at him.

"You'll learn to submit, Little Lamb," he snarled, eyes cold. "You were raised to submit to me. Just like I was born to rule these men. To take over the Ward Empire."

Jesus, did this man hear himself?

Villain monologue, here we come.

There was no truth to his words. I hadn't been raised to

submit to anyone. I'd been raised to fear and obey, and fuck if I was going to do any of that. Not anymore. I'd let myself be the victim before and look where that got me.

Absolutely nowhere.

Submission needed to be earned, and I chose who I gave it to. Fuck all if I was giving it to this prick.

Christian still had a hold of my hair as he droned on and on about how he was meant to rule the family. How his father couldn't see the big picture like he could. That the man who was backing him had promised him everything. All he had wanted.

Keep talking, idiot. The more he talked, the more I listened, the more I learned. Christian wanted to believe I was nothing, so I let him. Let him think that his rant was going in one ear and out the other. He believed I wasn't getting out of here. He was wrong.

"My men are loyal. Uncle Dante has already sworn his allegiance to me," Christian rambled, his grip on my hair loosening. "Everything will come out into the open soon. I will protect this family, ensure our legacy lives on, you'll see. I will rule this city like my father never did."

I couldn't stop the dark chuckle that moved through my chest, permeating the space between us.

"You really are an idiot, Christian." He stopped his ranting mid-sentence, his cool eyes narrowing. "Do they know? Your men. Do they know what you did to your *family*? I mean...killing Elias was one thing but this...who did you hire, Christian? Anatoly?"

Christian's free hand wrapped around my throat, pressing into the delicate flesh. There'd be bruising by morning, I would guarantee it. But it didn't matter because I'd knocked him off kilter. He hadn't realized I knew his secret. My *brother* wasn't the only one who had secrets.

Christian's expression was all thunder and hatred. His eyes flashed in a silent warning, his grip on my hair becoming almost unbearable.

But I ignored it.

Pain meant I was still alive.

Meant I was under his skin.

"Shut your mouth, Avaleigh." Pure venom dripped from his words. He was a rattlesnake, prepared to strike, but so was I.

"I don't think I will." I dismissed him with a painful shrug of my shoulder before continuing on. "Anatoly wouldn't have done it, and he would have ratted you out to Dante. I'd say—it was probably Marko, wasn't it? He's always desperate for money, and god knows you wouldn't have had the balls to pull the trigger yourself."

Neil stepped forward, his gaze darting between us, confusion etched in every line of his face. He had loved Libby like she was his own sister. Same with Kenzi. He'd doted on the pair of them like an older brother should. He didn't have any siblings of his own, and Christian had never bothered to pay the twins any attention unless it garnered him something.

"What is she talking about?" Neil questioned his cousin, his gaze boring into mine, seeking out the truth.

"Nothing," Christian sneered. "She's playing us. Thinks she has something over me. She doesn't."

I smiled with my teeth, my head still craned far back enough that I no doubt looked feral. Or like a deranged idiot. It wasn't like there was a mirror nearby.

"Okay. Sure. I'm bluffing." The words came out somewhat choked, despite my snarky smile. "If that's the case, you won't mind if I tell them, right? Tell them how you had your sister murdered at my wedding."

"What?" Neil stared at Christian in disbelief. Even

Archer took a step away from him in shock. Redness was seeping up Christian's neck, the vein in his forehead pulsing. I had him right where I wanted him. There was one thing he'd never learned from his father.

Control.

"Shut the fuck up, Ava" he screamed, tightening his grip on my neck a fraction more in a silent threat. Yeah, I was ignoring it. "I'm warning you."

"What was her crime, Christian?" I gasped out, struggling to get the words out around the iron grip he had on my throat. "That you would kill someone as sweet and innocent as Libby. What the fuck did she ever..."

"She betrayed this family!" The hand on my neck disappeared as he dragged me to my feet by my hair. I could feel chunks of it beginning to separate from my scalp and winced at the thought of having a giant bald spot.

The pain didn't help either.

My hands clawed at the one in my hair, fingernails digging into his skin, but it didn't matter. His grip was too tight as he dragged me against his body.

"She took off the moment she could. No contact. Nothing. I knew she was a traitor. A whore, just like our mother. Just like you. Her loyalty should have been to this family, and those who aren't loyal will die at my hand."

Time to poke the bear.

"Too bad it wasn't at your hand though, huh?" I taunted him in my raspy voice. Fuck, my throat hurt. Douche. "You would've been too busy shaking and trembling in your little suede shoes like a crying little boy. Just like you did when Matthias held a gun to your head. Nothing but a coward. A..."

"I am not a coward!" he roared in my face. "I am going to lead this family into a modern era. Become more powerful than even Uncle Dante. This will be my city, and you will either stand at my side or I will shackle you in the *stables* and use you as my fuck toy until you give me what I want. That is your choice."

I snorted.

"I'd rather slit my throat than have your diseased little pickle anywhere near me." I batted my eyelashes at him in faux flirtation. "Or maybe I'll slit your throat, you fucking—"

"No, wait—"

Well, shit.

Archer's voice was the last thing I heard before the pain and the subsequent darkness that followed tumbled over me like waves against the shore.

CHAPTER THREE

Vas

B<i>lyad.</i>
Fuck.
I combed my fingers through my hair, an exasperated puff of air leaving my lips as I paced back and forth in the bunker's comms room. It was late. Almost midnight, but sleep hadn't been something I'd bothered with lately.

There was a lot to be done, and seeing Libby's sweet face with a bullet between her eyes whenever mine closed didn't shake the insomnia.

It had been two weeks already. Two weeks since Matthias and Ava's shamble of a wedding, and I was nowhere near getting my boss out of jail or finding out where the hell his wife was.

After Matthias's arrest at the venue, I'd rushed back to the penthouse, expecting to see the fiery redhead waiting. Crying. Rampaging. Anything, but she was gone.

The penthouse was empty.

A few hours later, we found her assigned SUV in a ditch with a dead driver behind the wheel. A driver who wasn't one of ours. It had been a setup. The SUV was banged all to hell. Windows broken, blood sprayed across the back seat, caved-in doors. It was like it had been in an accident.

Only, there was no sign of one.

The ground wasn't disturbed; there was no debris. The only thing left behind was a set of nearly washed-out tire treads.

The vehicle had been planted. But why?

And that had been the start of my problems.

If the shit storm hadn't been bad enough, video evidence of Matthias killing Elias in cold blood had surfaced from an anonymous source. It was impossible. The paperwork Ben had been given during discovery listed the coroner's estimated time of death for Elias while we had all been at the compound.

Not that it mattered.

The fucking douche of an FBI agent didn't care that we had video evidence of Matthias sitting in on one of Ava's classes, as well as more than a dozen eyewitnesses. Claimed we could have doctored the time stamp and paid off the witnesses.

The only fake footage was what he'd given the judge.

He was a filthy fucking liar and didn't seem to care that I knew.

If there was one thing I hated most, it was dirty, cheating asshole feds.

The entire situation was still un-fucking-believable.

Plus, I was pretty sure Matthias had gone off the fucking

deep end, so to speak. He was starting to lose it. Cuckoo for Cocoa Puffs, as the Americans say. There was no way in hell I was going to follow his orders. Not this time.

Keep telling yourself that.

I had an ample amount of respect for Matthias. The man was not only my leader, but a brother to me. I'd left Boston to follow him to Seattle as his *Sovietnik*, his second in command, almost five years ago, giving up my claim to the Ivankov Bratva throne in the process. Matthias had never asked me to do it. He'd never had to.

I was proud to stand alongside him.

The six of us—Matthias, Nikolai, Maksim, Leon, Dima, and I—were a brotherhood. Soldiers who'd been to war together, who'd been through hell. We'd always had each other's backs.

We always would.

I'd known I was never meant to lead. My father had tried his best to form me into a leader who was worthy of holding his title, but he knew it wasn't ever going to be me.

It couldn't be.

There had been no uncertainty when I gave up my title. No regrets when my father removed me from succession to give the title to my younger brother, Pavel. While I'd been busy screwing, fighting, and drinking my way through Moscow after my eldest brother's death, he'd studied. Listened. Learned.

He deserved to one day hold the title of *Pahkan*. It just wasn't who I was. Or who I ever wanted to be, and now that I'd been thrust into that unwanted position, I knew I never would be.

This shit was stressful.

With Matthias behind bars at the small federal detention center, it was my job as his *Sovietnik* to step into his shoes as temporary *Pahkan* to ensure everything continued to run smoothly.

I didn't like it one fucking bit.

Especially after his latest set of orders.

I may be the *Pahkan,* but it was in name only. Matthias's orders were still meant to be followed. Even if I didn't agree with them.

"Is everything secure?" Matthias asked from where he was sitting, his large frame barely contained by the small metal chair they gave him to sit on. His scarred, tattooed hands sat folded congenially on top of the scratched metal surface of the table, wrists cuffed to a large ring welded to the top.

Fuck.

Even chained, he was a threat. The FBI weren't idiots, but if they honestly thought some handcuffs and a secured room would contain a man like Matthias Dashkov, they were naïve and living in a world of fairy tales.

The only thing keeping me from busting his ass out of the dismal room was his orders.

He was needed here. It was the only way we could get access to the building to flush out where the false video came from.

"Secure as it can be." I sighed. It was our code phrase. Well, code phrase was stretching it a bit.

I paced the small room, sweat beading on my forehead as I waited the extra few minutes for our comms specialist to work his magic. Confinement and I weren't known to get along, and although I knew, realistically, I was not a prisoner, my body wasn't getting the message.

Pussy.

Two long beeps sounded in my ear, one tone after another.

Perfect.

Rolling my shoulders to ease the tension that had settled there, I lifted my eyes to the camera in the corner before waving my middle finger back and forth at it like a twat.

Nothing.

Good. The loop was set.

"Subtle." *Matthias snickered. Turning back to him, I caught the corner of his lip turning up just a fraction at my antics. All I did was shrug.*

"Okay, now that I know we're not being monitored," *I sat down across from him, my face souring a bit,* "we have a few problems."

Matthias lifted a brow. "You think?"

I chuckled at his attempt at humor. To the world around him, Matthias was a cold, unfeeling leader of one of the States' most powerful Bratvas. To those who knew him, there was a small slice of dry humor he let show every now and again. A very, very small slice.

That was dry.

Very dry.

"The FBI is refusing to state where they got the anonymous video, and Judge Hardtford let it stand." *Again, they weren't idiots. They knew what we would do with that information. It didn't help that they had the one judge who wasn't in our pocket playing on their side of the field.*

"We already know who it is," *Matthias hissed. His eyes darkened as he leaned forward on his elbows. The table shifted under his weight.* "You saw the footage yourself. She was with him. Handed the fucking thing over herself."

Kristos. He could be a fucking idiot sometimes. And bullheaded.

Running a hand down my face, I struggled to count to ten before speaking. "You saw what he wanted you to see," *I tried to point out. "How would Ava know how to manipulate footage? Where did she get the SD card? We don't know the full circumstances. Now, I've been compiling some resources—"*

"Stop." It was a command. His tone harsh and unrelenting as he banged his fist down on the table. "Stop looking. Stop compiling. For all we know, she's part of this and has been the entire time."

"I don't think..."

"It doesn't matter what you think," Matthias snarled. "What matters is that I am giving you an order. I don't want any of our men wasted on finding her. She betrayed me. She betrayed the Bratva. Simple as that."

He was dead set on this. The man really believed Ava had betrayed him. I knew better. There was nothing in it for her. Sure, she'd given the FBI douchebag an SD card, but she hadn't looked happy about it. Then there were the obvious questions glaring at us like a neon sign that Matthias refused to think about.

Who the fuck gave her the SD card?

How did she know the FBI agent?

"Matthias..."

"The fucking agent knew his name, Vas," Matthias growled, but it sounded more resigned than before. "He knew... he said my brother's name. The fucker whispered it in my ear as he led me away."

"How would he know..."

"Ava," Matthias snarled. "There are only four people who know about him. You, your father, me, and Ava." Sighing, he leaned back in his chair, looking exhausted. "I confessed it to her one night. She'd been having a nightmare..."

"It doesn't mean she betrayed you, brat,*" I tried to argue. "He could have..."*

"Enough. Vasily," Matthias pressed the button on the table to signal the guard. *"This conversation is over."*

"What's the story?"

Lost in my own thoughts, I'd been careless. The door to the bunker had managed to open and close without me blinking an eye.

Shit. I'm losing my touch.

My four comrades piled into the room, avoiding the large curved wooden table that sat facing the monitors in favor of the smaller round table just beyond it. None of us felt right sitting in our normal seats without our fearless leader.

And there was no way in hell I was sitting in his chair.

We'd started building the compound years before making our foray into Seattle. An operation on this level required detailed and militaristic planning for everything to run smoothly. It was how we managed a nearly bloodless coup of the underground.

No one saw us coming.

To the outside world, the compound was nothing more than a boarding school for orphaned children, generously run and funded by a non-profit called Funding for a Better Future. It was part of the Dashkov Corporation. No one knew that, of course. Just like no one knew what truly went on behind its walls.

The children here were mostly the children of fellow Bratva brethren. A place where they could grow up in relative safety. To learn skills and lessons no school was capable of teaching them.

They learned to survive.

To strategize.

They were taught comradery and investment. Nearly

every student who graduated would go out into the world equipped with more than half a million dollars.

Some of them would go off to college before coming back to join the ranks of their brethren. Those were typically the children whose parents still served the Bratva. While the others, mostly the orphans, chose to be inducted into the Bratva straight away.

We'd yet to have someone walk away.

"Where to begin," I muttered lowly as I poured myself a whiskey neat.

"The beginning, obviously," Maksim deadpanned as he grabbed a beer from the small fridge just under the bar. Leon snorted, his head shaking in mild amusement at the large Russian. For an Italian, he wasn't half bad.

Most of the time.

Leon was the more refined of us all. Minus Matthias. While the rest of us sported jeans and T-shirts half the time, maybe a polo here and there, he wore a suit.

Downtime? Suit.

His first camping trip? Suit.

Fuck, I'm 99 percent sure the pretty boy came out of the womb in a suit.

He drank wine and ate at upscale restaurants whose names I could barely pronounce. Unlike the rest of us, Leon had grown up with a silver spoon in his mouth. Didn't make him any less our brother, but it certainly made for good entertainment.

"Insightful as ever, my friend," Leon chuckled under Maksim's glare. Even from across the table, that shit made my skin crawl. Maksim was no teddy bear wrapped in bulking muscle like Dima.

He was a killer. End of story.

The fact that his glare, that I'd personally seen reduce

grown men his size to tears, didn't bother Leon told me how much of a psychopath the posh Italian really was.

"Children," Nikolai admonished with a smirk, dragging out what Matthias had dubbed his professor voice. "Settle down so we may listen to our fearless usurper."

Fucking old-timer.

"All hail Vasily the Fearless." Maksim held up his beer in mock salute.

"I thought it was Vasily the Fearful? Running from the seat of power since 1988," Leon cracked as he took a sip of his wine, eyes gleaming.

"No, no," Dima crowed. "Vasily the Drama Queen."

Har-fucking-har.

"It's going to be 'Vasily with his boot up your asses' in a moment," I threatened, but there was no real heat behind my words, and the three men howled with laughter. They all knew how much I was loathing being in this position. "Now, report."

"Spoilsport," Dima muttered somewhat petulantly, still chuckling under his breath as he lifted his beer to his lips. After taking a long swig and a deep breath, he set the bottle down on the table and up a map on the small screen that sat nestled in the middle of the table facing upward.

"We've been tracking all of Ward's known associates, including the Romanos," Dima began as a slew of red dots popped up on a map across Seattle. Each one of them was a tracker of a targeted individual. It was late, just past midnight, and most of the dots were inactive, but there were a few still moving along the streets. "The Romanos have been the most active since the wedding, but as far as I can tell, they haven't strayed outside their normal routine."

"Are we sure they don't suspect they're being followed?" I asked. If Ward's people had a suspicion they were being tracked, they'd be more careful to keep their movements the same. But even that was a pattern we would be able to detect. No one did the same exact thing each day, every day.

"We've come up with some...creative ways to ensure they remain unaware they're being followed," Dima assured me. Not that it helped. Dima's plans, although solid most of the time, usually ended up with me paying someone off.

Or murdering someone.

Or disposing of a body.

"Do tell," I encouraged him with a raised eyebrow. Maksim and Leon chuckled. I could have sworn I heard Maksim mutter something to Leon about paying up.

"Well, those we have following them are less likely to be noticed than most," Dima hedged. All I could do was blink at him stupidly.

"Less noticeable?"

"They're small," Dima continued. He was hedging around giving the full answer.

"Like children," Maksim butted in happily. My eyes narrowed at Dima.

He wouldn't. The motherfucker.

"You're using the children for surveillance?" I roared. "Are you fucking kidding me, Dima?"

The man before me shrugged unapologetically. "They wanted to help get their boss out of jail, and I needed a group of people who could surveil without drawing attention. Hence, children, or more *technically*, young adults."

"Matthias is going to kick your ass when he finds out you sent some of the students on an unsanctioned surveillance mission."

"Pay up," Maksim whispered to Nikolai, who handed him a crisp hundred-dollar bill just like Leon had. *Jesus, I'm working with toddlers who have gambling addictions.*

"We'll be coming back to that later, Dima," I warned the still smiling Russian. "Did you happen to find anything useful while using our students to do your dirty work?"

"You make it sound like I wasn't doing anything at all," he feigned hurt. "I'll have you know I am your hardest worker."

"Bullshit," Maksim coughed under his breath.

"You call sitting in your pervert van sipping Fanta, doing something?" Leon snorted at the same time. Dima growled at the man but remained silent as he dragged the screen feed to the side, the map rushing from view, replaced by a photo of a man I'd never seen before.

"This is Marko Cane." Dima narrowed his eyes at Leon, ignoring his jibe. "He *was* a low-level hitman for the Romano family. Since Dante took over, he's more of a runner than anything else."

"And I care about him, why?" Niko cocked his head to the side.

"Well, before the wedding, Marko was in debt up to his eyeballs," Dima informed him, pulling up the man's financial records on the screen. "The Irish, the Greek. Hell, he even owed the Lords of War."

"And why do I care about the finances of one of Romano's hired thugs?" *I was beginning to sound like a broken record.*

Dima smirked. "Because less than twenty-four hours after the wedding, his debt of more than 1.5 million was cleared, and he's been spending like a high roller every night at Club Mezzanine."

That was news to me.

"And tell me, Dima," I tilted my head, eyeing him curiously, "how does a member of the Italian Mafia know about one of our super-secret, super-secure strip clubs?"

"Pay up," Leon muttered to Maksim with a smile.

Toddlers.

We had several legit businesses around the city that cleaned up our dirty money. Ones that were open to members of the public and ones we kept hidden in the shadows. The fact that one of Romano's hired thugs managed to gain entry meant he'd been led there.

"You invited him, didn't you?" The urge to groan and throw my head back was pretty fucking strong right now. So was the urge to strangle him.

"Yep." Dima popped the *p* like a fucking douche.

"Why?" I grilled.

"Why else?" Dima raised an eyebrow at me like an idiot. I had to resist the urge to throw my fist in his smug little face. "Information. Men talk when they're drunk and horny."

"And you found out…"

"Well, nothing from him directly, but I did manage to break into his accounts."

I was going to strangle this motherfucker. Fuck the code.

"Jesus," Maksim snorted. "Stop being an ass. Three million dollars was wired into his account less than twenty-four hours after the sniper hit on the wedding. Do I need to spell the rest out for you?"

Choosing to ignore the insult, I turned my gaze back to Dima. "Why would Romano pay one of his men to kill his own niece?"

The Italians had a code. *Family doesn't kill family.* Dante Romano had made that code after the death of his father. The father he'd killed. He wouldn't break it.

Unless he didn't.

Pizdets. Dammit. How could I have missed that?

"You think Christian hired Marko to kill his own sister?"

The three of them simply stared at me as if it was the obvious conclusion. Conflict smacked across their face, shining from their eyes like fucking beacons, but they all knew better.

I didn't need their pity.

"Why?" I asked, somewhat dumbfounded. "What would Christian Ward have to gain from killing her?"

"Nothing," was the simple response from Leon. "From what we could tell, killing Libby wasn't part of any grand scheme. She didn't have any insider knowledge or passcodes. Libby was sharp, and her insights into how her father behaved were helpful, but from what we can tell, nothing worth killing over."

"So why do it?" No one had an answer to that. "Do you think we could use Marko? Shake him down?"

Dima shook his head. "Marko has been on the outs since Alfonzo Romano's death," he informed me.

"Maybe he wasn't aiming for Libby," I surmised hopefully. "Maybe he was aiming for me."

None of my brothers looked convinced.

"You said he was a low-level hitman," I reminded Dima. "He could have just missed the shot."

"No, *brat*." Leon frowned. "Evidence on his computer testifies that he was aiming for Libby. And he may be a low-level thug now, but he wasn't always. Not until Dante took over for his father. Before that, Marko Cane was his top hitman. Marine sniper. Top marks."

Damn it all to hell. Why did it have to be Libby? Sweet, naïve, innocent Libby. The only woman in the world who'd managed to knock me off my high horse and get my blood boiling. I could still taste her on my lips from our first kiss. Cherry Chapstick.

She'd fought it at first, but by the end, she'd been meeting my passion with her own. It was like nothing I'd ever experienced before. There'd been women before Libby, but I doubted there would truly be any after her.

Libby had been fireworks and confetti. Now, she was nothing more than flesh to rot away beneath the dirt.

"Do you think Romano knew about the hit?"

Leon shook his head. "No," he replied assuredly. "Christian knows what would happen if anyone found out. He likely chose Marko because of how isolated Dante had made him. Not to mention, if Romano found out about his debt, he'd be dead. Christian saved his ass."

"We don't think anyone knows he killed Elias either," Nikolai spoke up.

That made sense. Christian would be a dead man if anyone did. Patricide was looked down upon in the Italian Mafia. The only one to ever pull it off successfully without repercussions was Dante Romano himself.

His father had been a right douche though. No one was missing him.

The question was, who had helped Christian manipulate the footage of Matthias killing Elias? It had to be someone with access to the FBI. Or millions of dollars, because Christian sure as hell didn't have all that money lying around. Not since the raid on the port. Mark had confirmed that all the Ward assets were frozen.

Someone was funding the little bitch.

"What do we do about Ava?" Maksim approached the elephant in the room. He knew I'd gone to talk with Matthias about his wife to try to put together a rescue plan.

"Nothing."

The three of them stared at me, mouths open, eyes blinking. It was as if they were having a hard time processing what I'd just said.

"Beg your pardon?" The shocked look on Leon's face sent

a pang of guilt rippling through me. "I might've just gone stupid, because I'm pretty sure you just said we weren't doing anything."

Swallowing past the lump in my throat, I nodded. "Matthias has branded Ava a traitor. We aren't to utilize any of our men to rescue her. Our focus is to get him out of jail and make these false charges disappear."

The men didn't have time to protest what I'd told them before a low, unhurried voice spoke up from behind me.

"I can help with that."

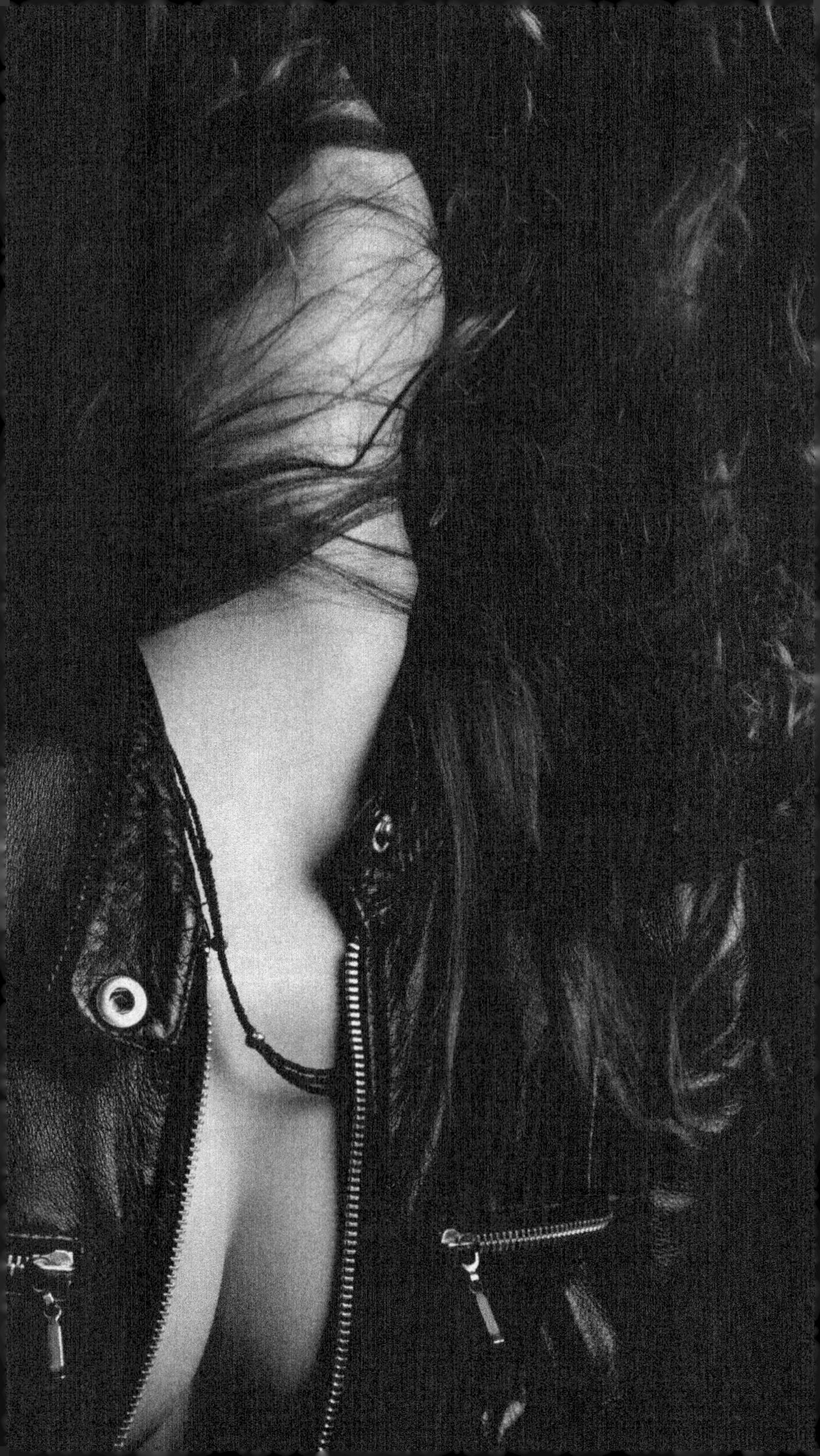

CHAPTER FOUR

Vas

There was a rush of commotion as the five of us jumped from our seats, spinning to face the intruder, guns drawn. The large heavy door to the bunker was wide open, the coded alarm blinking in hues of colors I'd never seen it cycle through before.

"I can't believe this shit," Mark, the unwanted intruder, commented in awe as he took in the vastness of the room before him, eyes wide with wonder. "This is like some *Justice League* shit right here, man. I'm talking some real Bruce Wayne's Bat—"

"Finish that sentence," Maksim growled, making a show of cocking the hammer of his gun, "and you're a dead man." Niko and Leon snickered. It took every ounce of training I had to hold back my own bark of laughter.

I kept telling him this was the Batcave.

Now wasn't the time to rub it in the burly Russian's face, however.

I'd see to that later. Mark being here was a serious breach of security.

"Okay, man, calm down." Mark grinned at my enforcer before turning his gaze to me. Maksim growled, but at least he'd put his gun away. The others followed suit.

"How the hell did you—"

"I swear to all that is holy, Mark..."

Jesus, what the hell was happening here? Roman had come barreling into the room, red faced and out of breath like he'd just run a marathon.

"Chill man." Mark smirked back at Matthias's cousin. "Cardio is good for your heart."

"If they don't kill you, you little shit," Roman panted, leaning against one of the chairs near the main table, "I sure as hell will for making me run like that."

Mark opened his mouth to rebut, but I got there first. "What the hell are you doing here, Mark?" I shook my head. "Scratch that. How the hell did you even find this place? Let alone gain access?"

The little hacker fuck full-on grinned at me, teeth and everything, mischief dancing behind his shining eyes. "It wasn't all that hard," he admitted with a shrug of nonchalance. Like finding a secret bunker out in the woods was the easiest thing in the world. "This is the worst well-kept secret on campus. Everyone knows there's something out here. Some think it's your hideout. Others think you're coming out here to have wild Roman orgies together."

Well, that was a piece of information I could have lived without.

"Orgies?" Nikolai pinned the hacker with a glare, his

voice deep and thunderous. "They think we're out here fucking each other?"

Leon chuckled. Of course he would find this amusing. We all knew how he viewed sexuality.

"Well, some of the girls do." Mark winked at the man. "To be fair, they've been reading a lot of romance books lately. I'm sure the men don't think that. Probably...Maybe."

"Fuck me," Nicolai growled as he sat back in his chair, guzzling down the rest of his beer like it was water.

"Apparently one or more of them are."

The hacker was digging himself a hole. A giant one. Nikolai was the eldest, but he also tended to be the most volatile when provoked. Even more than Maksim, at times. Maksim's rage was easy to see coming. Like standing in front of a freight train with its whistle blowing.

Nikolai—well—Niko's rage snuck up on you from behind. He was unpredictable, and the aftermath wasn't something I liked cleaning up.

"How'd you get in?" Leon gratefully steered the conversation in a more pertinent direction. "Those doors are coded."

Mark smirked, holding up a small device in his right hand. It was barely the size of a credit card and looked like something he had put together himself from spare parts without bothering to perfect or refine it.

"It's a decryption device. Works twice as fast as the older, more traditional 16-byte model and is wireless. Don't have to hook it up to the door or anything. The range is sweet too."

"Fucking hell," I muttered, taking a long draw of my whiskey, or what was left of it, at least. Something told me I was going to need a refill. Or two. "Told Matthias we should have gone with a thumbprint or retinal scan entry."

"So you broke in here. Why?"

"Isn't it obvious?" Mark questioned, tilting his head curiously.

"If it was, would I be asking?" I retorted hotly, pouring myself another generous helping of whiskey.

Mark huffed. "I have a way to get Matthias out of jail."

"And you didn't think to come to us before?" I grilled. Mark shrugged, a habit of his when he didn't know how to word something properly. The kid was brilliant. Top marks on all his tests in school. IQ off the charts. He was a mechanical prodigy, but like many, he was another kid just thrust through the system.

It didn't matter that his scores were well above average. He didn't do his homework.

No one cared that his IQ rivaled Einstein. He didn't show up for class.

The system only cared if he could fit into their nanoscopic social construct, not that he could build something that could literally topple the American construct.

And it was sad.

"I didn't really have a solution until a few hours ago," he admitted sheepishly before adding, "Also, I need a few assurances first."

My brows raised at the mention of assurances. The only people who needed those were people who'd done something wrong. Something they weren't supposed to.

"And what would those assurances be?"

Mark gulped, his Adam's apple bobbing up and down as he visibly trembled. "One, you can't kill me when you find out exactly what happened, and two...I need you to help safeguard my mother and sister."

There was no mistaking the implication. Mark had betrayed us, but there was something in the way he stood, the way he pleaded, that told me it hadn't been willingly. Not by a long shot. Still, Matthias didn't tolerate betrayal.

I, however, was not Matthias.

And I was currently *Pahkan*.

"Sit down and tell us what happened," I snapped at the hacker. There was a need to be firm. He needed to understand that although I wasn't likely to kill him, he'd still suffer the consequences. I couldn't be his mentor in this situation. Lines needed to be drawn. "And don't you dare fucking lie to us, or I'll let Maksim show you what happens to men who betray us."

The boy nodded furiously, eyes alight with fear, but there was something else behind it. *Respect*. A weaker man would have killed him without explanation. But I wasn't a weak man.

Not anymore.

Taking my own advice, I sat down with my chair facing Mark after having refilled my tumbler. I was going to need a lot of alcohol for this. I could already tell by the way he was twitching.

"Okay," Mark breathed, his body bouncing slightly, psyching himself up. "What do you want to know?"

"Start from the beginning," I ordered roughly, not bothering with niceties. That would come later. Once he confessed his sins. Mark nodded and leaned forward in his chair; elbows braced against his knees.

"That would be about a week before you tracked me down."

Maksim whistled, raising his eyebrows at the boy's confession. A fucking week before? *Khristos*.

"A man showed up at my door and identified himself as Jonathon Archer, FBI."

Nikolai growled, and even Leon's feathers looked ruffled.

Shit. He'd been working with the very agent who'd arrested our boss. This wasn't going to end well.

"Wait," he exclaimed, sensing the sudden tension in the room. It was so thick it could have easily been cut with a blunt knife. "I had nothing to do with Matthias's arrest. Neither did Ava. When he came to my door, he only wanted two things. He wanted to know where she was and..."

"You told us you didn't know her location." Dima's eyes narrowed. "That's why you led us to Maleah."

Mark flinched at his friend's name.

"You knew her location all along, didn't you?" Maksim snarled at him. Mark didn't need to confess; the overladen guilt was written across his face in bright neon ink. "Why the fuck would you give us Maleah if you knew where she was all along?"

"Look..." Mark tried to interrupt, but Maksim, who'd been the first to see the video of Maleah being beaten and raped, wasn't going to let up. This was too close to home for him.

"No," he nearly roared, his thunderous voice filling the space like a heavy thunderstorm. "You saw what they did to her. She was sold, and you what? Wanted to save your own skin while hers was bloodied and bruised by those—"

"Ava never told us!" Mark screamed at the top of his lungs, his chest heaving as he stood angrily from his chair, eyes wet. "She never told us the full extent of what Elias did to her or about what he was capable of. No one knew. Not even Libby. We thought maybe he smacked her around a few times. We all knew he locked her up like some kind of leper, but none of us knew how far his reach was or how sick and twisted his mind was.

"Archer threatened me, all right?" Mark continued, his voice dialing back a few notched as he paced in front of us, a hand running through his unkempt hair. "He said he'd send my mother to prison for her old drug charges. Charges I thought I'd buried. She's been sober for over ten years, and I... I couldn't let my sister be put in the foster system. So, I told him where Ava was, and he said that when the time came, I was to give you Maleah's name."

"We didn't actually track you down, did we?" I asked calmly, trying to ease the suffocating atmosphere his confession had created. "You led us to you."

Mark nodded. "He told me you'd come for me," he admitted, his voice shrinking, eyes red. "When I asked why I was giving you Maleah's name, he told me not to worry about it. That she'd be safe. I had no idea what Elias would...I still can't..."

Words failed him, as they had all of us. This went deeper than any of us thought it did.

"What was the second thing he wanted?" Nicolai questioned.

"He wanted me to clean up a video and decrypt some files," Mark confessed as he sat down again. "Then, I was to give the SD card to Ava and have her deliver it to him."

We'd been wondering how Ava had managed to get the small SD card. Had she planned the entire charade when she fled the penthouse that day? Or had that merely been a coincidence?

"So, you gave Ava the evidence of Matthias killing Elias." I'd stated it as a fact because I couldn't think of any other plausible reason the agent would have given him the SD file. Mark shook his head.

"No," he assured me firmly. "That SD card had nothing to do with Matthias's arrest, trust me."

Leon scoffed but held back his retort.

"When I asked why I had to be taken by Matthias, he'd told me that the only way he knew I could access the files was within the Bratva database," Mark kept explaining. "Then I asked how he was supposed to know when Ava had the SD card and how she was going to get it to him, but he didn't answer. Just shrugged like it was no big deal when she got it to him, just that it needed to be *her* who gave it to him."

The pieces were slowly starting to fit together bit by bit, a picture forming. Ava hadn't betrayed Matthias. Not in the way he believed, anyway. She was trying to protect her friend and his family. It wasn't much of a leap to think that Ava herself had most likely been coerced into working with this agent as well, long before she'd been brought back to Seattle.

"What was on the drive?" I asked curiously. Mark smirked.

"Let me show you."

One moment he'd been sitting with his hands free, and the next, he was holding his cell phone and had hijacked the main display system. The screens filled with a dark, grainy footage I immediately recognized. *Fuck.*

"I was barely able to clean it up." Mark scrunched his nose. "It's old. Like late eighties to early nineties old. Plus, it's Russian, which means the quality was even shittier than what it would have been had it been made in America." He paused and looked back at us sheepishly. "No offense."

Before I could protest, he pressed play.

"From what I can tell, it's two young boys, probably in their teens," Mark narrated the grainy footage I knew so well. I didn't need to see the footage; I'd heard the story many times before. "The taller boy, the one who looks older and somewhat more trained, comes at the younger one. They tussle, they fight, then..." He didn't need to explain the rest. The younger boy won, then cried before shakily dumping the body of the other teen into the river flowing beneath the bridge. His body would never be recovered.

At least as far as I knew.

"Why is an American FBI agent interested in a fight between two homeless boys that happened twenty-odd years ago in Russia?" Nicolai questioned. He wasn't connecting the dots. He didn't have the full story. Nor did he recognize the younger boy. No one did.

"It wasn't just the fight he was curious about." Mark tapped his phone before bringing up a grainy image of the boy's wrist. "It was this...birthmark? That seemed to hold his attention."

I didn't have to look back to know that all the men were staring at me, Roman included. They all recognized that mark because we'd all been there the day Matthias had gotten the tattoo that covered it up.

Roman hadn't been there. He'd been too young, but he knew exactly who was on that footage. He had the same mark. It was familial.

There was no going back now.

So I told them the story of the boy who killed his brother after he ambushed him. How, even after his death, the attacks never stopped. One after another after another, until the boy wised up to the ways of the world and began to fight back.

"Explains why the fucker was in the gym all the time." Nikolai shook his head in disbelief. "I thought maybe he'd just wanted to be a fighter. I never realized he was learning to fight to survive."

None of them asked why he never told them.

They didn't need to.

Killing a brother, even one who'd tried to kill you, was a pain no one could express. If only that were the end of the secrets.

"What about the documents?" I asked, steering the

conversation back to the present. "What was on them, and why did you need the Bratva network?"

Mark frowned. "They were mostly birth and death records. Even when I decrypted them, I couldn't read them. They were all in Russian. However, I made a copy of them so you could."

"Okay," Roman finally spoke up. "We know what the agent wanted from you, but why use Ava? Or arrest Matthias? You said you had a plan to get him out of jail, or did you lie about that too?"

"Nope." Mark's frown morphed into a wicked grin. "I'm not sure why he had Ava deliver him the SD card, not when I could have easily sent it over a secure channel. My only thought is that he *wanted* her to look guilty. *Wanted* Matthias to question her loyalty. She only did it to protect me, and she had no idea what was on it."

"And what about Matthias?"

"Oh, that's already done," Mark assured the room. "I may have hacked into the FBI mainframe and deleted the evidence and left a...surprise."

"What surprise?" Leon asked. Mark's grin widened.

"Oh, the kind of surprise that will have them chasing their tails for a good couple of weeks looking for someone who doesn't exist."

"So the video doesn't show who actually killed Elias?" I pondered about what that could mean when Mark shook his head.

"The entire video was staged." He curled his nose up. "I'm not sure who did it, but he was good. All I can think is whoever manipulated the footage deleted any background information. He took Elias's body and managed to manipulate it enough so that it looked like Matthias had slit his throat. There are some discrepancies, but it was easier for me to just purge all the evidence than to try to get your lawyer buddy to point that out."

I could understand that. "Good work," I told him. "It doesn't mean you're off the hook, but you showed that you are loyal to us. Even though you were forced to betray us, you did it in a way that could bring it back around to help."

Mark swallowed hard, redness creeping up his neck as he looked away sheepishly. "I've never been a part of a family," he admitted with a small shrug. "My mom was drunk or high most of my childhood, and when she did get sober, I was the one...anyway, you could have killed me in that warehouse and instead, you saw potential and helped me. So, I kinda owe you."

"Fuck yeah you do, kid." Nicolai beamed at the hacker. "And mark my words, you will answer for what you did, but I'm proud you came forward. We all are. You could have kept everything to yourself or fled, but you didn't. You faced us knowing damn well we might have killed you. That is what makes you a Dashkov."

"Now that we have that settled." Dima raised his glass. "How about we work on finding Ava?" The men around me cheered before stopping short when they took in my grim expression.

"You got to be shitting me," Maksim growled.

"Matthias ordered that we are not to use any of our men to rescue her." My jaw clenched as I recounted my conversation with our burly boss.

"Dammit," Leon swore. "He thinks she's actually in cahoots with them?" Roman shot Leon a weird look.

"Cahoots?" Roman snorted. "Who the fuck says that?"

"You're about to be able to say nothing at all when I punch your teeth out," Leon snarled. Roman held his hands up in mock surrender, but the smirk still held. Those two never got along, but I didn't have time to worry about that.

That was a problem for future Vas.

"Vas, we can't just leave her to them," Mark begged. "She didn't do anything wrong. Not really."

"I know that." I sighed, leaning back in my chair. "But my hands are tied."

"Did he say not to go after her or just not to use *our* men to do it?" Maksim queried, stroking his beard as a plan formed in his mind.

"He said, '*Our* men'..." I replayed the conversation in my head. "He also said to stop looking and compiling."

Maksim grinned. "Great." He pulled out his phone. "Then we don't use any of *our* men. We use someone else's. Someone who would want to get her just as much as we do. Plus, we have an inside asset we can use."

I knew I wasn't going to like where this was going. Maksim's plans were just as bad as Dima's.

"We can't burn him. Matthias will be pissed," I warned. "We wouldn't have an inside man anymore, and he doesn't have enough men at his back to ensure it works."

"So we form an alliance," Leon added, no doubt already knowing what Maksim had planned in his devious mind. "Maksim's right. There is someone out there who would want her out of Christian's clutches just as much as we do. They just don't know it yet."

I was too afraid to ask, because I could already tell where this was going. *Matthias was going to toast my ass.* "Are you proposing what I think you're proposing?"

The men at my table smirked, and I knew whatever they were planning would have my ass in a sling.

Matthias was going to be pissed.

CHAPTER FIVE

Ava

The sky was beginning to darken as the hour grew late. Storm clouds threatened to drop rain on those who had come to pay their respects at the gravesite. The days were growing colder, the forecast taking a turn for the worse as the briskness of fall began to fade into an icy winter.

I'd known this day was coming the moment Christian had so callously informed me of Elias's death.

Standing over the closed casket of the man I'd once called father, I hugged my jacket closer to my body, staving off the chill of the winter wind that bit viciously into my exposed skin. The gazes of the men around us drifted between Christian and me, their faces a mix of anger and confusion as they took in my position at his side.

Some of them knew who I was. Their places in Elias's inner circle granted them privileged information not available to the masses. The others, well, the only thing they knew about me was I'd been stolen from Matthias. None of them knew me as Elias's fake *daughter*.

To them, I was just a spoil of war. An enemy. Someone close to the man they believed responsible for their leader's death, as well as his daughter.

I hadn't thought Christian would allow me to accompany him. It was a risk to have me out in the open. Now that I was here, I knew exactly why he had brought me.

A power play.

He was telling the *Famiglia* he had me on a tight leash. That I was where I belonged.

Under his control.

God knows he didn't deserve my tears. Hell, he didn't even deserve this funeral. No, my unshed tears were for Libby, whose own closed casket lay next to his, completely identical, from the solid cherry poplar wood exterior down to the plush red velvet interior in a French fold design.

It was sickening.

Libby had always said she wanted to be cremated and spread out on a cliff where the wind could take her on a new adventure. Instead, my little sister would be buried next to a monster.

The thought of her being laid to rest here, with the likes of him, broke my heart.

Her death, I knew, was not my fault. The burden of it shouldn't have weighed down my soul. But it did. Christian's perverted obsession with me was what had ultimately led to her execution. There had been a small moment, just one second in time, when I had prayed that I'd been wrong. That what I'd seen at the wedding had been part of the ultimate plan and that maybe, just maybe, she wasn't really gone.

I should have known better than to pray to a god who never listened.

The bitter truth of her death was laid before my eyes, and all I felt was the intense urge to gut Christian and his men from stem to stern.

To paint the town red with their blood.

To make everyone understand my pain.

They would get theirs. I'd be sure of that.

Father Bianchi recited his prayers, but the words were nothing more than rushing water through my mind as I pulled my attention away from the monotony of his useless eulogy. I'd let my gaze wander over the graveyard, taking in the attendees with rapt attention. If there was one thing Elias had taught me, it was that information was power.

The more of it you had, the more power you had over people, the more you could manipulate them. Play them like pawns on the chessboard. A ready sacrifice.

The problem? People were unpredictable, easy to shift alliances at a moment's notice. Elias had once had power over many of the men here. He'd even had power over Christian. Look where that had gotten him.

Murdered by his own son.

Most of the people in attendance were made men. A few of them attending with their wives by their sides. Children had been strictly prohibited.

Neil was nowhere to be found, and neither was Archer. Their absences didn't put me at ease though. They were the only two people who'd been able to temper Christian's rage.

I winced, the pounding in my skull that had finally started to ebb shot to the forefront of my mind as I thought about the last time Christian had lost control. Had it not been for Neil and Archer, I most likely would have been beaten to death.

Another reason people were staring.

My face and neck looked like a Picasso painting of black and blue. That was just the part people could see. The skin beneath my dress was worse.

Eyeing Kendra, I let my thoughts shift away from the past and back to the present. Elias's widow stood on the other side of her husband's grave, the picture of the perfect Italian wife in mourning. Her long raven dress was fit more for a Paris fashion show than a funeral. Her face was partially masked by a thin black lace veil, and every now and again, she brought her white handkerchief up to wipe at her dry eyes.

Oscar-worthy performance, in my opinion.

Standing stoically next to her, his youthful face pinched in irritation, with his hand around her too thin waist, was Dante Romano. The man I'd grown up believing to be my uncle.

His dark eyes were narrowed at his brother's casket as it was slowly lowered into the ground. I'd never seen him so on edge before. There was a perplexing look behind the anger, and I could almost see the gears in his head whirling and spinning. I wondered if he knew that his brother's killer stood among them.

Had he been in on Christian's plan?

Plotted his kin's demise?

I wanted to believe he wouldn't. He was the one who created the code *La famiglia non uccide la famiglia.* Family doesn't kill family.

It was the look of fleeting sadness that painted itself across his face as his gaze landed on Libby's casket that puzzled me. I'd never seen him show much affection to either of the twins. Oftentimes, he'd gone out of his way to avidly avoid them.

The twins had been born a year after his wife's death. Luisa, my *aunt*, had died during the birth of their firstborn, Luca. I attributed his violence to the sadness surrounding him at constantly being reminded of Luisa's death.

Kenzi had been named after her.

Then again, he should be deflated; she had been his niece.

She'd also been Christian's sister, and that hadn't stopped him from having someone put a bullet in her head.

"The loss of life in the Ward family is a tragedy. It is always sad when death takes one so young and another before his time is truly finished," the priest droned on. "We hope justice finds whoever took them from us so early."

"Could take justice right now if they knew the killer was right here," I muttered under my breath, not expecting anyone to be able to hear me. Christian's sudden bruising grip on my already tender side told me he had.

"I'd keep quiet if I were you, Avaleigh." He leaned down to whisper in my ear. "Or I will happily repeat our session from the other day if you want to disobey."

Cowed by the thought of another beating, I meekly nodded my head. Inside, I was seething, my blood boiling as he kept his grip firm, his fingers digging into my tender skin without restraint.

"...In nomine patri, et fili, et spiritus sancti," the priest finished, his free hand making the sign of the cross above each casket as they finished being lowered into their final resting places. A whisper of amens rose among the attendees, including my own. Pressure had begun to build behind my eyes, the tears threatening to fracture like fragile ornamental glass, shattering into millions of tiny pieces. But the last thing I wanted to do was cry in front of these people. The ones who had done nothing but lie and beat me down.

"Let's go," Christian huffed impatiently as he led me from

the graveside. I didn't push him; he was already on edge at having been forced to attend the funeral of the people he'd murdered in cold blood. Instead, I followed him obediently, weaving through the small crowd until he stopped abruptly at the sound of someone calling his name.

Cursing, he turned to face his uncle, who'd silently approached us, leaving Kendra to mingle with the other wives.

"Dante." Christian's tone was informal, if not a bit biting, and I could see his uncle's eyes narrow at the informality. No one spoke to the *Don* that way. Not even family. "What can I do for you?"

Dante's gaze momentarily shifted to me, his expression unreadable as he took in the sight that was my face, before pulling back to Christian. "A few of the men want to talk to you about our next step."

Christian snorted derisively. "I don't need to discuss anything with them." His upper lip twisted in disgust at the thought. That was the problem with Christian. He didn't play well with others, especially those he thought to be below him. He was entitled. A trait Elias had unfortunately encouraged through the years. "My men's job is to follow my orders. Not question them or discuss them. That's it."

"They aren't your men, Christian," Dante reminded him with a snarl. "They are *my* men, and if you don't discuss with them *our* next steps, they won't be following your orders much longer. Understood?"

His nephew's shoulders stiffened at the obvious rebuke. I listened carefully, my eyes trained on the ground as I attempted to make myself appear small. Christian wasn't much different from his father when it came to his views on women or me. He either thought I was too dumb to comprehend the conversations, or his pride wouldn't allow for him to believe I would ever get away and use that knowledge. The latter thinking is what had gotten Elias into trouble in the first place.

Never underestimate a woman scorned.

I stood aside as the two men batted words back and forth like ping-pong balls for several moments, their words becoming heated, before Christian finally huffed out a colorful curse, tugging on my arm sharply.

"No need for the girl to hear all that," Dante told him. "I'll stay with her while you tell *my* men our plans."

Sure, just poke the bear, why don't you?

Christian shot his uncle a scathing glare before he let go of his unforgiving grip on my arm to stomp off toward the group of men who waited none too patiently near Elias's fresh grave.

A beat passed. Then another. Neither of us spoke, letting the tense silence hang between us and fester like an infected wound. I was content to keep it going for as long as necessary. Nothing I had to say to this man would be considered civil.

For a moment, I contemplated making a break for it. The cemetery, although remote, was still a better place to chance an escape than the *stables*. Theoretically.

"Ava." Dante broke the silence with my name, his smoky voice low, as though he didn't want to be overheard. My gaze drifted up to his face, and I could see that his eyes held the same sadness and regret I'd seen earlier when he'd watched them lower Libby's corpse into the ground.

"Dante," I kept my voice flat, my gaze held his. He huffed out a small breath.

"What happened to uncle?" he asked.

I couldn't help the snort that left my painted lips. "Were you ever my uncle?" I tilted my head up to get a better look at him, and for a second, I was caught up in how much he resembled the twins. He had the same dark hair, although his was a few shades lighter, and the same faint olive complexion. Unlike Elias, he was toned and muscular, the lines of his muscles visible beneath his well-fitted suit.

Pale scars littered his hands, and if he were to remove his jacket and roll up his sleeves, he'd have ink snaking up both arms.

Dante Romano was a man to be feared.

When he didn't say anything, I had my answer. "Exactly," I hissed. "Tell me something, *Uncle* Dante," I spat out the word like it was a curse. "All of these years feeding me chocolates and bringing me goodies. Did you know what your precious brother was doing to me? What his plans were for me? Did you turn a blind eye because you needed his business? Or because he was your brother, and I was nothing more than a dead woman's kidnapped daughter?"

At least he had the decency to look somewhat ashamed of his inaction over the years. Not that his interference would have done any good. In fact, it might have made the situation worse, but color me selfish. All I'd ever wanted was for one person to stand up for me.

No one ever had.

Even Libby and Kenzi had remained quiet. No one dared to openly defy Elias Ward. Not even his own brother, apparently, even if he was the Don of the largest Italian Mafia Family in the Pacific Northwest.

"It's true," he whispered as he ran a large hand through his trimmed hair. "I suspected there was more going on than what Elias let on, but you and I both know confronting him would have only made things worse for you."

"So what?" I scoffed, folding my arms against my chest.

"You thought smuggled candies and goodies with a few smiles would make up for all the abuse?"

Dante shook his head. "No," he said firmly, his tone somber, leaving no room for argument. "But I'd hoped my kindness and sincerity would help ease some of your loneliness, at least a little."

And it had. There was no denying that the small acts of kindness he showed me over the years had indeed eased the pain of loneliness and despair that would often settle over me in the dead of night. Knowing that at least one person, one family member, cared at least a small amount, held some of the shadows at bay when darkness surrounded me. He was the one person I thought had seen me as human and not as a whipping post.

Anger and understanding whirled in my mind like a category five hurricane, fighting for control, and I wasn't sure which side I wanted to win.

"Are you glad he's dead?"

My eyes widened at his sudden question, but I didn't hesitate to answer. "I'm not going to be shedding any tears any time soon, if you really want to know." My brutal honesty seemed to surprise him, but it was quickly masked, his eyes darting to where Christian stood with his back to us. "But that doesn't mean I wanted him dead. He was still the one I called father for the last fourteen years. Those feelings don't just go away."

Dante nodded as he took a second to gather his thoughts before straightening his shoulders and taking a step toward me.

"I want to know who did it." His smoky voice had taken on a menacing edge that caused the hairs on the back of my neck to stand on end. He may have been Uncle Dante for most of my life, but this man was still a predator. Just like my husband. "Tell me which of Dashkov's men pulled the trigger on Libby."

Libby.

Not Elias, his brother, but Libby.

"None of Matthias's men killed her," I strongly assured him, holding his gaze, refusing to look away. He needed to see that I was telling the truth.

Dante's lips curled in obvious disdain. "You're lying," he growled, eliminating the small space that was left between us. My neck strained back to look at him. He towered over me by nearly half a foot, but I didn't dare step away. Now was not the time to cower. "Christian told me what happened at the wedding. How one of Dashkov's men shot her point blank when she wouldn't cooperate."

The Don took a step back in surprise at my sudden hollow burst of laughter.

"You really shouldn't listen to a fox who's gotten in your henhouse," I told him, struggling to keep myself together. Only a fool would take Christian's word as truth. I'd never thought the man before me to be easily fooled, but here he was, proving me wrong.

"Give me a—"

"You want a name?" I asked with a sneer. "Why don't you take a look at some of the men under your own command or take a look at the fucking autopsy report instead of relying on an untrustworthy source for information?"

"You're saying I can't trust my own nephew?" he asked. "My own flesh and blood? You think he'd honestly—"

A short cry of alarm burst from my lungs as his body tackled mine to the ground abruptly, shielding me as the distant sound of screams and gunfire erupted around us. Instinctively, I buried my face in his chest as he covered me while barking orders at his men.

"Set up a fucking perimeter," Dante yelled, struggling to be heard over the sound of gunshots and terror. There was a flurry of commotion outside of the bubble Dante held me in, his grip on my head tight as he fought to ensure I was not harmed. "Get moving."

Slowly, the panic began to subside as the chaos dimmed. Dante eased his grip on me and stood, his head still on a swivel as his men rushed to surround him. I took his offered hand, gently brushing the dirt from my skirt before looking around.

The graveyard was in chaos as Christian and Dante's men rushed back and forth, guns drawn as they hurried the women from the gravesite to their cars. I was mildly shocked I hadn't heard Christian screaming my name yet. Then again, I doubted he cared if I was shot or not. He was also probably too busy cowering behind a headstone and peeing his pants to really give me much thought.

"Avaleigh," Christian hollered, his face red and thunderous as he stormed toward us.

Damn. I was kinda hoping he'd gotten shot.

He was like fucking Beetlejuice, but worse. Just think his name and he'd appear like an unwanted cockroach in a Motel Six bathtub that just won't die.

Dante shifted slightly in front of me as his nephew approached, something that wasn't missed if Christian's glower was anything to go by.

"Let's go, Avaleigh."

"You're not going anywhere," Dante hissed. Christian snarled at his uncle; hackles raised like a dog protecting its bone. *Fuck me, I was the damn bone.* "You wanted to lead the men, then you need to be here to lead them. She goes, but you stay." With that, he walked away without even a backward glance, leaving me alone with an irate Christian.

I was a dead, dead duck. This wasn't going to end well for me.

"Eduardo." Christian motioned for his second in command. Fuck a duck. That man was foul. Like sewer living foul. He looked like someone dressed up a warthog in an ill-fitting suit and said, "Have fun at the banquet. Be back before midnight." The trousers he wore were stunted, hovering well above his thick ankles. His white button-down was covered in faded yellow stains, the buttons straining against the fabric that barely held in his rotund belly.

In short, he was repulsive.

"Yeah?" Eduardo tilted his head up to his boss in recognition. Hardly a sign of respect.

"Take the little lamb here back to her cage and make sure she behaves." A small smirk formed on his lips. "You know what to do if she doesn't."

Eduardo smiled at Christian, showing a mouth full of yellowing teeth. "Got it, boss," he said with a wide grin as he took my upper arm in his grip and proceeded to drag me toward Christian's SUV. His quick pace had me stumbling after him, the slim heels of my shoes getting caught in the soft grass. "Move it, girlie. Stop messing around or I might have to punish you right here." He delivered that line with no shortage of glee.

The thought of this man doing anything to me had my body shivering repulsively. My skin already felt like ants were crawling just beneath the surface at the way his beady eyes kept roving my body every time he looked back at me. Not wanting to give him a reason to try anything, I quickened my pace, trying my best to keep up with his long strides while nearly walking on my toes.

Bile churned in my gut and panic swelled in my chest when I looked back to find Christian's gaze on me. A dark, twisted smirk spread across his lips as Eduardo all but tossed me into the back of the waiting SUV.

That look was all too familiar. Whatever he had planned wasn't going to be good. I needed to come up with a way to escape, and fast, because I doubted I would survive whatever came next.

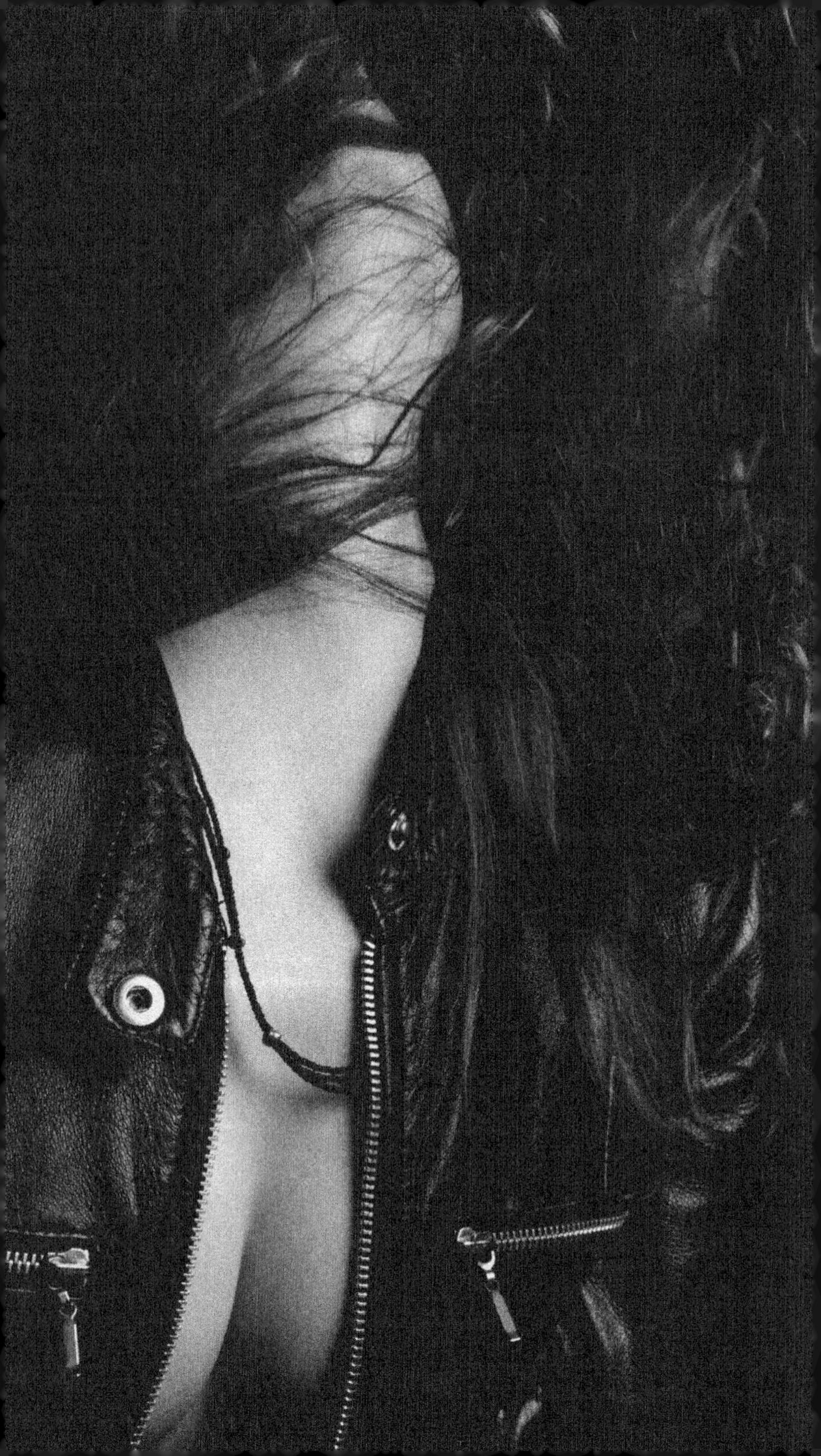

CHAPTER SIX

Ava

Eduardo dragged me along the empty corridor of the *stables* toward my cell.

It was quiet. Almost too quiet.

There was usually some kind of noise here, whether it was the other women sobbing or Christian's men walking the halls or whispered conversations.

Now, there was nothing but the portly man's stomping footsteps, heavy breathing, and the click of my pesky heels against the concrete floor.

I stumbled into my cell, caught off guard by Eduardo's rough shove, mumbling under my breath.

"What was that girlie?" he asked, his head shifting a bit to hear me better, mocking me. *Dick*. "I'd be careful what you say." His eyes roamed the length of my body. The immediate outward repulsion that radiated from me at the gesture caused him to sneer.

"Think you're too good for me, *Little Lamb?*" he mocked. "Women like you were born to be whores. Just like that little friend of yours. I got a real good taste of her before they sent her off."

Well, he had that slap coming.

A bubble of gleeful smugness came over me at the sight of my handprint slapped across his shocked face. Then it popped, cold fear washing over me at Eduardo's narrowed eyes. His hand came up to touch my cheek, the gentleness bellied by the rage streaked across his face.

"You're gonna regret that," he snarled as he turned and made his way toward the cell door.

Shit. Shit.Shit.

Maybe he was leaving? *Fat chance of that moron.*

"Do you know the instructions my boss gave me to punish you?"

I didn't have to see his face to know the fucker was feeling rather jovial about the turn of events. He'd been looking for a reason to use Christian's threat of punishment, and I'd given him the perfect opening. It didn't take a rocket scientist to read between the lines and know exactly what the pig had in mind.

"Said I couldn't touch that sweet pussy of yours, but everything else was fair game."

My eyes widened at his threat, throat constricting in fear as my hands grew clammy, and my breath became short. "Don't." I internally winced at the tremors that racked my voice as Eduardo slammed the cell door shut. He turned to face me, a sick, twisted grin on his dry lips. I swallowed past the lump in my throat. "Please."

"I love it when they beg." He stalked toward me, licking

his lips in what I was sure he considered a seductive manner. His heavy footsteps filled the room. All I could do was shake my head and back away from his advance as far as I could manage.

Which wasn't far at all.

A small gasp left my lips when my back collided with the cold stone wall of my cell.

Fuck.

He stopped right in front of me, his hand coming up to caress my cheek. I flinched as his offensive odor spilled over me. Choking me. Eduardo smirked as he grabbed my arms, pulling me flush against his body as he buried his face in my hair, inhaling deeply.

Futilely, I pushed against his large chest, turning my head away from him in an attempt to create distance where there was none. One hand traveled to the tie that held my bun in place, roughly pulling it out, causing my hair to spill down my back and over my shoulders.

Then both his hands began to roam my body, tugging and pinching to the point of pain.

He smelled like alcohol, sweat, and sewer waste. I held my breath as I fought against him, trying my best to ignore the putrid stench wafting off him.

I squealed in pain when Eduardo's hands grabbed at my breasts roughly, squeezing hard enough to no doubt leave significant bruising. Where were the other guards? Had Christian authorized this stank of a man to violate me? He'd always been so possessive. It didn't make any sense.

Unless—I thought back to the cruel smirk he'd given me as Eduardo led me away.

Had he planned this as a way to break me?

Taking a deep breath, I sucked as much air into my lungs as I could. My intent had been to let out an ear-piercing scream to alert someone. Anyone. Eduardo must have sensed my plan because my sudden scream was cut short, muffled by his meaty hand pressing tightly against my mouth while his free hand hitched up the short skirt of my dress.

His stubby fingers pried at the folds of my opening, forcefully finding my entrance. Christian, that rat bastard, hadn't given me any panties to wear.

Panicked, I wiggled and kicked against him, twisting and turning my body against the wall, trying to dislodge his hold. It wasn't enough. The gluttonous pig outweighed me by a hundred pounds at least. The only thing I had managed to do was lose my heels.

"Just give it up, whore," he spat at me, spittle landing in my eyes. *Nasty.* Who knew what fucking diseases he had. "We all know you gave it up to that Russian cur, so don't be such a fucking prude."

My blood simmered beneath my skin at his insults. With all the strength I could muster, I managed to rip my mouth from under his hand and chomp down on the tender skin between his thumb and forefinger.

"Puttana," he swore at me in Italian, calling me a bitch. His face darkened as he pulled his body slightly away from mine. *Sure, I'm the bitch for biting him when he was trying to rape me. Makes sense.* It was hard to believe that I was the first female to snub his unwanted advances. Although, I might have been the first one to bite him.

With the practiced precision born of a man who was well acquainted with beating women, he backhanded me across the face hard enough my teeth rattled. I pitched to the side, a small whimper escaping me as my body hit the hard, unforgiving ground.

Eduardo wasted no time in climbing on top of me, a psychotic grin slapped across his hideous face.

"Fuck what Christian ordered. You want rough? I'll fuck every hole until you're fucking bleeding, and I still won't stop," he mocked, slamming his lips against mine as I struggled underneath him. I tasted blood as his thick, slimy fish of a tongue pushed past my mouth roughly. He pulled back, a hazy lust clouding his eyes that stirred the panic inside me.

"What do you know about rough, shrimp dick?" I mocked him back. "Fucking a woman isn't the same as fucking one of those sheep you've been practicing on."

One day I'll learn to keep my mouth shut, was the thought to go through my mind as the pot-bellied man landed a punishing right hook across my cheek that had my vision exploding into nothing but blackness for a short moment. Vomit rolled in my stomach at the sudden disorientation, and I willed my body not to black out.

Unconsciousness would not be good.

Momentarily stunned, all I could do was lie there trying to right my vision and regain use of my limbs while the man pulled at my dress, rolling it up toward my chin to expose my naked body to his lustful gaze.

When I looked down at him, he just grinned proudly as he ran his filthy hand over the bare skin of my waist. I shook my head, trying to clear the fog that had descended over my mind. *I won't be a victim. I won't be a victim.*

Eduardo must not have considered me much of a threat since he didn't bother to restrain my hands as he hastily worked to undo his belt.

I will not be a victim.

The sound of his zipper opening was all it took to shake me from my stupor.

Without thinking, my left hand shot up into his face, palm striking a direct hit underneath his nose. The sound of snapping bone was followed by a strangled "*oomph*" that puffed out of his mouth as he jolted backward. He sat up slightly, his hands covering his bleeding nose, a slew of colorful curses filling the space between us.

His face turned thunderous, eyes shifting almost midnight as he snarled down at me. A bloodied hand left his nose, poised to strike.

Then all hell broke loose.

Threads of gunfire erupted from outside the cell window, followed by a deafening explosion that shook the building. My arms shot up to protect my face as dust and debris rained down around me. I turned my face away, spying my opportunity for escape.

My freedom.

I will not be a victim.

Seizing the opportunity, I struck.

One moment he had me pinned beneath his hips, and the next he was lying flat on his back next to me, a large gaping wound on his head.

The stone was heavy in my hand, covered in his blood, but I ignored it.

I am not a victim.

I could feel my chest tightening, my breathing shallow and labored as I shifted to my knees. Eduardo groaned, his body slowly shifting. That's when something let loose inside me.

Rage surged through my veins like boiling lava as I struck at him again and again until I was panting and out of breath, my body covered in a light sheen of sweat, his face nearly unrecognizable.

The hollow thump of the stone hitting the ground echoed through the cell as I struggled to keep from panicking. My hands shook as I held them out before me, the panic coursing through me rapidly increasing as I took in the sight of his blood splashed across them.

Eyes widened in horror as my mind began to process the carnage I'd created.

Leaning to one side, I vomited up what little was in my stomach, dry heaving for several moments when there was nothing left. *What had I done? What had I done?*

My vision darkened around the edges, my chest rising and falling with short, shallow breaths.

I'd killed him.

Murdered him.

I sat back on my heels as horror and revulsion washed over me, the waves of despair threatening to suck me under.

Faintly, in the dark recess of my mind, I heard the door swing open, the heavy metal hinges groaning against the heavy weight. It was probably Christian. He'd kill me for this. Of that I had no doubt, but still. I couldn't move. I was frozen in place, my eyes glued to the corpse of the man I had murdered.

"See? Told ya she'd be fine, Seamus."

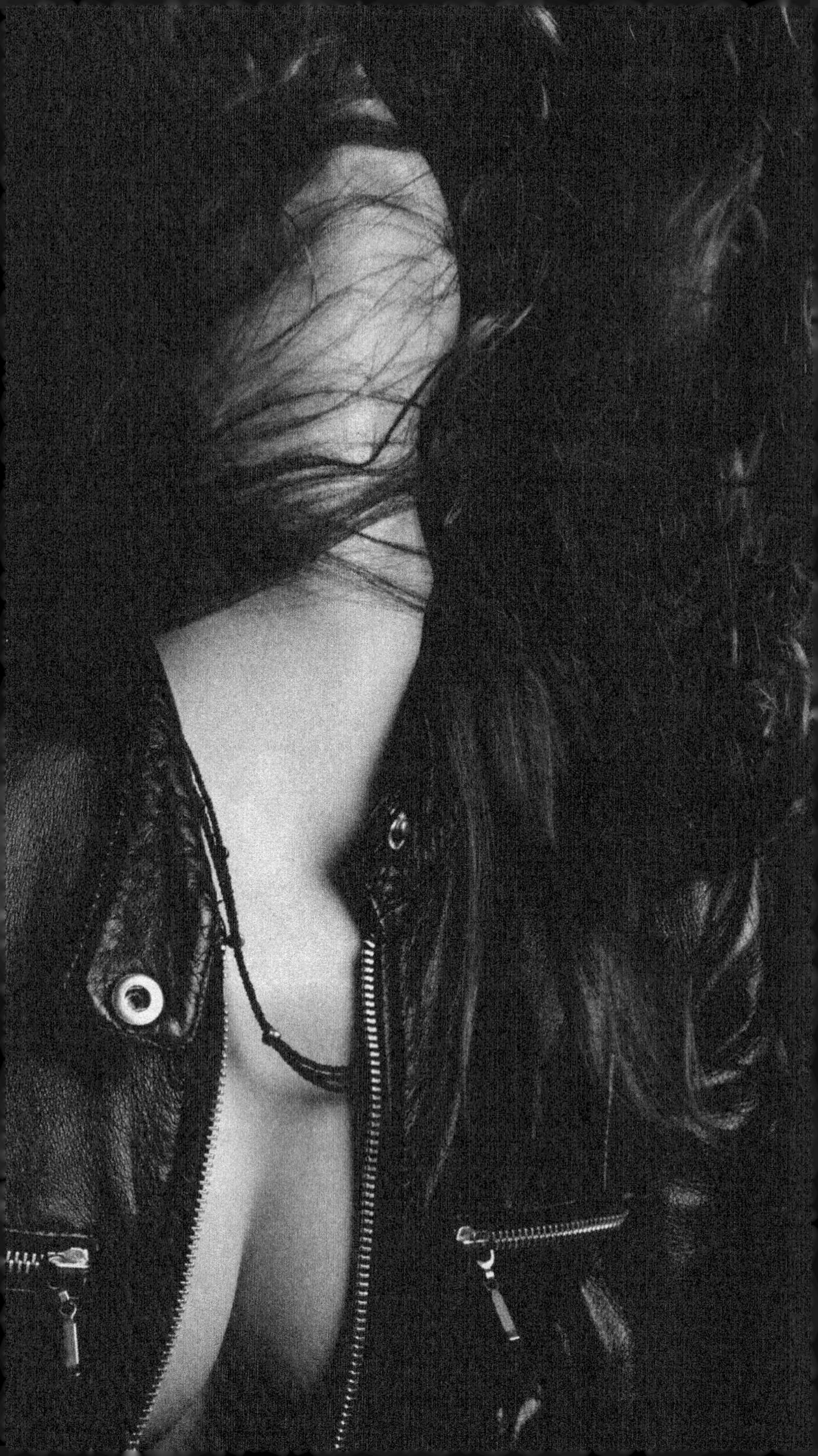

CHAPTER SEVEN

Ava

A deep, thick Irish brogue shifted through the space around me, filling the silence.

"That doesn't look fine to me." Another voice, one almost indistinguishable from the first, joined in. "She looks like she's about to keel over."

Footsteps approached, their heavy soles crunching the debris with each step. They stopped just behind me, the heat from their presence pressing against my back. Slowly, the fog that had swarmed my mind began to lift as if sensing they were there to help.

Or kill me.

One of them whistled as he crouched down on my right side, a gun hanging casually between his legs as he leaned in to get a better look at the chaos I'd created. At whom I'd killed.

Murdered screamed the little voice in the back of my mind.

"Looks like our damsel is a wild one," the one next to me joked. "Kiernan, come help with her, would ya?"

The other man grumbled under his breath as he crouched down on my left side.

"Come on, lass." He held out his hand in front of me. It held a white handkerchief. "Get that blood off your hands, and let's get out of here before the fireworks go off."

Sharp emerald eyes met mine when I lifted my gaze to his. My breath caught in my throat as I took him in. It was almost like looking in the mirror. His jaw was sharp, angular, and seemed to be more pronounced with his ginger hair tied in a man bun at the back of his head. Freckles dotted his lightly tanned skin, and I could see a swirl of inked artwork riding up the collar of his T-shirt.

Carefully, I took the handkerchief from his hand and began to vigorously rub at the blood I'd stained them with. A desperate sound filled the room. A haunting wail. Where was it coming from?

Me.

It was coming from me.

"All right," the man I believed Kiernan called Seamus stood, dragging me along with him. "That's enough of that."

They were twins. The wailing stopped as my head cocked to the side to examine him. The only difference was that Seamus had a beard. Everything else was a mirror image, even the tattoos.

"Well, that was easy." He smiled down at me, showcasing a row of pearly white teeth. "Whatcha say we beat it and get out of here, eh? Not much of a resort spot, if you ask me."

I couldn't help but smile at his attempt at humor. Swallowing hard, I nodded my head and was greeted with another wide smile. He nodded at Kiernan, who took my hand, leading me from the room, Seamus hot on our tail.

"Where is everyone?" My eyes darted back and forth, taking in the empty hallways and quiet rooms. "What did you do with them?"

"Them?" Kiernan asked without looking down at me.

"The girls," I pointed out. "Where are the other girls? They would have felt the explosion. They could be hurt or..."

"All the women here are being transferred," Seamus spoke up from behind me. *Transferred?* Did they deal in human flesh too? No, I wouldn't be a part of that. I wouldn't allow myself to be dragged into that. Even if these men were related to me.

Pulling against Kiernan, I planted my feet firmly on the ground, catching him off guard. He stumbled slightly. His grip on my hand faltered, and I yanked it from his grasp.

"What the fuck, Avaleigh?" Kiernan growled as he righted himself and turned to face me. I winced at the use of my full name. "We need to get the fuck out of here."

"Where are the other girls?" I demanded, stepping out of his reach when he went to grab at my hand again. My gaze hardened as I stared at him, arms crossed against my chest. Out of the corner of my eye, I could see Seamus biting back a smile, his eyes dancing with mirth as he took us in.

"I already told you..." Kiernan stopped, assessing me before he let out a prolonged breath as his gun-free hand came up to pinch the bridge of his nose. "For fuck's sake, Lass. They're being transferred to a damn women's shelter. We don't deal in human flesh like these lowlifes."

I dropped my arms to my sides and softened my gaze a bit. Lips twisting, and heat creeping up my cheeks, I took in the raw disgust on Kiernan's face and the sincerity in his tone. My eyes darted to Seamus, and the twin nodded his assurance.

"We don't sell women," Seamus's soft voice was warm but sincere. "We'll tell you all about where we sent them later, but right now, we really need to get out of here."

Taking a deep, elongated breath, I nodded and mumbled a small "Okay" before I let Kiernan take my hand again and lead me down the corridor. It didn't take long for the three of us to reach the end of the corridor, where a set of creaky wooden steps led to the topside of the *stables*. Where the actual livestock were kept. Seamus went first, the gun in his hand at the ready as he slowly ascended the stairs.

Before he had a chance to turn the handle on the door, it swung open, the cocking of a gun filling the void of quiet. I made to scream, but Kiernan's hand had let go of mine to cover my mouth. His own gun pointed at the top of the stairs.

"Christ, Da," Seamus muttered as he lowered his gun. "What the fuck were you thinking just opening the door like that?"

The man at the top of the stairs raised a brow at Seamus, his face stern. If I had doubts about the twins being related to me, I didn't any longer. They were nearly a younger carbon copy of their father. Same shining emerald eyes, strong cut jaws, and a head full of ginger hair.

Liam just happened to be older, his fiery red hair graying slightly at the edges and along the stubble that graced his chin. He held a black rifle in his hand, his stern gaze drifting from one twin to the other before landing on me.

"You're late and we're behind schedule," he scolded them, his eyes still on me. "We need to move."

Kiernan huffed, pulling me along behind him as he ascended the stairs. "Blame the damsel here." He shook his head and sighed. "Decided to dig her feet into the ground when she thought we'd stolen the girls to sell."

Liam chuckled darkly as we moved past him and into the dim light of the open barn. The air was fresh, tinted with the smell of hay. I could feel my biological father's eyes roaming over my blood-stained body, taking in the splatter across my face and my dress. His face twisted in anger and disgust, and for a moment, I thought he might be furious at what I'd done.

Murderer.

His hand swept up from his side, and out of instinct, I whimpered and melded slightly into Kiernan's side. Hurt and what might have been concern flashed across Liam's face as he lowered his hand.

"He dead?" He turned his attention to Kiernan, whose hand I was currently gripping on to for dear life.

"Yep." Kiernan full-on grinned, an oddity for such a serious man. "She took care of him all by herself."

Liam nodded. "Good." Then he strode away. "Let's get the hell out of here before word gets back to Ward."

The twins nodded as they followed after him, eyes searching, guns ready. Everything was quiet, even their footsteps on the harsh dirt floor. They reminded me of Matthias's men.

Trained. Quiet. Deadly.

They were a force, the three of them. A silent, lethal hurricane, and for the first time in a long time, I felt safe with someone other than Matthias. The large swinging door to the barn was already stretched wide open, two men with rifles, one with his back to us, waiting dutifully on guard.

Snap. Snap. Snap.

It sounded like a broomstick snapping. My heart lurched, and a scream caught in my throat as the two men at the entry dropped like flies.

"Fuck," Kiernan cursed as he ducked us behind one of the barn's large wooden pillars. "Keep your head down."

I didn't need to be told twice. My hands went to cover my ears as he released a few rounds from his gun, the sound echoing in my ears with his closeness. The smell of gunfire wafted around me as screams and shouts rent the air.

The sobs were caught in my chest as the scenery around me faded away until all I could hear was the steady thrush of my blood rushing through my ears. My heart was working overtime as I struggled to control my breathing, my gaze darting around the space, taking everything in.

Kiernan had his back turned, so he didn't notice the odd shadow sneaking up from behind us. He must have come in through one of the horse stalls.

The shadow didn't see me crouched behind the pillar at Kiernan's feet, nearly eclipsed in the darkness myself. My eyes widened as the man stepped out, a wicked smile on his face as he raised his gun, pointing it at Kiernan's back.

The fucking coward.

His finger went to the trigger, steadily beginning to pull.

My body moved of its own accord, never once hesitating when I tackled Kiernan to the ground as the man's gun fired.

All that mattered was that I saved him.

Even if it ended me.

CHAPTER EIGHT

Matthias

Freedom never tasted so damn good.

The rich amber liquid slid down my throat, and I savored the subtle taste of vanilla and notes of caramel as it assaulted my senses. After weeks of fucking stale water and what the FBI considered food, this was heaven. Or as close as I would ever get.

I should be celebrating my release with my comrades.

Instead, I was pacing the length of my office behind my desk in an attempt to burn off some of the anger I had building thanks to the five idiots in front of me. The grip on my tumbler was so tight I could feel the crystal beginning to crack under the pressure.

"I gave you an explicit order not to use any of our men to

rescue her," I snarled at Vas. "Is that not what I fucking told you?"

I expected my *Sovietnik* to look chastened, not smug.

"What do you mean, *Pahkan*?" Vas sat easily in his chair, relaxed, one leg crossed over the other. "I obeyed your instructions to the letter."

"You call shooting up Elias Ward's funeral to retrieve Ava obeying my orders?" I roared, throwing the crystal in my hand into the lit fireplace. The crystal shattered against the marble; the fire shot up as it lapped at the liquor. None of my men blinked. None of them flinched. They weren't afraid of my ire.

Maybe I should change that. Make them cower beneath my blows for defying me. Whip them until they understood my word was law.

Blyad.

Where had those thoughts come from?

I shook my head to clear the darkness that seeped in from beneath the barrier I'd erected so long ago. That was not me. My father was the one who beat his men into submission. It was the same for Elias. They ruled with fear and pain.

I was not them.

I would never be them.

Tomas showed me a different way. A better way.

"We didn't know Ava would be there," Nicolai spoke up, eyeing me warily as I resumed my pacing. "Our sources told us he wouldn't be stupid enough to drag her out in public. Then again, he wouldn't have known our plan for getting you released. He probably thought it was safe to parade her around like she was a spoil of war and he was Caesar."

My jaw clenched, fists tightening at the thought of that pervert's hands on her, touching her. I shouldn't care about that. She'd betrayed me. Ava had sealed her own fate.

Or so I wanted to tell myself.

The minx was still under my skin, affecting me in ways no woman ever had before. And many had tried.

Ava was never meant to mean anything to me. I'd meant to keep my distance. To keep her at arm's length, but even the best laid plans paved the road to hell. I'd ordered Vas to abandon her, and I had felt that decision tear me down to the core.

I was torn between my duty to my men, my empire, and the woman I'd made my wife. The woman who'd betrayed me.

Only she hadn't.

Not really.

It was that failure that was making me irritable and bitter.

"If you didn't rescue her," I questioned my men, "then who did?"

The five of them eyed each other, their faces twisting guiltily, like toddlers with their hands caught in the cookie jar.

"Well, when you ordered me not to use our men to rescue Ava, we might have used...a mutually interested party instead."

I raised an eyebrow at him. "A mutually interested party?"

Dima covered a cough with a laugh.

"Are you pausing for dramatic suspense?" I questioned. "Or are you too afraid to tell me?"

Vas mumbled something beneath his breath I didn't quite catch.

"I'm sorry. What was that, Judas?"

Everyone but Vas snickered.

"The Kavanaughs." Vas cleared his throat. "We struck a deal with the Kavanaughs."

"And you found her how?" I had my suspicions, but I wanted them to come clean. They burned an asset to get her back. They would have had to. The only place for Christian to hold her would have been where Elias kept his women, and only a few people knew where that was.

The question was whether burning that asset was going to hinder us.

"We didn't have a choice, Matt," Nikolai spoke up from his spot near the fireplace. "About a week after Ava went missing, he started sending us photos. He said if we didn't get her out soon, she'd be dead, and he made sure to show us exactly what Christian was doing to her."

The older Russian dragged out his phone, fiddling with an app before he handed it over to me.

Shit.

I'd wanted so badly to believe she hadn't betrayed me, and this proved it. The gruesome evidence before me caused my stomach to churn and bile to rise in my throat. Ava's body was covered in bruises, her fair skin cut in several areas. Blood dripped down her pale, nearly lifeless face.

The more I scrolled, the worse the evidence became, until I was forced to look away.

I was no stranger to violence. I'd cut, stabbed, hacked, and maimed more men than I could remember, but never a woman.

And this was my woman.

My woman.

I swore to myself a long time ago that I'd never let a woman get close to me. Not after Katerina, whose deception I'd been so blind to it had nearly cost me everything. I'd let my emotions blind me to her betrayal, and I'd promised myself I would never let myself feel that way again.

And then came Ava.

Ava, who wore her emotions like a shield. Whose emerald eyes were a sea of torment and innocence that could swallow anyone whole. Unlike Katerina, Ava wasn't practiced in the art of seduction. She'd never been taught how to lure men to her bed. Hell, she'd been a virgin on our wedding night.

Still, she'd betrayed me in the end. Even if she hadn't meant to. Even if it had been to help someone else, she'd ultimately betrayed me, and that was something I couldn't easily forgive. Vas was sure there had to be another way the FBI agent had known my brother's name, but I wasn't yet sold.

The real problem was that as much as I wanted to pretend that she meant nothing to me beyond a pawn I could move across the chessboard, I knew that wasn't true.

Even after her apparent betrayal, I feared losing her.

Ava was the chink in my armor.

My Achilles heel.

That had to change.

She could stay with the Kavanaughs for all I cared because there was no way in hell she was coming back here. The last thing I needed was a weakness, and Ava was the greatest weakness of all.

I wouldn't let a woman destroy what I had worked so hard to build.

Even if that woman was my wife.

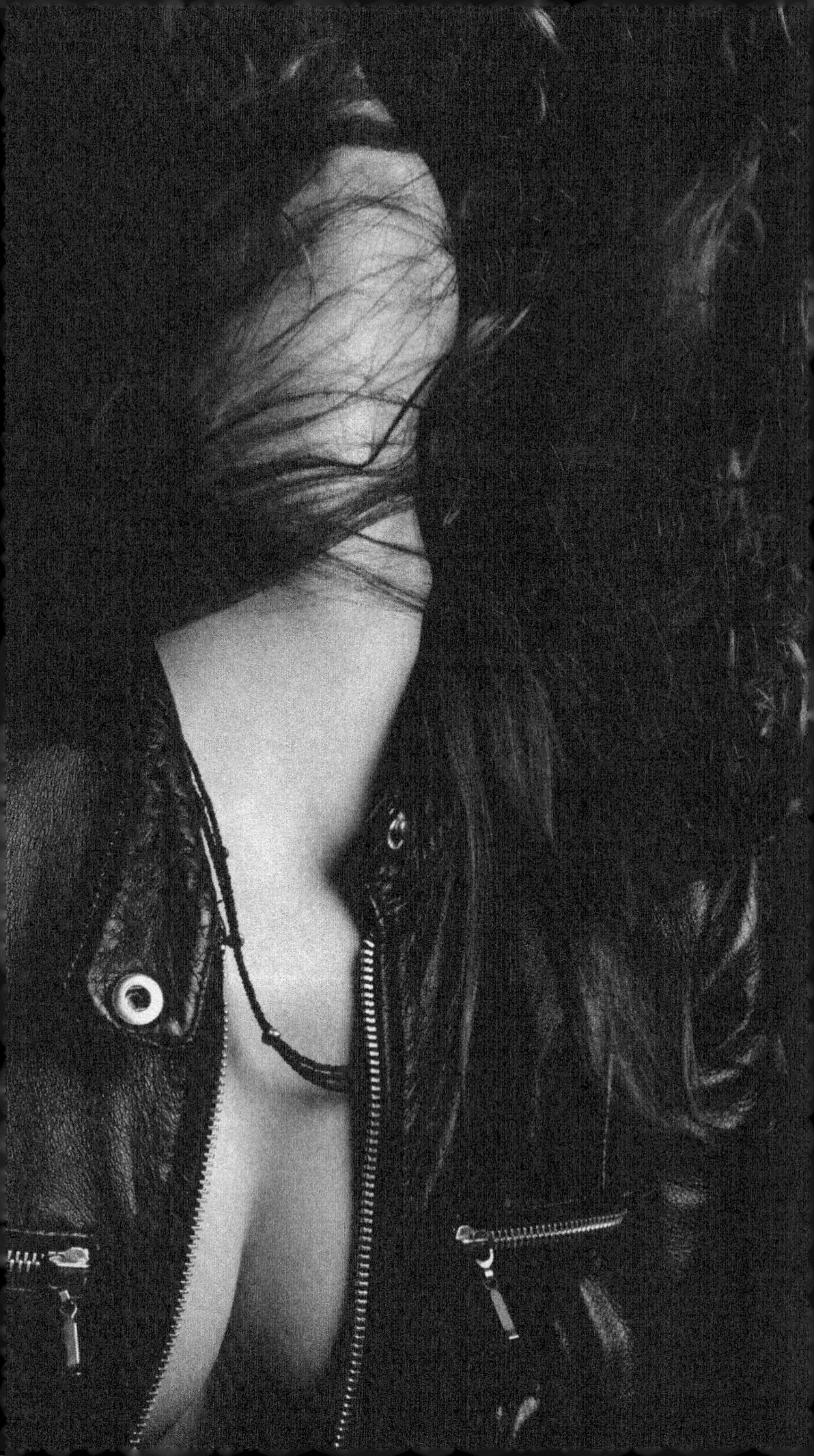

CHAPTER NINE

Ava

The first time I woke, I had no sense of time or reality. The world around me shifted, my eyes too heavy to open, my brain too foggy to register the sway of my body.

Warmth enveloped me, but I was still cold and shivering. There was no part of me that was unaffected by the rage of pain coursing through my body. Someone was screaming. Crying.

I could hear it.

No.

I could feel it.

It was me.

Hushed conversation surrounded me, and gentle hands

caressed my face, but I couldn't concentrate on them. Not when everything hurt so much.

What was the fire in my stomach?

Was I dying?

Was this what dying felt like?

Thousands of needles digging into the skin.

Poking...

Poking...

Then it was gone. Replaced by a deep, smooth voice that was warm like a summer wind, but with the bite of a winter chill. The scent of orange and cedarwood washed over me as well. A juxtaposition of sensations that calmed the frenzy gripped my mind.

A low thrumming filled my veins as I listened, the pain ebbing slightly at the rich tones of lyrics I knew all too well. Wetness gathered on my cheeks, the warmth a stark contrast to the chill of my skin, but I welcomed it eagerly.

"Hó bha ín, Hó bha ín.
Hó bha ín, mo ghrá.
Hó bha ín, mo leana,
Agus codail, go lá.

Hó bha ín, mo leana,
'Is hó bha ín mo roghain.
Hó bha ín, mo leana,
Is gabh amach a bhadhbh badhbh.

Hó bha ín, Hó bha ín.
Hó bha ín, mo ghrá.
Hó bha ín, mo leana,
Agus codail, go lá."

Those hauntingly familiar lyrics were the last thing I remembered before darkness rushed up to greet me.

Over the years under Elias's roof, the memories of my mother had begun to wane, and I often wondered which of them were real. There were times, when I'd been left in the dark, confined space of the shed, that many of the moments that came to me felt—fake. Like I had somehow conjured them up in my imagination to stave off the repressing darkness.

Hó bha ín, Hó bha ín.

Sleep, my child. Sleep, my child.

The familiar tune tugged at the edges of my fraying memory, the tapestry of my mind slowly unraveling to reveal the pattern beneath.

I'd forgotten those words.

Those lyrics.

She used to sing them to me every night before I went to bed.

Is breá liom tú, mo laoch beag.

I love you, my little warrior.

Those were her last words to me as she shoved me into the small crawl space just beyond the kitchen.

Our secret hiding place.

I'd always thought it was a type of game when she'd make me practice time and time again, getting in and out of the crawl space without being heard. Without being seen.

Knowing what I did now, it was clear there was something much more urgent behind it.

Hó bha ín, Hó bha ín.

Who had been singing those lyrics? Lyrics to a lullaby that my mother once told me had been passed down from generation to generation among the women in her family.

Before I could put much thought into it, that same voice had begun to hum the tune from beside me. Was I dreaming?

No, I was in too much pain to be dreaming.

Then what was happening?

Did it even matter? The warm bass of the voice humming mother's tune caressed the air around me, filling me with a sense of peace. A sense of home, and once again, I slipped into the depths of unconsciousness.

***

THE NEXT TIME I WOKE, I had no idea where I was.

The stale smell of hay and urine was gone, and the bed beneath me was soft and warm. There was a blanket draped over me, its heaviness providing a comfort I wasn't aware I needed.

My eyes were heavy, and I didn't need to open them to know I was alone. I'd spent a lot of time over the years getting to know what an empty room sounded like. Taking a deep breath, I inhaled the fresh scent of the room.

Orange and cedarwood.

What an odd combination.

My mind was too foggy to recall where I'd smelled that scent, but my body seemed to understand it meant safety because the tension in my muscles began to uncoil.

Slowly, I pried my eyes open; the lashes were nearly glued shut. The room was blurry, and I carefully brought a hand up to wipe away at the conjunctiva that had settled over them. I took a deep breath, fear washing over me before I had a chance to clamp down on it.

What if this was all a dream?

No, it couldn't be. I remembered them, the men who'd rescued me. The ones who bore features similar to mine.

My brothers.

Or had that all been a figment of my imagination?

Pain tore through the left side of my abdomen when I tried to sit up, and I gulped back a scream, tears stinging my eyes.

Then it all came back to me.

I'd been shot.

Rescued and shot all in one day. Karma really was a bitch.

"You're awake."

I turned my attention to the door, where an elderly woman stood smiling, a small tray of food in her hands. She stood tall, her shoulders erect, head slightly raised as she took in my current state.

Sweat dotted my forehead as I struggled to stay composed on my side while she made her way into the room. My stomach was killing me in this position, but I knew I wouldn't be able to sit up fully without help, and I didn't want to show weakness by lying back down.

"You might as well give it up, dearie." She smiled softly at me as she set the tray down on the dresser opposite the bed and approached me. "Either lie back or ask me for help."

Was she a mind reader?

"Not a mind reader. Just perceptive." *Oops. I hadn't meant to say that out loud.*

The woman held out a strong, wrinkled hand and raised an eyebrow at me. Like she was challenging me to deny it. With a small sigh, I took it, letting her help me into a sitting position against the headboard.

I had to admit, that had been much easier than trying to do it on my own.

"I'm Siobhan, dear, but you can call me Nan," she introduced herself before turning to retrieve the tray. "Your grandmother."

My grandmother? I had a grandmother. That was a novel idea. I'd never had a grandmother. Elias's parents had died before he'd taken me. Rumor was that Dante and Elias's father had killed their mother in a fit of jealous rage, which led to Dante killing him.

That was how he had ended up as Don so young.

Something warm stirred in my chest at her gentle gaze and soft smile. Not even Libby had looked at me with such warmth, and this woman barely knew me.

The hearty smell of stew filled my nose as she set the tray on my lap, and my stomach grumbled.

"Thank you," I mumbled between small spoons full of soup. "This is delicious."

Nan beamed at my praise as she fussed around the room while I ate. The stew was heaven on my tongue, and I had to resist the urge to moan in ecstasy at the bits of steak that melted in my mouth. The bread she gave me was thick, crusty, and smelled homemade. I dipped it into the stew and brought it back to my lips.

After weeks of water and barely digestible food in the *stables*, there was nothing better.

The silence between us as she worked was comfortable, and I couldn't help but sneak a peek at her every now and again as she moved about. She was taller than my five-foot-five frame and willowy. Long legs peeked out from under a billowing bohemian skirt, and on her feet were a worn pair of Birkenstocks. She wore a white peasant blouse and several layers of necklaces in all shapes and sizes.

Nan reminded me of my mother. Wild and free.

Her graying red hair hung in a smooth bob just below a strong, angular jaw that made her look younger than she was. This was a strong, natural woman. The opposite of Kendra's plastic, manufactured beauty. It was refreshing.

The quiet of the room was suddenly disturbed as the door swung open harshly, revealing a slender woman with long straight strawberry blond hair holding a stack of clothes. She'd aged since the photo I'd seen of her laughing with mother, but I recognized her all the same.

Marianne McAlister

"Ever heard of knocking?" Nan's brusque tone astounded me. Her radiant eyes were narrowed at the woman, hands on her hips, a scowl on her lips.

"Why would I knock in my own house, Siobhan?" Marianne sneered at Nan as she thrust the clothes at her before turning toward me. Her mud brown eyes widened at the sight of me.

"Jesus," she gasped, a hand flying dramatically to her mouth. "She looks just like..."

"Remember something, Marianne," Nan growled. "You may stay here, but this is not your house. It is mine, and you will show me the respect I am due."

Well, shit. Nan has some golden balls.

The pair fell quiet, their gazes locked on one another in a silent battle of wills, giving me time to study the woman my mother had once called her *best friend*. Her posture was stiff as she continued to stare Nan down. There was a history here I didn't understand, but one thing was glaringly obvious.

This was the twins' mother.

My encounter with the duo was short, but I could see pieces of her in them, even if they had been subtle. Their fair, flawless skin matched her own almost perfectly. The same for their angular noses and long eyelashes.

The rest was all Kavanaugh.

So, my mother's best friend married the man she had been in love with. Is that why she didn't follow up with the police? Because she wanted what she couldn't have?

Or was that just my cynical paranoia showing?

Matthias was a bad influence on me.

Lost in my thoughts, it took me a moment to realize that Marianne had been talking to me.

Scrunching up my nose, I looked up at her. "I'm sorry, what?"

"I asked if your mother ever mentioned me." Marianne's eyebrows furrowed. "Marianne McAlister?"

I shook my head. It wasn't a lie. Mother had never talked about her life before Portland. Not once. So, it was easy for me to act like I had never heard anything about her. Marianne seemed to buy it, but the glint in Nan's eyes told me she hadn't bought my BS.

Marianne's face fell, and a small feeling of guilt overwhelmed me.

"I didn't know about…" Marianne visibly swallowed before giving her head a small shake and pasting a fake smile on her painted lips.

"You can go now, Marianne." Nan dismissed her with a wave of her hand as she approached the side of the bed with the clothes.

"I can help," the blonde insisted, her smile stretching even wider. "I'll…"

"No," Nan bit out without offering any further explanation.

Marianne's smile slipped into a scowl before it was once again replaced by her Malibu Barbie smile. Fake and plastic.

"Well, if you ever want to know anything about her, just come find me. I have all kinds of juicy stories to tell you."

I pasted on a fake smile and nodded my head enthusiastically. I didn't trust her. There was a look in her eye that caused my body to stiffen and my heart to race as she gave me another once-over before walking from the room. I'd seen looks like that before, and it was never good.

"Watch yourself around her," Nan murmured in warning as she took the tray of finished food from my lap.

"You don't trust her?" My head tilted a bit as I watched her for her reaction. Nan snorted.

"She may have been your mother's best friend, but that woman has always had an agenda." She rolled back the blankets, holding out her hand to me. "You recognized her, *an leanbh*, and didn't say a word. Tells me you don't trust her either."

I shrugged my shoulder without answering. She may be my grandmother, but that didn't mean she automatically had my trust. I'd been burned before, and I wouldn't let that happen again. My gut told me I could trust her, but my brain hadn't caught up with that. It was still leery, even of family.

"We can talk more about that while you get in the shower."

Carefully, I slid off the bed with her help, the bite of pain a grim reminder of my mortality. I'd willingly thrown myself in front of that bullet for Seamus, a brother I didn't even know, who'd come to rescue me without knowing me either.

That meant something.

I'd lost the one I'd called sister. I couldn't stop her death, and I had no idea where Kenzi was or if she was okay. There was no way in hell I was going to risk losing another family member, one whose eyes lit up when he looked at me.

Like I was something special.

Something precious.

Even Matthias hadn't looked at me that way before. Eyes full of lust and desire, yes. But he'd never looked at me like he couldn't live without me.

Because he could.

My jaw trembled as Nan helped me out of my borrowed button-down shirt. The woman in the mirror was nearly unrecognizable. Her long red hair was dull, covered in dust, a matt of knots on top of her head. Dark bruises covered her from head to toe, varying from deep purple to a jaundice-looking yellow. She was thinner; her curves lessened, ribs showing, face gaunt. The brightness in her emerald eyes was gone, replaced by a wary darkness that had crept in.

All of this damage was caused in just a few weeks.

A white bandage with blood just barely seeping through covered the right side of her abdomen just below her breast.

This couldn't be me.

"It's all right, *an leanbh*," Nan's voice was low and soothing in my ear. "It's merely a graze, and the rest will heal in time. There's no need to cry."

Cry?

Who was crying? Me?

I brought my hand up to my cheek, and no mistake, the wetness of my tears soaked the fingers I traced along their path. I was crying, but all I felt was numb.

"My mother once said, '*Briseann muid ionas gur féidir linn a chur ar ais le chéile níos láidre fós.*'" Nan recited, her Irish accent thickening as she spoke. "It means *we break so we can be put back together even stronger.*"

I swallowed back the lump in my throat.

"I killed him," I whispered, my eyes lowering to the marble tile of the counter. "I'm a murderer."

"Are you talking about the man who was trying to rape

you?" Nan asked. Obviously, someone had filled her in on what happened at the *stables*. All I could do was nod, a fresh wave of tears falling. Nan's slender finger dipped beneath my chin, forcing me to look at her. "There is a difference between murder and survival, my child. The guilt you are bearing is not needed for a man like that and will only weigh you down until it consumes you, and you drown in it."

Dropping her finger, she moved away from the counter, and a moment later, I heard the squeak of metal and the sound of running water. The room began to fill with steam, the heavy presence of heat at my back stilting my anxiety just enough for me to breathe.

"Death in our world is nothing new, and you will need to learn to accept that," Nan continued as she led me to a glass-enclosed shower. The walls were covered in a mystic green hexagonal tile with the glass flanking it on one side. A large, golden rain showerhead with vertical jets took up one side; a perfect complement to the exotic-colored tile below it.

"It sounds harsh," Nan closed the shower door behind me, "but it is necessary to survive."

"What if I don't want to accept it?" I asked curiously as I gently ran a bar of soap along my battered body.

"Then the guilt will consume you and drive you mad," was her simple statement.

I turned her words over in my head, the wheel spinning and spinning as I robotically went through my shower routine with some help from Nan.

She was right. It had been about survival. It was him or me, but wasn't everything in this world? I thought back to the shootout just a few weeks before the wedding. I'd felt such guilt for those men that it affected my sleeping mind. One nightmare after another, their faces flashing before my mind's eye like a broken record.

I doubted they would have felt the same.

No, I knew they wouldn't have.

My whole life, I had allowed myself to be a victim. I'd allowed myself to be used and hurt and broken because I didn't want to be like them. I didn't want to murder or maim or torture. Fighting back meant I would have to hurt someone, and if I hurt someone, I'd be no better than they were. Animals. Killers without a conscience.

But they weren't all that way.

Matthias.

I'd never seen him torture anyone for the fun of it. Never seen him kill because he felt like it. He could have killed Mark after he was done loosening him for information, but he didn't. Elias would have killed everyone in his inner circle for talking to him like Matthias's men did. They weren't disrespectful. They were comfortable, and Elias hadn't allowed his men to be comfortable.

He hadn't wanted comradery and respect built from love and loyalty. Elias wanted respect built from fear, but men who feared you never truly respected you. They'd never be blindly loyal.

Dante's words at the funeral stirred something inside of me.

They aren't your men, Christian.

The tension between the pair had been palpable. Christian didn't respect his uncle or his men, and that was an opening I could work with. Dante wanted the name of Libby's murderer, and I'd give him just what he wanted.

I just needed solid evidence to present to him.

Without Dante's men, Christian had nothing. Elias's men had fled after the Port was seized and his assets frozen.

A dark smile formed on my lips as a plan formed in my head.

I was done allowing myself to be the victim. Done playing the damsel in distress.

Nothing was going to stop me from bringing Christian's empire to the ground, and god help anyone who got in my way.

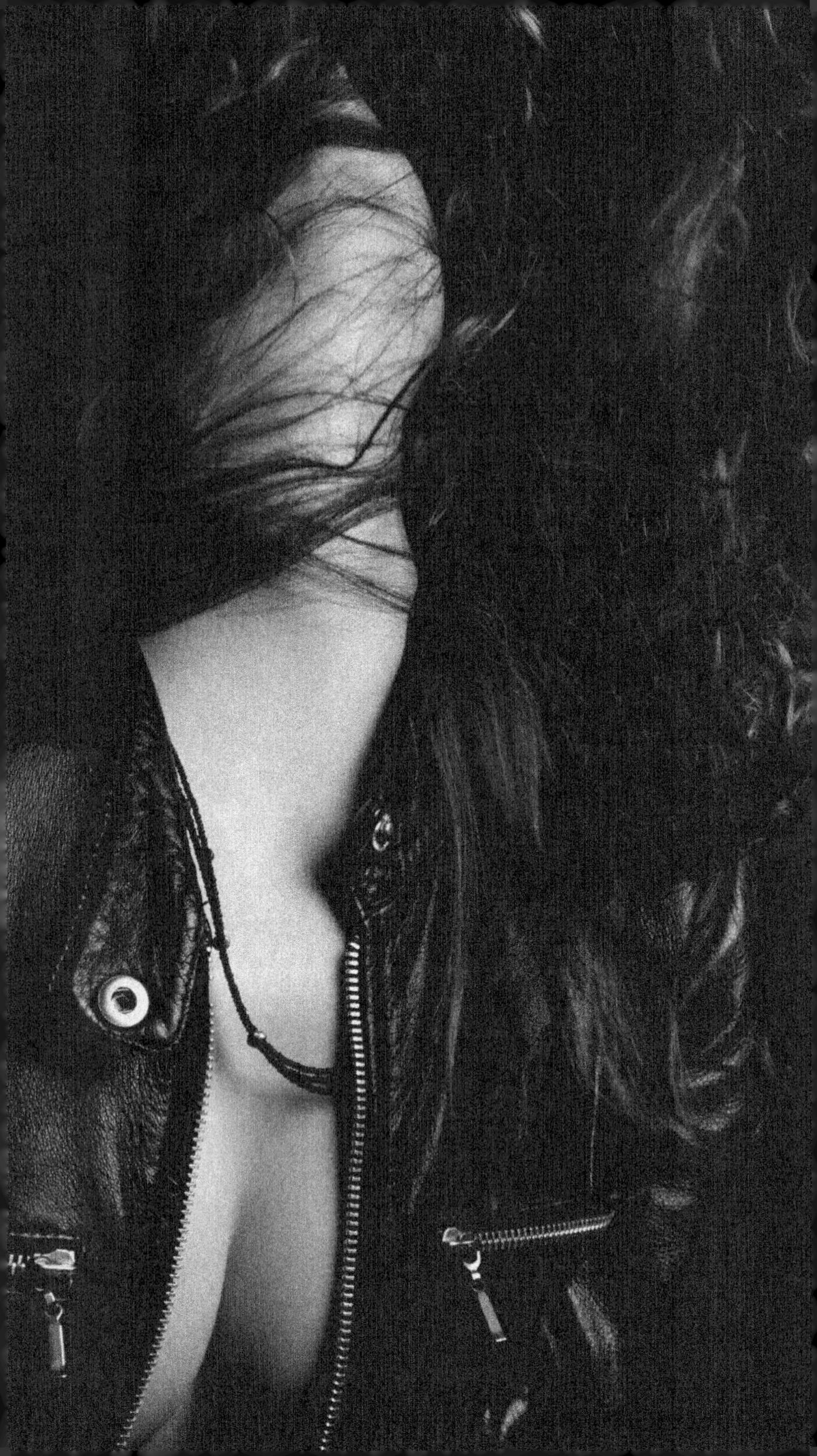

CHAPTER TEN

Ava

Nan helped me dry off and dress in the clothes Marianne had brought. We didn't say any more about the subject of killing or murder. Instead, she busied my mind with talk of her family.

Our family.

I had to keep reminding myself of that.

The twins, Seamus and Kiernan, were the oldest of Marianne and Liam's children. Born barely three months after me. Then Connor and Saoirse, who came a few years later, fraternal twins. The last one was Jack, who was still in high school.

The family, she told me, was split between Boston, Ireland, and Seattle. Liam became the head of the Seattle branch after his father had a stroke. His brother Declyn ran the Ireland branch and their cousin Cian had Boston. All three branches of the Kavanaugh family worked together for the most part but had independent autonomy in their respective cities. They were equals. No one leader answered to another.

Once she was done helping me get ready, she nudged me toward the door and told me to head down to the bar. Someone wanted to see me.

Taking a deep breath, I took one stair at a time down the small stairwell until I hit the bottom. Voices filtered back from the main room, the sound of glass against wood, hushed conversation. I peeked my head around the corner.

I'd never been to an Irish Pub before, but I imagined it probably wasn't too dissimilar to any other one around the city. Or maybe it was. How was I to know?

The space was large, larger than I would've guessed it to be from the outside. A massive wooden bar sat against the wall to one side, lined with crowded green cushioned barstools. A strip of draft handles sat to one side, and just beyond that was a wall covered in a scattered mix of liquor bottles and menus highlighted by a subtle green glow.

A row of pool tables sat up on a dais that extended the length of the bar, accompanied by several dart boards along the back wall. An Irish flag and an American flag were pinned to the ceiling above.

It was a comforting space. Unfamiliar, but it somehow still made me feel—safe.

It was early afternoon, and the bar was nearly empty. A few men I'd seen at the *stables* sat huddled together in one of the booths, beers in hand.

A few tables away sat Liam and the twins. My brothers. *I had brothers, and not the weird, creepy type either.*

I hoped.

There was another man at the table, his back turned to me so I couldn't see who he was.

I hung back, hovering at the threshold, half tempted to flee back to the room I'd woken in. There were still so many unanswered questions. Why had they come for me? How had they even known I was there? Where was Matthias?

I'd thought he'd have been the first one I'd see when I woke up.

Questions swirled in my mind, a strong current dragging me down into the ocean until I was lost in its dark depths. Taking a deep breath, I shoved the anxiety aside, straightened my shoulders, and stepped from the shadows of the doorway.

The minute I did, Liam looked up, his emerald eyes shining with something I couldn't decipher. He stood, the legs of the chair scraping against the wooden floor. The rest of the table followed his gaze, including a pair of eyes I hadn't expected.

"What the hell is he doing here?" My tone was brusque, eyes hard as I took in the man I'd called cousin.

Liam frowned at my tone. "Neil is the one who helped us get you and the other women out of the *stables*."

Good for him.

"Did he also tell you he's the one who put me there in the first place?"

Neil's jaw clenched, his gaze turning to look down at the bottle of beer in his hands.

"Avaleigh—" I cringed at the use of my full name. A reflex. I'd been conditioned to hate it over the years because the only time it was ever used was when I was being punished. Then again, maybe that was how Elias had planned it.

Avaleigh was an Irish name. A reminder to him that I was not his. I'd just never known that.

"Ava," I told him through gritted teeth. "Just Ava."

A sadness seeped into my biological father's eyes, but he didn't say anything more about my name.

"Ava," he amended. "Neil is here under my protection. He risked everything to rescue you. A thank-you should be in order, don't you agree?"

"No," I hissed. "He dragged me from Texas, then forced me to watch my best friend get raped by the man I thought was my brother, which he blamed me for. Then, he ran a truck into the side of my SUV, kidnapped me, and let that motherfucking psycho cattle prod, stun gun, whip, and nearly drown me. So forgive me if I'm not in the mood to say *thank you*."

The twins snickered from their chairs, burying their faces in their beer when Liam shot them a glare.

"First off, watch your language, young lady," Liam turned his attention back to me. "Second, I understand the resentment, Avale—" He cut himself off. "Ava. But you must understand that Neil was in a compromising position. He couldn't help you without letting on that he was passing information."

Neil was a spy? That was news to me.

"He's been spying for you?" I asked incredulously. Liam shook his head.

"No," he said. "He's been spying for Dashkov. Has been for some time."

That couldn't be right. Matthias would have told me if Neil was spying for him. That was our agreement. No secrets when it came to taking down Elias and Christian.

Looking back at the confrontation with Christian before the funeral, Neil had silently warned me not to mention my marriage to Matthias. The only people who knew we were married were Matthias's inner circle and the man who had officiated our shotgun ceremony. Not even his men knew. They all just thought I was a spoil of war.

"That can't be right," I whispered, mostly to myself. "Matthias would have told me."

Kiernan snorted; his face twisted in a way that told me he didn't think I was the brightest crayon in the box.

"You think that man would have given you insider information?" he scoffed. "He'd be an idiot to tell the supposed 'daughter' of the man he was hauling money out of that he had an inside man."

"Since we're married—" I narrowed my eyes at him "—Yes. And watch the tone, *brother*. I took a bullet for you. A *thank you, big sister* would be nice."

Seamus howled with laughter. Even Liam's lips twitched, but Kiernan wasn't having any of it.

"And how stupid was that, aye?" he questioned.

"Stupid?" I asked, dumbfounded. "I took a bullet for you, you bigheaded ginger. That man would have shot you, and you'd be dead."

"I was wearing a bulletproof vest, you moron," he snapped. "The worst I would have gotten was a bruise. You, however, would have died if he'd been aiming any higher."

I blinked.

Shit.

"But...I didn't see a vest."

Kiernan rolled his eyes. "That's the point. If a man sees a bulletproof vest, he automatically aims for weaker points like the head, the legs, or the arms," he informed me. "If they don't think we're wearing them, they aim for the chest. Hurts like hell, but I would've lived."

I'm pretty sure my mouth was popping open and closed like a guppy.

A big fat frickin' guppy.

"As entertaining as this all is," Liam interrupted, pulling out the chair next to him. "I'm tired of standing. Ava, take a seat, please. It appears we have a few extra things to discuss."

Feeling like a chastised child, I did as I was told. Seamus smiled warmly at me as I sat down, then handed me a bottle of water.

"Can't drink while healing." He winked at me before turning to his father.

That seemed unfair.

"You remind me of your mother," Liam told me proudly, his emerald eyes shining with unshed tears. "But I can see my genes have certainly taken over."

I couldn't help but laugh at that.

"It is kind of like looking in a mirror."

"Don't we know it," the twins exclaimed at the same time before bursting into what was no doubt their drunken cackles.

"Did your mom ever..." Liam awkwardly left the sentence hanging, unsure of how to proceed.

"Talk about you?" I finished for him. He nodded, his neck reddening slightly to match his hair.

He was nervous, I realized, and the thought made me smile.

"No." His shoulders slumped forward slightly in disappointment. "But my mother didn't talk about a lot of things. I think, for her, talking about the past was probably a painful reminder of what she'd had to run from."

Liam's brows furrowed in confusion.

"Run from?" he asked. "What do you mean run from? She left. Twice."

Neil coughed awkwardly from his chair before taking a large gulp of his beer. So he hadn't told them anything about my mother.

"My mother didn't run," I snarled at him. "She was kidnapped. Then sold. Then raped and abused."

The table was silent. Even the men in the corner booth had stopped their hushed conversation to look over.

"She never said anything." Liam held my glare. "Not once when she came back after being gone for months. She never once said a thing, and then she was gone less than a week later."

"And so you think she ran? My mother may not have ever talked about you, but that doesn't mean I didn't notice things," I told him. "Like the way she looked at you in every picture I've been able to dig up. Or how she used to say no to the single dads at my school when they asked her out on dates because she'd already met her soulmate. Elias used her as a hostage to keep her parents from expanding into Seattle. I didn't put two and two together at first because all I'd ever grown up knowing was that he was my father. That my last name was Moore."

"How could you possibly know that?" Liam argued. "Just because Elias used you doesn't mean he had..."

"She's telling the truth." Oh, goodie, Neil was finally growing a backbone. "Elias Ward had Katherine McDonough kidnapped and sold at a private virgin auction three days after her disappearance. Originally, his plan was to rape her and give her back once her father backed off the port contracts, but he became—obsessed with her. Took out his sick, twisted fantasies on her."

"And how do you know this?"

Neil sighed. "My father was the one who set it all up, and both of my parents were the ones to help her escape the first time."

"Your parent set it up and then what? Felt bad?" Seamus sneered.

"My father was in debt up to his eyeballs to Elias after a failed business venture," Neil started. "Elias told him that he'd forgive all of his debt if he did him this one favor."

"Kidnap my mother."

Neil nodded at me solemnly.

"From what I've gathered from my father's journals, he hadn't known Elias's full plan or that he would become so entranced by her," Neil continued. "Not until he was invited to a private party, and Katherine was the entertainment. They did things to her that—well, let's just say it wasn't pretty. Two weeks later, my mother stopped by under the pretense of meeting with Kendra. With my father's help, she managed to help Katherine escape without being noticed.

"Elias didn't know how she escaped, and he went searching. Offering a large bounty to anyone who brought her back to him and found out who helped her escape."

My heart was racing and my stomach churning at what Neil was saying.

"Your parents' deaths weren't an accident," I whispered in horror. "Were they?"

Neil shook his head.

"No," he turned to face me fully. "Elias executed them without permission from the Don and set it up to make it look like they died in a car crash."

"Oh my god, Neil." I could feel the tears running down my cheeks.

He didn't let me continue.

"Someone turned Katherine in," he informed Liam. "Someone close to you. She didn't come back under her own power."

"How did she escape the second time?"

"Kendra." Her name poured from his lips in disgust. "She

never liked your mother, and she knew what her having a Kavanaugh baby would mean."

I could sense there was more he wanted to say, but for some reason, he kept quiet.

"I didn't know." Liam's lower lip trembled. I'd never seen a man show this much vulnerability before, especially not in front of his men. "Fuck."

"We can't linger on that anymore." I laid a gentle hand on his shoulder. The motion felt natural, and he didn't pull away. "What we need to focus on is taking down Christian and whoever is pulling his psychotic puppet strings."

Liam stared down at me, our twin-colored eyes meeting in silent acceptance, before shifting his gaze away.

"Okay, little one." He took a deep breath in, letting it out slowly. "What's your plan?"

"We hit him where it hurts, and we use his own family against him," I told my biological father. "He'll never see it coming."

The men at the table nodded as they scooted closer to hear the plan I'd been putting in motion since the funeral.

I realized something in the small, dank cell Christian kept me in. My entire life had always been chosen for me. I'd always been someone's pawn. Elias's, Christian's...Matthias's.

No more.

It was time to take back what I'd never had before.

It was time to become the queen I was always meant to be, and fuck anyone who got in my way.

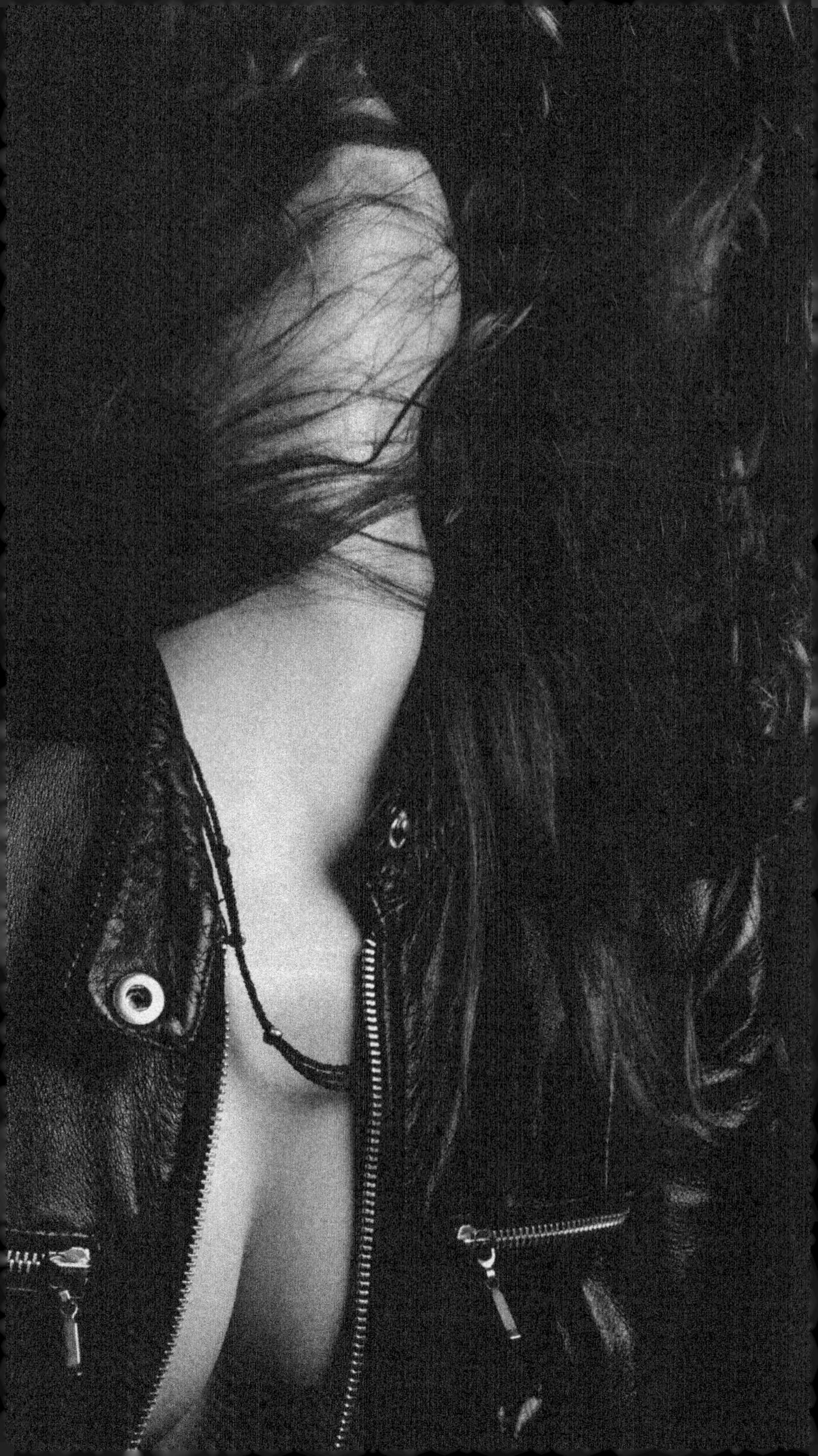

CHAPTER ELEVEN

Ava

I wrung my hands nervously as the phone on the table taunted me.

Coward, it seemed to say. *Pussy.* It wasn't wrong. The plan I'd come up with and we'd begun to perfect hinged on his cooperation. His willingness to help take down Christian and his puppeteer.

What if he didn't want to?

He thinks I betrayed him. That was why he hadn't come for me. The man I'd fallen for who could never love me back.

"You're gonna have to do it sooner or later, lass," Liam leaned the bar on the opposite side, arms crossed against his chest as he fixed me with a knowing look. "Might as well get it over with."

"You don't sound too thrilled about it." I picked up the

shiny black iPhone, running my fingers along the edges, marveling at how light it was. I'd never had a phone of my own before. Not even Matthias had given me one. I thought it was because he hadn't trusted me, even after everything I'd done to show him my loyalty, but I'd come to realize it was a form of control. Like everything else.

Liam snorted. "Am I thrilled at the fact that my daughter, who I hadn't known existed for the last twenty-four years was forcibly married to one of the strongest Bratva *Pahkans* in the nation?" he chuckled mirthlessly. "No. But I learned a long time ago there are no changing things that happened in the past that were out of my control. The only thing you can do is be in the present and take control of the things you can. Like making that phone call."

Without saying another word, he left, leaving me somewhat stunned as I watched him walk away. My biological father was the fucking Irish version of Ghandi.

Christ.

But he was right. I was running scared. Afraid I'd fall back on old habits. It was too easy to become the docile submissive I'd always been. Too easy to let him take control.

It was my turn to captain my life.

Sighing, I unlocked the phone, dialing the one number I knew by heart.

It rang. Once. Twice. Before the telltale sign of someone picking up pitched through the speaker.

"You got a lot of nerve calling here, Avaleigh."

I winced at the use of my full name. He rarely used my full name unless he was upset.

"Some people call it initiative, Matthias," I snarked. "And why give me a number you never wanted me to call?"

"That was before you betrayed me," he growled into the phone.

"I never betrayed you," I whispered sadly. "Not intentionally."

Matthias's laugh was cold. "You honestly expect me to believe that?" he questioned. "You honestly expect me to believe that you weren't working with that FBI agent?"

"I was—" I hesitated. "At first. But he never asked for anything other than that SD drive. I never told him anything about operations or the training center. Or even about us."

"You expect me to believe that?" Matthias scoffed. I could hear the sound of ice clinking against crystal. He was drinking. "You expect me to believe that you didn't give that FBI agent my brother's name? Because he knew it, Avaleigh. He whispered it in my ear and you're the only one who could have told him."

What was he talking about? I'd never given Archer any information on his brother. I'd only ever met with him once before I was taken and even after, I never gave up anything. I wouldn't.

"Fuck you, Matthias," I whispered. "You know I would never do that."

"Well, darling *wife*," he spat out the word like it disgusted him. My chest tightened painfully, tears gathering in the corner of my eyes at his darkened tone. "I don't believe you. Now, if this is all you called for, I have better things to do."

Better things to do.

Fuck him.

"Christian is moving two containers of ammunition in one week," I told him, forcing my tone to go flat. Let him think I'm unaffected by his words and that I don't care.

Because I don't.

Two can play that game.

"And I care why?"

I've never wanted to punch someone so badly before for being a fucking twat.

"Kavanaugh wants to form an alliance against him," I kept going. "If we can start taking out his convoys and find out who is supplying him, we can start taking down whatever he's been building."

"He shouldn't be building anything," Matthias growled. "The DEA froze every Ward asset. There is nothing left for him to build."

I barked a laugh. "Wow," I breathed. "The great Matthias doesn't know everything. How cute."

"Ava." His tone was a warning that I didn't heed. I no longer had to. He had no control over me.

"No, just let me soak in this moment for a second." Letting out a long, happy sigh I counted to five before finally moving on. I didn't have to see Matthias on the other end to know his jaw was clenched, eye twitching, no doubt ready to paddle my ass.

Too bad for him.

"Christian mentioned that there was someone backing him." My breath hitched as I pushed the dark memories to the back of my brain. I could still feel the pain from his beating ghosting along my face and body. The punches. The bruising. That damn cattle prod. "Not only that, but the FBI agent who tried to *blackmail* me, is in on it too. But..." I paused as I searched for the right wording. "He's playing Christian, too I think."

"You think?" The man probably had his eyebrows raised in disbelief, mocking me, even through the phone. I resisted the urge to bite back.

I was the bigger person.

Or so I told myself as I held the phone away from my ear and stuck my tongue out at it.

It's not like he could see me.

"Mark confirmed that Agent Jonathon Archer was real," I continued like I hadn't just acted like a four-year-old who hadn't gotten her lollipop. "But Christian is under the belief that it had all been nothing but a façade. A trick to lure me in."

"He's definitely a real FBI agent," Matthias murmured.

"Christian is also the one who killed Elias." I wondered if Matthias knew that. "And Libby..."

Matthias was silent on the other end for a moment before he let out a long sigh.

"Vas told me about Libby," Matthias murmured, not unkindly. "I didn't know about him killing Elias. Did he tell you why?"

"Because he gave me to you," I answered.

"Makes sense," Matthias sighed. "Christian was obsessed with you and Elias just fed on that obsession."

Wasn't that the truth.

"Whoever was supporting Elias behind the scenes in stealing your shipments is behind it." It made me wonder if it was that mysterious person who also put it in Christian's head to murder Elias. After we took down the port, whoever was supporting him would have been furious and looking for the next best thing.

"You think that same person is backing Christian?" Matthias didn't sound convinced. "Why? What's his motivation?"

"You."

Crickets.

More crickets.

Maybe I'd short circuited his wiring.

"Whoever is pulling Christian's strings is connected," I didn't wait for him to respond, plus, the silence was making me uncomfortable. "And has enough money to fund the operation without any of the Ward assets."

"You're sure it isn't Dante?"

Fair question, but Matthias didn't know about the tension between the uncle and his nephew.

"Definitely not," I assured him. "At the funeral, Dante was ready to pull support from Christian. The only reason he hasn't is because he thinks someone under your command is the one who killed Libby."

"And you didn't think to tell him otherwise while you were talking at the funeral?"

I smiled. So, he'd checked up on me.

"I hinted that it was someone in his own organization." I smiled smugly. "But without solid evidence, he isn't going to take my word that his own nephew had both his brother *and* niece killed."

Matthias huffed out a frustrated breath.

"So, what do you need from me?" he asked. "I assume that's the reason why Kavanaugh had you call. Thought you'd relay his plan better?"

Anger bubbled in my veins. It wasn't my biological father's plan. It was mine.

My plan.

I came up with it and everyone helped fine tune it.

"No," I grit my teeth. "He wanted me to call because it is *my* plan, and it unfortunately needs you."

"Oh, really?"

Smug bastard was smiling. I just knew it.

"Yep," I smacked the 'p'. "So, feel free to come down to McDonough's tomorrow night and have a chat with us. Might even get some free drinks while you're at it."

Matthias chuckled. Actually chuckled. Not a fake one or a humorless one.

"You think I'm dumb enough to walk into an Irish bar unarmed?"

"Did I say anything about weapons?" I asked him as I stood from my stool and walked around to the opposite side of the bar. A drink was definitely needed after this conversation. "Bring a hoard of weapons for all I care, just be here at seven. I'd deflate that ego of yours too a little before you come. Doorways a little narrow so you might not fit in if you don't."

Then I hung up, a small triumphant smile on my face before letting it slip. Sighing, I took a sip of my beer and wondered if he would actually show.

One thing I did know for sure though—everything was about to change.

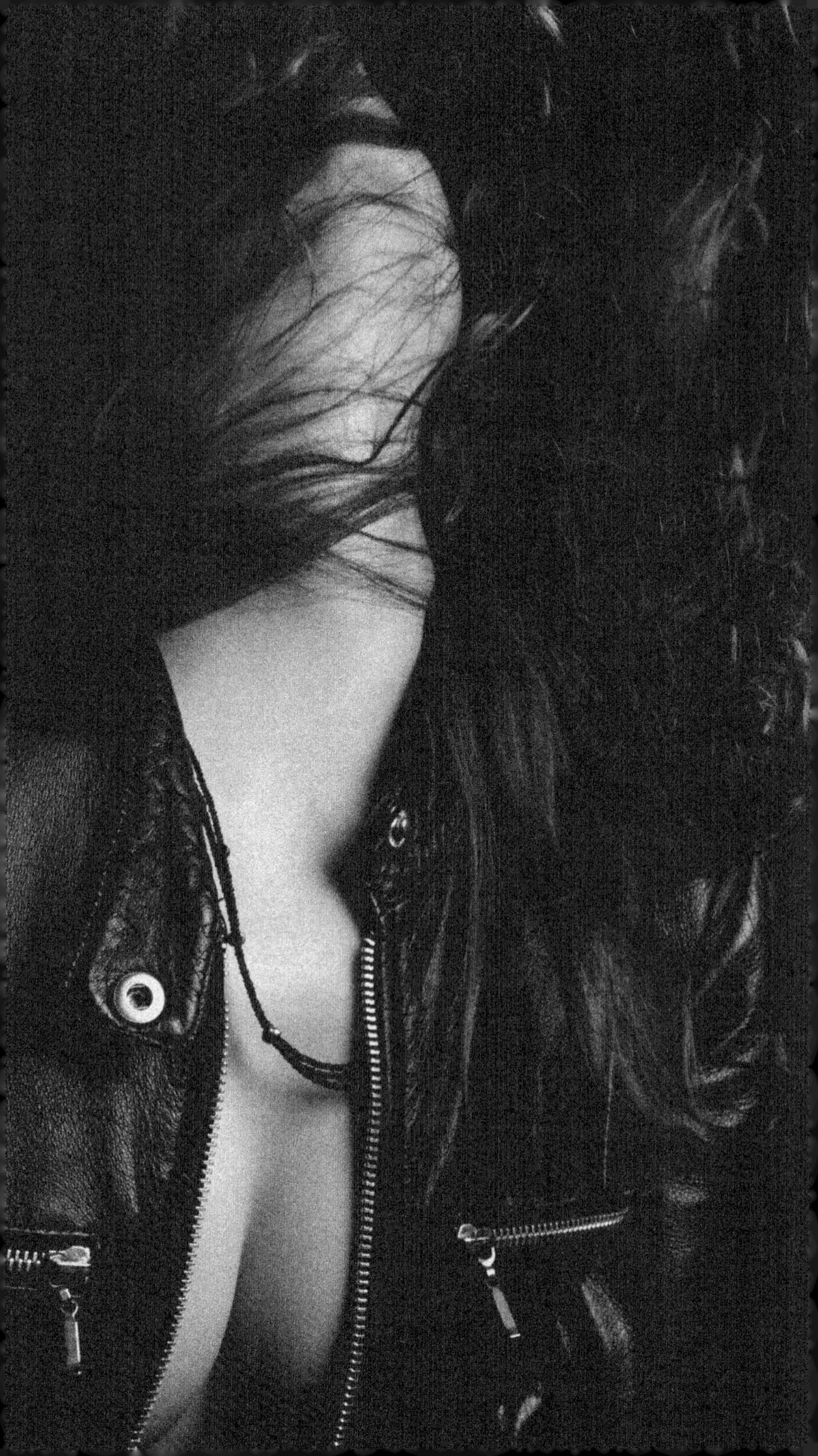

CHAPTER TWELVE

Ava

"You need training, Lass," Liam scolded as I glared at him over a hot cup of coffee. It was the only thing saving my biological father from getting his eyes clawed out at the moment.

Four a.m. Who dragged someone out of bed at four in the morning for training practice? Even six in the morning would have been pushing it but at least I wouldn't have been shooting death glares at him.

The meeting with Matthias and his men had gone surprisingly well. If by well, it meant that he'd practically ignored me the whole time, only speaking directly to me when he needed to and even then, his eyes were never on me, but on some faraway point in the distance.

The others, however, had been excited to see me. Wrapping me up in their warm embraces, fussing over my cuts and bruises. Maksim, who was Matthias's medic on most things, refused to leave without making sure he gave me a full check-up.

"He'll come around." Vas had whispered in my ear as they left. "It's easier to believe you betrayed him than it is to admit he cares for you."

Yeah. Okay.

It hurt me that he'd barely acknowledged me or the plan I'd put into motion. The entire meeting I'd struggled to keep my expression blank and not show the frustration and anger I felt toward him.

All I wanted to do was scream and rage at him. To show him the scars I'd endured and would carry for the rest of my life because I refused to betray him. He said I betrayed him, but I was the one who felt betrayed.

Liam told me why Vas had come to him. Told me that Matthias commanded Vas to stop

"Admittedly, I was a little shocked when the lad showed up at the bar with his men," he told me with a laugh. *"I'd never seen anyone more determined than that man. And to learn you were my daughter. I'd had my suspicions, but to have it confirmed."*

"He broke down crying," Seamus cracked, elbowing me lightly in my uninjured side good naturedly. *"In front of those Russian pricks, nonetheless."*

I ground my teeth against the insult.

"Those Russian pricks are my friends, asshat."

Seamus grinned broadly.

"Oh, I know," he teased. *"But you're so easy to wind up."*

Kiernan snorted.

"Alright now," Liam scolded, but there was no heat behind his words. Instead, he had a glint in his eye that told me he was enjoying the banter. *"Leave her alone, now. We got bigger things to worry about than who she decides to associate with. Even if they are dogs."*

"Hey!"

"Look, lass," Liam fixed me with a stare. *"I don't have anything against the Russians. We've never had any problems with the likes of them, but that doesn't mean this is going to be an easy partnership. I'm willing to put things aside for you. Doesn't mean I like it. Understood?"*

I nodded my head mutely.

For me. That's what he'd said. Not, 'for the greater cause' or 'to get rid of Christian'.

For me.

"This is ridiculous," I muttered as I laid down on the mat covered floor of the gym. McDonough's was larger than I thought. Well, not the bar itself. Looking from the outside McDonough's appeared to be surrounded by several separate businesses. When in fact, they were all connected.

Two doors down, but connected by a long wooden corridor, was a small boxing studio. On the other side was a gun store with an underground gun range and the Kavanaugh Clan owned them all. Plus, a few of the other businesses surrounding the bar.

"It isn't ridiculous if it saves your life," Kiernan growled as he threw a leg over my hip and straddled me, his knees pushing into me on either side. He noticed my wince of pain but ignored it. Instead, he smirked and said, "You're not always going to be in the best fighting shape. You need to learn to move through the pain."

Easy for him to say.

He grabbed a hold of both of my hands in one of his and stretched them above my head.

"This is awkward," I mumbled uncomfortably.

"Only because you're making it awkward, sister," he snapped heatedly. "We're related and I'm teaching you a skill that could not only save your life but one of ours."

"Well, excuse me, Mr. High and Mighty," I hissed. "But my last so-called *brother* wasn't nearly as chivalrous with his wandering hands. So excuse me if it takes a little time to rid those images out of my head."

"You need to get over that," my biological brother growled, his hand tightening on the ones he held within his grasp. Yeah, sure buddy. Getting over psychological and physical trauma is like snapping my damn fingers.

Poof.

Lola's gone.

Wrong.

"Fuck you," I hissed at him as I struggled beneath his body weight. "Let me up you fucking asshole."

"You want up?" He smirked down at me. "Then fucking get up, princess. Work for it. No one is coming to save you and there isn't a stray piece of rock for you to use to bash my skull in."

I let out a strangled howl of rage as I struggled to move my hips beneath his, bucking my body in a vain attempt to dislodge him. It didn't take long for me to tire myself out and my side was aching something fierce.

Once I was panting and sweating, he eased up a bit, one of his ginger eyebrows raised at me mockingly.

"You done?"

Taking a deep breath, I nodded, letting my body relax beneath his. He proved his point. I was useless.

"Good," he smiled down at me genuinely. "Now, I want you to raise your knees, shift your feet towards you."

Doing as I was told I bent my knees until the bottom of my feet were positioned where my knees had been resting. The weight of him dug into my hips a bit harder causing pain to flare in my side, but I could still focus.

"Grab my right wrist with both of your hands," he demanded, and I shifted to comply quickly, wrapping my small hands the best I could over his larger wrists, tightly.

"This next step needs to be done all at once, understand?"

"Okay." Despite my strong assurance, I was unsure and vulnerable. This was completely new to me. No one had ever taught me to defend myself before. Why would they? Elias didn't want me fighting back when he beat me, neither did Christian. Even Matthias hadn't taught me self-defense. Though, I never asked why.

"Using your legs as leverage, you are going to arch your back while keeping your shoulders firmly planted on the floor," he instructed seriously. "Then, you're going to suddenly drop your weight while pulling on my arm with yourleft hand and pushing with your right. If you do this correctly, you'll be able to roll me off you and follow my momentum, reversing our positions. Understood?"

Wow. He was good at this.

Not that I expected him to be, but I hadn't expected him to be such an amazing teacher. Kiernan, I'd come to realize, was more serious than Seamus. I expected it was because he was being groomed to take Liam's spot as the head of the family, but I couldn't be sure.

"I think so."

"Go," he ordered.

I tried not to overthink the moves he'd just given me. I knew the moment that I did I would easily falter and fuck it up. Taking a deep breath, I cleared my mind and imagined the weight pressing down on me was an attacker and not my younger brother.

Using my legs, I braced myself with them for leverage, managing to just barely lift my hips off the ground as they strained against his weight. I clenched my jaw, my teeth grinding as I tried to remain focused. Without thinking, I dropped my weight when my knees began to shake and simultaneously pulled and pushed on his arms ripping his hands from where he'd placed them on my neck before we'd begun.

Kiernan let himself be rolled off me and onto his back, landing on his waistline instead of his hips where I should have.

Whatever. It was good enough for me.

"Good job," Kiernan's voice was filled with pride, a tone I'd rarely heard in my life.

"Now," he grinned as he tackled me to the ground, his hand back on my throat. "Again."

TURNED OUT, I was pretty good at defensive training.

The three of them, Liam, Seamus, and Kiernan rotated when it came to training me. It seemed like they were all versed in different forms of fighting, and one was often better at a particular aspect of training than another.

Kiernan was highly adept at what they called *Dornálaíocht,* which was an Irish style of boxing as well as *Bataireacht,* a form of Irish Martial arts that utilized sticks. Over the past few days this had become a staple in what he had begun to teach me.

"The further away you can keep your opponent, the better chance you have," Kiernan had said. "You can keep them at a distance, tiring them out while still delivering damage."

The first few days, the only damage getting dealt was to me. My welts had welts. That was no joke.

Seamus was more skilled with knives and weapons. He was also a much calmer and more patient teacher than his twin. He broke down each weapon, their purpose, their function, and their pieces, making me take them apart and put them back together again before he'd even let me anywhere near a target.

Same went for the knives. He'd spent what felt like days, but was probably hours, working with a wooden blade, concentrating on my form, technique, and how to tell if a blade was properly weighted, before he finally let me touch one.

Then it was another day or two, okay, hours, of form work with a real blade before he finally deemed me prepared enough to hurl it at a target.

If he wasn't careful, that target was going to be his head.

By the end of the second day, I was exhausted. Run ragged. In desperate need of coffee. Liam's grueling training schedule was going to kill me, and I hadn't even started working with him yet. He hadn't even told me what we would be training on.

Today was the day I would find out.

Eventually.

Right now, it was eight in the morning, and I was dying for a cup of coffee and a hearty breakfast. My stomach growled as Nan busied herself in the kitchen behind the bar, her humming reaching me through the double doors.

When the door to the bar opened, I put on a wide smile, expecting to see my biological father strolling through the door. With my hectic training schedule, I hadn't had much of a chance to do any sort of bonding with him, and I'd been simmering with excitement for whatever he had planned today.

Instead, a scowling Marianne stalked through the door, her eyes narrowed as she huffed and puffed, muttering under her breath. She wasn't usually here this early, or at all. One thing I'd learned over the last few days is that Marianne didn't like to put in the work, she just liked to reap the benefits.

"I don't know what you're playing at, girl," she hissed at me as I took an innocent sip of my coffee. "But don't think you can just waltz in here and change things."

My eyebrows shot up at her acidic tone. I hadn't been trying to change anything aside from my mission to eliminate Christian. I didn't much care about the daily running's of the Irish mob. I'd done everything to keep my nose out of everything that didn't involve my mission. As far as I was concerned, it wasn't my business. I was a Kavanaugh by blood, but that was it, and Liam hadn't made it seem like he wanted to include me in anything, anyway.

"I don't know what you're talking about," I sighed, setting down my coffee. "I haven't tried to change anything. All I care about is my mission. That's it. If you think otherwise, then you're just being delusional."

Marianne glared at me, her jaw clenching so hard I swore I heard her teeth crack.

"Play the innocent act all you want," she hissed. "But I'm not stupid. You're just like your mother. Sticking your nose where it doesn't belong."

Her glare diminished slightly at my sudden burst of laughter.

"What do you think is so funny?" she asked, her tone dripping acid.

"For someone who said they were my mother's best

friend," I told her. "You sure are quick to villainize her. I wonder why that is?" My head cocked to the side to examine her.

She'd done nothing but avoid me since our first meeting in my temporary room upstairs. For someone who'd told me she could tell me stories about my mother growing up, the only time I'd ever seen her was for dinner. The Kavanaugh's cherished their nightly family dinners but even then, Marianne had done nothing but avoid conversation with me.

"I don't know what you're talking about," Marianne denied, her throat bobbing nervously. "But I do know that you walk into our lives and suddenly Liam has all these grand ideas. Ideas he doesn't need to put into *my* children's heads. And let me tell you..."

"I wonder why someone who'd been my mother's best friend since childhood wouldn't follow up on her missing persons case." I held up my hand to interrupt her, not caring for whatever she was about to say next. "Or how about how you didn't file that report sooner."

"I didn't know she was missing," Marianne shrugged, but I could see the stiffness in her shoulders.

"When people lie, it shows not only in their face, but their body." Matthias's voice rang through my mind. *"Their face tightens, they'll look you straight in the eyes, their fists might clench with no signs of real anger. Their shoulders will stiffen as they try to hold themselves erect. Making them look more honest. It isn't just about micro expressions. It's about examining their body as a whole and using it against them."*

She was lying.

"Really?" My head tilted to the side, eyes widening. "Katherine McDonough never missed a class, and she couldn't have been with Liam because he'd been out of town with his uncle that week. Not to mention that you conveniently forgot to report the fact that your dorm had been broken into the day she went missing."

"I don't know—"

"Now, you were either just being a negligent friend *or* you had a hand in her disappearance," I leaned forward, bracing my elbows on the sleek bar top beneath them. "Trust me when I say that if I find out you had anything to do with my mother's kidnapping...I will kill you and I'll be sure you see it coming."

Marianne's face darkened, her hazel eyes glaring daggers as her lips turned into an ugly sneer. This was the real Marianne. The demon beneath the motherly, caring façade.

"Listen here, you little bitch," she snarled. "If you think you can threaten me, think again. There's more here at work then you will ever know, and I can't wait till you end up just like your..."

"Breakfast is ready, dear," Nan's smiling voice sliced through the bitter tension as she swept into the room carrying a large quiche and a small plate of fruit. She sat them before me, pulling a slice of mouthwatering quiche from the pan and placing it on the small plate of fruit in front of me. "Eat up. You're going to need it to deal with your father."

Your father. She said it so casually. I hadn't even called him that. Just Liam. But it wasn't like he called me his daughter. Barely even referenced me being that. It didn't hurt my feeling that he didn't refer to me as his daughter or introduce me as a Kavanaugh.

Because I wasn't.

I was a Dashkov and the two of us barely knew each other.

Seamus and Kiernan, however, went around telling everyone I was their big sister. The twins seemed to enjoy not being the eldest.

"Marianne," Nan turned to her daughter-in-law with a scowl on her face, finally acknowledging her presence after she'd put away her own healthy dose of breakfast. "Shouldn't you be doing inventory? I know you rarely deign yourself to come and help out down here, but you can at least do that, right?"

Marianne let out a frustrated growl as she slammed her own cup of coffee down on the bar, the liquid sloshing over, before stomping into the back room, leaving the two of us to giggle conspiratorially at her departure.

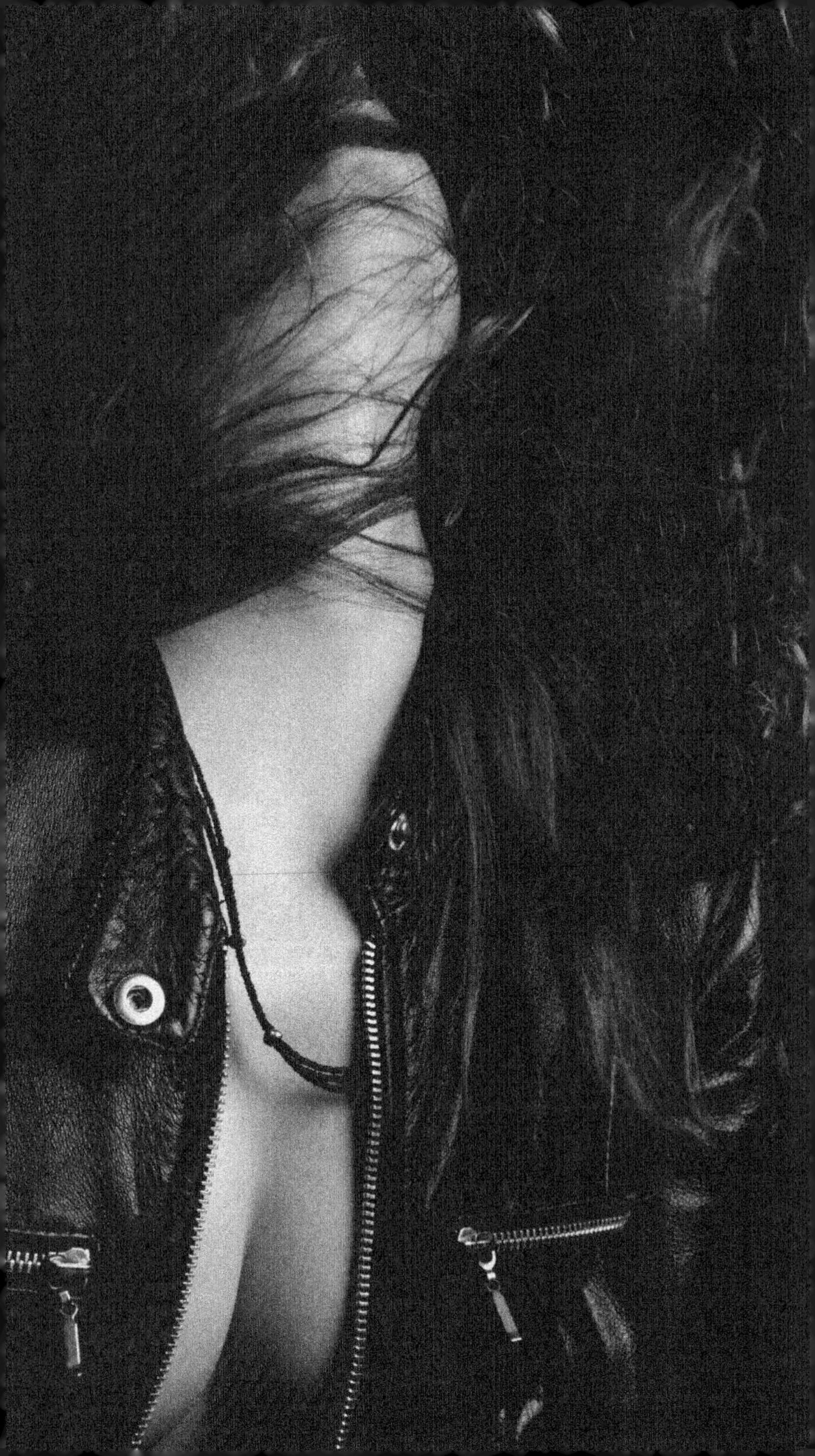

CHAPTER THIRTEEN

Ava

"Where are we going?" I asked Liam as he drove through the streets of the city toward the port. Not long after Marianne huffed her way into the back for inventory, Liam walked through the door with a wide grin stretched across his face.

"You'll see." He smiled over at me as he pulled into a large barren parking lot strategically dotted with orange traffic cones. It looked like a course, but I couldn't make out what each station was for.

Liam parked his black Porsche Panamera in front of a painted-on white line, similar to a racer's starting line, and killed the engine. "Come on." He motioned for me to get out, and I easily obeyed, excitement thrumming in my veins as I took everything in.

"Each set of cones is designed to guide you through different situations you may encounter on the streets," he told me, his hands slipping casually into his jacket pockets. He looked completely at ease, like he'd done this a time or two. Or four, since that was how many siblings I had that had reached driving age. "It's designed to not only teach you the rules of the road but also how to evade, how to lose a tail, and a few other maneuvers we will do as you become more confident behind the wheel."

I stared out at the course, dumbfounded. "You're teaching me how to drive?"

"Neil mentioned that you were never taught." Liam looked down at me. There was no pity in his gaze, just a warm kindness and a lingering sadness. "Every father should have the opportunity to teach their children to drive. You're my daughter, Ava, and I am honored to have this chance."

Well, balls.

What does a girl say to that?

Nothing. Because I had no words. Instead, I smiled up at him, nodding my head with tears dancing in my eyes as he handed me the keys and motioned his head toward the driver's side. An embarrassing squeal left me as I practically flew to the other side of the car, eagerly encasing myself inside the powerful machine.

"All right now, lass," Liam's deep tone was intense as he buckled himself into the seat next to me. "There are a few things we need to go over before you can hit the course."

I nodded my head. Smart idea. I was aware of where the brake and gas pedal were, but that was about the extent of my knowledge. At least he wouldn't be giving me an in-depth history lesson on cars.

"Now, the first car was made in 1886 by a man named..."

I couldn't help the frustrated groan that left my lips, and

when I looked over at Liam, he was beaming at me, his eyes twinkling with mischief as he took in my expression, which no doubt said, *are you fucking serious, dude?*

"Oh, Seamus was right," he chuckled. "If looks could kill, lass, I'd be burning in my seat right now."

Shaking my head, I rolled my eyes heavenward before taking a deep breath and relaxing into my seat. He continued chuckling under his breath at his little joke while he explained each button, switch, signal, and pedal.

I listened with rapt attention, taking in his calm, assuring tone as he taught me. He was patient, more so than either Kiernan or Seamus, and answered my questions without making me feel stupid or useless.

The only thing missing was the one person besides my mother that I wanted to share this experience with, and if that didn't tell me how bleak my life was, I didn't know what would.

"CAN I ask you something about my mother?"

The comforting silence of the ride back to the bar was blissful. We'd spent hours on the course as he ran me through drill after drill. I was by no means Richard Petty, but I could at least perform the basic functions of driving.

For the most part.

A few cones might have been sacrificed for the greater good.

I turned my gaze reluctantly away from the orange and pink that streaked across the sky as the sun settled itself behind the tall steel trappings of the city. Liam kept his eyes on the road, his face calm. The only thing giving away his discomfort at the mention of my mother was the white across his knuckles as he gripped the steering wheel tighter.

"Of course." The words were tight, his jaw clenched.

"The police report stated that you were out of town the week of her disappearance," I began, twisting my fingers in my lap nervously. "Where did you go?"

Liam sighed, running his free hand through his graying hair.

"Your mother and I were one of the lucky ones," he started. "A betrothed couple actually in love with one another. The contracts were already signed. It was all set that as soon as we finished college, we'd be married. That week, your mother's father, your grandfather, wanted me to investigate a business offer in Portland."

"What kind of business?"

"Ground transportation company called Lion's Share," he told me without hesitation. "If we bought the company, it would provide another way to transport drugs and weapons across the nation and Mexico without raising suspicion."

"Because the trucking company itself was legit?"

Liam nodded. "Yes. It isn't uncommon for Mafia families to buy established, legit companies to move their illegal products. But it also provides an income that is legal."

"That's why Matthias targeted Ward Enterprises, isn't it?"

"Yes," he acknowledged, a stunned look crossing his face. "The difference is that Matthias didn't buy out the company. He bought out Ward's debt instead, because as a newer power in the city, at the time, it would have been more suspicious."

"Whereas quietly buying Ward's debt let Matthias stay in the shadows," I pondered thoughtfully. "And then any kind of heat would come down on Elias and not him."

"Exactly." Liam smiled. "It was smart on Matthias's part,

but there is always a small caveat when you don't fully own and operate a business."

"Elias got greedy." Everyone knew that. "He didn't want to keep giving up part of his profit, so he tried to cut Matthias out by stealing his shipments and reselling them. He probably thought he could blame the thefts on another gang."

"You're pretty perceptive."

I smiled sheepishly at the compliment. "I paid attention. People talk when they think you're too stupid to listen. Or when they believe they have a firm hold on you."

"Well, they're the stupid ones if they didn't see the snake hidden in their grass." He said it with a proud smile on his face; being called a snake didn't irritate me. It was true. Elias never saw me coming when we hit the port. Never bothered to consider what I might do with the information he so freely talked about in front of me.

"Who told you she ran away?"

"Ava." Liam pursed his lips together, his forehead furrowed.

"Was it Marianne? She lied," I pointed out desperately. "I have proof that my mother was kidnapped a full week before she filed the police report and—"

"Enough, Avaleigh." His booming voice filled the small space as he parked the Porsche in the back parking lot of the bar where the employees kept their cars. I flinched at the use of my full name. "I will not have you throwing accusations at people. She is my wife, and you will therefore resp—"

"Respect her?" I sneered at him. "You people are all the same. Respect is earned, not freely given. I've lived my whole life having 'respect' beaten into me. There is only one person I respect, and he—"

"Isn't here, is he?" Liam interrupted coldly. "Barely looks at you. Didn't bother to ask if you wanted to come home with him. He left you here, face that. You may respect him, but he doesn't respect you."

"Neither do you," I hissed, unbuckling my seatbelt. "I'm telling you that something is off with Marianne. Whether she was involved in my mother's kidnapping or not, she is hiding something."

"You don't know anything, little girl," he seethed. His emerald eyes bored into mine, a mirror image. "I went into that police station every day waiting to hear something. Waiting to either identify Katherine's body or welcome her into my arms. Nothing. And then she suddenly shows up months later, and you expect me to believe she was kidnapped?"

"She was!" I insisted, my voice pitching in desperation as I pleaded with him to believe me.

"She left a fucking note!" he roared. "Two weeks after Katherine miraculously appeared back in my life, I woke one morning to find her gone and a note left on the bedside table. She didn't want to be with me. She didn't want this life."

"Then why didn't she go back home?" I asked. "Why run away to Portland and change her name? Why hide me? None of it makes any sense, and Marianne—"

"Enough about my wife!"

He leaned forward like he was going to slap me, and instinctively, I shoved myself against the passenger side door, covering my face with my hands and clenching my eyes tightly shut.

Silence.

The blow didn't come.

Cracking an eye open, I peeked between the slits of my fingers to find him staring at me, eyes wide, mouth slightly open as he took in my defensive position. He mumbled something under his breath before hastily exiting the car, slamming the door behind him.

I waited.

One moment.

Then another, before following behind him, being sure to keep my distance. The alleyway behind the bar was quiet, the streetlamps just beginning to flicker on as darkness descended. I followed him through the large metal door, through the kitchen, and into the bar, where I watched him stalk angrily up the stairs without a backward glance.

So much for that relationship.

I was pretty sure I bombed that worse than my tenth-grade calculus test.

Wonderful.

"I take it driving lessons didn't go so well?" a voice asked from beside me.

"The driving lessons went great," I muttered petulantly. "Then I had to go and open my big mouth."

"You always did have a hard time keeping shit to yourself."

"Fuck off, Neil," I growled. "I'm still furious at you."

Neil ignored me. "What did you say that made him so mad?" he asked curiously as he slid behind the bar like he owned the place. "Liam Kavanaugh has always been known to be pretty levelheaded, and he looked like he was about two seconds away from a nuclear explosion."

"I asked about my mother."

"And?" Neil pushed as he took down two-pint glasses and began filling them with beer.

"I may have insinuated that his wife had something to do with my mother's disappearance." Saying it out loud made me cringe.

"That'll do it." Neil chuckled as he came back around the

side of the bar, beers in hand. "Here. Let's sit and down, and you can tell me why you think your stepmother is evil, little Cinderella."

I snorted at the reference. "If anything, I'd be Rapunzel," I pointed out, taking the beer from him but making no attempt to move. "And second, I'm not telling you jack shit until you tell me what the hell you were doing straddling both sides of the fence."

"Look, Ava..." Neil started, but I wasn't hearing any of it. Not anymore. I wanted answers.

"No, Neil," I bit out. "You suddenly want to bond and talk after what you did to me? After what you let Christian do to me? To Maleah?"

His face darkened at the mention of my best friend's name.

"You don't get to pretend like everything is all right," I fumed, holding the beer glass tightly in my hand to steady my raging emotions. "You were one of the few people I thought I could count on. The one who always made things better after they got worse. The one who let me cry on his shoulder, who helped nurse me back to health, and then suddenly you're this emotionless cunt. You want to bond? Start with how the fuck you started spying for Matthias."

"We're gonna need more beer."

***

"Elias went mental when you disappeared," Neil began. We were sitting in one of the back corner booths, away from prying eyes and ears. Not that there was anyone at the bar besides the opening staff, but Neil was on edge. "He had every available man out searching for you day and night, and after a week, when nothing came of it, things turned for the worse."

Neil took a shaky breath.

"I'm not sure what he had over Uncle Dante, but whatever it was must have been big and damaging enough to get him to drag in every family member who'd refused to be inducted." Neil took a gulp of his beer. "Anyone who refused or tried to run and hide was beaten down. Made examples of."

"What? Dante would never do that."

It was one of the things I loved about the man I'd called my uncle for so long. He and Matthias had similar ways of running their organization, especially when it came to forced induction.

"If you force a man to do your bidding, he will never be truly loyal," he told me once. *"The first chance he gets, he will stab you in the back for his freedom. True loyalty and respect are earned. Loyalty and respect caused by fear of death are false."*

Neil shook his head. "Not Dante." He gritted his teeth. "Elias."

That made more sense.

Man had been a sociopath.

His son was a psychopath.

Soon one would be joining the other.

"One night, Elias took all the younger new recruits up to the *stables.*" Neil's jaw clenched, his grip on his glass tightening. My stomach clenched painfully at the thought of what was coming next. I knew Elias and how he thought boys should become men. "He stood us in the corridor and told us to pick a door."

Tears gathered at the corner of his dark eyes, his gaze dropping to the table as he tried to put some distance between himself and the memory.

"They made us..." Neil let out a small sob, a few tears dripping onto the wood of the table. "They watched, Ava. They fucking watched and laughed, and I couldn't let that go."

He let out a choked sigh as he rubbed at his eyes to clear away the tears. The weakness. The vulnerability. Everything he learned to bury had rushed to the surface, and now he was forcing it deep beneath the ground to rot and fester.

"What happened after?" I asked after he'd downed the rest of his beer and grabbed another.

Neil huffed out a breath. "I betrayed them. The *Famiglia*. I waited a few days before going down to the 85th Precinct. One that neither Elias nor Dante had control over. I'd thought if I could find a detective not associated with either of them, I'd get lucky. Give my testimony in exchange for witness protection or some bullshit. Instead, I got Detective Moreno." Neil scoffed. "A fucking dirty cop working for Dashkov. He told me we were going someplace without so many ears, and like a goddamn idiot, I believed him."

"He took you to Matthias." It wasn't a question. I knew that was what had to have happened. I was just a fan of stating the obvious, apparently.

"Yep." Neil popped the *p* gratingly. It's where I'd learned it, and I couldn't help the small smile that graced my lips at the memory. His answering smile told me he was thinking of the same memory. "He didn't threaten me or beat me. He and his men simply offered me an opportunity. If I spied for them and helped them take Elias down, I could leave scot-free and never look back. He said he'd give me money, a new identity, everything I needed to start over."

"That was a risky deal," I told him. "What would have happened if you got caught? You would have just been dead."

Neil shrugged. "I died the moment they made me pick a

door," he admitted. "And each time I was forced to look the other way killed me just a bit more. A small pick chiseling away at me inch by inch, and then when he took..."

"Maleah," I breathed. Neil's face darkened at my best friend's name.

"Yeah." He took another gulp of his beer.

"Are you out now?" I asked. "Did you get what you were promised?"

"He offered it to me," Neil admitted with a shrug. "But I'm waiting."

My brows snapped together as I tried to analyze what he was telling me. What was he waiting for?

"On what?"

Neil's lips twisted into a cruel smile. "To fucking kill Christian for what he did to Maleah. Then, and only then, will I leave this city behind. I don't care if I have to burn everything to the ground. I'm going to find her, and I'm going to rip him limb from limb until there is nothing left."

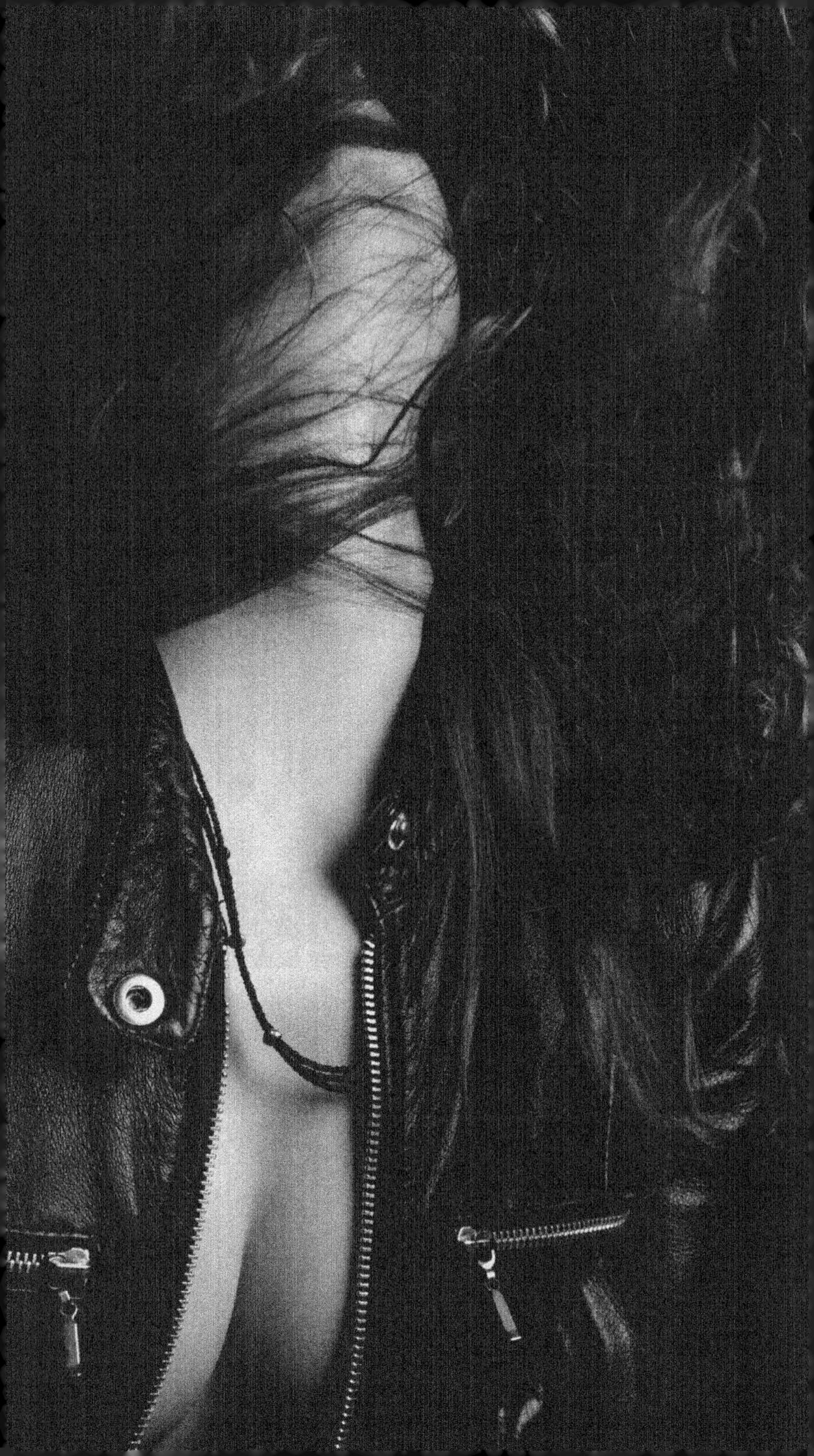

CHAPTER FOURTEEN

Ava

A few days later, I found myself pacing anxiously outside of Liam's car on the edge of one of the old shipping docks Dante used to secure his more illegal goods. It was a small port that rarely saw any traffic outside of fishing vessels, but it was the best place to hit.

I'd managed to piece a few of my more lucid memories together. I hadn't spent my entire time in that cell. Christian had dragged me to a few of his meetings in the main building not far from the *stables*. Parading me around behind him while I was nearly naked seemed to keep him in less of a foul mood.

"They're five minutes out." Seamus pulled the phone away from his ear.

Matthias was almost here.

"How many men?" Liam asked. His own men shifted uncomfortably in the background. Some of them had made their dislike about working with Matthias known, but that rebellion had been squashed pretty quickly.

The Irish were still growing in the Pacific Northwest, and unlike the Bratva, they didn't have large numbers to draw from. They were, for all intents and purposes, still considered a gang by most standards. Limited in number and assets.

In order to pull this off, we needed the skills and men that Matthias could provide.

"Fifty on site, plus two snipers and a hacker with infrared."

I smirked. Mark. Vas had told me that he was indeed alive, even after his betrayal, just grounded. Which meant he wouldn't be leaving the compound anytime soon and was being heavily monitored.

Better than dead.

Headlights bobbed in the distance, tires sloshing through mud puddles as Matthias's convoy approached. Jesus, I was sweating like a nun cornered in a whorehouse. Liam had tried to convince me to stay behind. He didn't like putting me in the line of fire, and neither did the twins, but I was set on this.

It was my plan, and I wasn't going to let them get into the thick of it without me.

"What the hell is she doing here, Kavanaugh?" Matthias's tone held a deadly edge to it that sent a shiver of wanton desire up my spine.

I never thought I'd say this, but—I needed to get laid.

"It's her plan, and she wanted to come along," Liam replied casually, without raising his voice.

"Fuck that," Matthias hissed angrily. "She doesn't have any defense training. She'll get killed."

Liam shrugged nonchalantly. "What would you have me do? Tie her up and put her in the trunk?"

"Yes," Matthias growled. My biological father laughed.

"Okay, Dashkov." He pointed a finger at me. "Have at it. Good luck, though. The twins made sure she was well prepared for tonight, and I doubt your wife will submit as easily now as she once did. By all means, go right ahead. Just don't come crying to me when she hands you your bollocks."

I struggled to keep my face impassive as Matthias scrutinized me, his forehead creasing as he stared me down, eyes narrowed. Liam was bluffing. Mostly. The twins had been teaching me weapons and self-defense, and according to them, I was a quick learner, but Matthias had something I didn't.

Time.

A reason to fight.

I was no match for him. But Liam had gotten one thing right. There would be no going down without a fight. Because, well—fuck him.

"She gets killed; it's on you." My husband pointed a finger at my biological father, who only smirked at the subtle threat.

"Don't worry, Mr. Russian," Seamus drawled. "Kiernan and I have Ava duty. You really should give her some credit though. She's more talented than you think."

"I don't need you to tell me about my wife, *kid*," he sneered. "I'm well aware of her talents."

Don't blush. Don't blush. Don't blush.

Shit.

I could feel the heat creeping up my neck at his words. I'm pretty sure the talents he was referring to were not how well I was doing with firearms.

Pretty sure, anyway.

"All my men are in position." Liam broke the tense silence that hung in the air at Matthias's last comment. "I've got men on the south entrance, and the rest are spread throughout the small port, disguised as security guards. Don't shoot any of them, please. They can be identified by a red ring around their left upper arm."

Matthias turned his hardened gaze to him and nodded.

"My men are covering the north entrance, as well as the high ground." He was all business now. "I've got several container trucks ready to go as backup on the water if needed."

"We're still not sure if it's human cargo or not," I spoke up, joining the small circle of men that had begun to form near the two mob leaders. "We need to make sure we aren't shooting into the containers until we know what's being transported."

Maksim, who'd come up behind me, made a disgruntled sound.

"I don't like going in with an unknown." His thick Russian accent startled some of Liam's men. A few of them were looking up at the Russian giant with wide, fearful eyes. I couldn't blame them. The man was massive and could snap half of the men here like twigs.

"Everything is solid," Kiernan spoke up. "The only unknown is the cargo itself. We've got tabs on every guard, hobo, port official, and tiny dicked Italian in the place."

Vas, who'd silently joined the group, snorted in amusement.

"No one here wants to be responsible for accidentally killing helpless women." My pulse wobbled when Matthias's gaze turned back to me. Warmth flooded my stomach, a tingling sensation building between my legs at his intense stare. His stormy eyes held mine, and I thought I saw a flicker of longing, but there was no way to be sure. It was gone faster than I could blink.

SHATTRED REMNANTS

"Fine," Maksim growled. "Clock is ticking."

Everyone nodded and filed back toward their respective cars, except Matthias. He was leaning in close and whispering something angrily to Liam, who just laughed and nodded his head at my husband like he was a puppy rather than a giant wolf.

Shaking my head, I made my way back toward Liam's SUV.

"Not you, Ava," Liam hollered to me, jerking his thumb back at my burly Russian husband. "Change of plans. You're going with him."

"Da!" the twins exclaimed at the same time.

"Don't *da* me," he scolded them. "He's better equipped to keep her safe, and the two of them have some marital kinks to work through. Don't you think?"

I cursed under my breath. If he meant that Matthias would ignore me the entire operation, then yeah, we were working through so many kinks.

"He promised me he wouldn't throw you in the trunk," Liam added, as if that small bit of information would help.

"Could still throw me in the water though," I pouted, grabbing my pack from Seamus's hand. I shot him a small smile before turning to where my husband and his entourage waited. Shoot me now.

"Let's go, Ava," Matthias barked. "Time is ticking."

Liam grinned broadly down at me as I shot him a glare, hoping it would melt his face off. No such luck. This was payback for our conversation about Marianne. I just knew it.

"Coming, darling." I smiled sweetly at my husband, my voice drenched in saccharine as I made my way toward him. Vas barked a laugh.

"Let's do this." The jovial Russian clapped his hands together in anticipation. Matthias simply grunted as he slid into the passenger seat of the vehicle, not bothering to open the back door for me first like he used to.

"In you go." Vas winked at me as he held open the door, allowing me to slide into the back seat.

"Everyone in position." Mark's voice crackled through the small radio that was mounted on the dash. "Keep everything in the shadows. You've got two large cargo trucks three clicks out from the north entrance."

Luckily it was one of our men on the gate.

We sat in silence. The tension in the car was stifling as we waited in the shadows for the trucks to pass through the gate. Once we knew where they were going, we could pursue. The plan was in place, set to near perfection.

Jake, our man on the gate, would routinely check their credentials while simultaneously sticking a small tracker on the side of one of the trucks. From there, we would be able to triangulate their position and follow them in.

Mark's infrared drone was hovering above the small port, giving him a real-time feed of the area. He'd be able to inform us of how many men were in the trucks, positions, and any surprises that might come up.

Easy as pie.

I hoped.

"You're staying in the car, Ava," Matthias finally spoke, his tone grave as he slid the slide of his gun back to double-check there was one in the chamber. Vas did the same with his. "There is no reason to be out there where you could get hurt."

I scoffed. "Thanks for showing concern," I sneered as I checked my own gun. A decently sized Smith and Wesson 9mm. Perfect for me. "But you won't be able to access the digitalized containers without me. I'm the one with the codes, and I'm not sharing."

Matthias snorted derisively.

"Assuming he didn't change the codes."

I missed him calling me Red. Or Krasnyy. Fuck, I wished we could go back to that. To before the staunch silence and titanium walls he'd erected between us.

"By all means, Matthias," I shot back at him, gesturing toward the port. "Feel free to conduct this plan without me. Let me know how that goes."

"We need her, boss." Vas leveled a hard gaze at his *Pahkan*. "You know that. Stop being so fucking stubborn." A beat passed before he tacked on a respective if not somewhat sarcastic "sir."

Matthias growled, the sound coming from low in his chest. It made me shiver, an unwanted flush creeping up my neck, heat suffusing my cheeks.

Fucking body didn't seem to be getting the message that we weren't on team asshole now. Traitor. But man, did I miss the sex.

So badly.

Goosebumps littered my skin as I recalled the gentle caress of his rough hands on my skin. His hot mouth sucking on my puckered nipple as he teased my clit with his fingers.

My body remembered what it felt like to be held by him. Dominated by him. Even when my mind wanted to erase the memories, they held on tight like a desperate man on a sinking ship. We were explosive together. Two broken halves of the same coin that didn't quite fit back together the way we had before.

"Trucks are coming your way."

Shit. Now was not the time to be getting sentimental about the past.

Or turned on by it.

The three of us tensed, holding our breath in anticipation

as the two trucks rolled by us toward the gate. Vas's hands tightened on the steering wheel as he watched the security feed from the small display they'd rigged over the radio.

None of us uttered a word as we watched Jake smile at them, his body relaxed and at ease as he checked the driver's credentials in the first truck. Then the second. This would only work if they didn't suspect him. It was a risky move, replacing the guard at the gate with one of our own. But it was necessary. One of Christian's men could have seen us sitting in the shadows or recognized any one of the men we'd used to replace the guards.

It was lucky for us that Christian used a private security firm to roam the port and not Dante's men. It would have required a whole new strategy. One that would have been riskier. I'd prepped Jake on how to act. What to say. He'd been the perfect fit with his coal black hair. We added caramel contacts to make him look more Italian, because green eyes were a dead giveaway, and made him watch a few horrible Italian movies to help him with the accent.

Not the best plan, but it looked like it was working, and that's what mattered.

A few moments later, Jake was waving the two trucks through the gate, and we were all set.

"We're a go," Jake whispered through the radio.

"Location thirty-six Alpha," Mark's voice crackled. "Twelve north, four east, five north, and eight west. Identification codes, 27-43-45 and 27-43-46."

Well, that was confusing as fuck.

"Let's move," Matthias ordered as he got out of the SUV.

Taking a calming breath, I moved to do the same, only to find him blocking my path as I went to climb out.

"You gonna move?" I asked.

"You stay between me and Vas," he whispered dangerously. "If anyone starts shooting, you fucking duck and hide."

"I can handle myself, Matthias." I attempted to push past him, but his large, calloused hand on my throat stopped me. My pussy clenched at the familiar action.

Hussy.

"I mean it, Ava." His lip curled up on one side.

"This isn't how it works, Matthias. You made your choice, husband. Showed your cards." I leaned forward against his hand, the pressure on my neck sending delicious tingles through my body, and whispered in his ear. "You don't control me anymore."

Before he could see what was happening, I grabbed the hand that held my throat and twisted before applying added pressure to his elbow and forcing it in the opposite direction. The large Russian stumbled back, eyes wide, pupils dilated as he took me in.

He should have seen the joint lock coming, but like most men I knew, he underestimated me.

Now he could clearly see who he was dealing with.

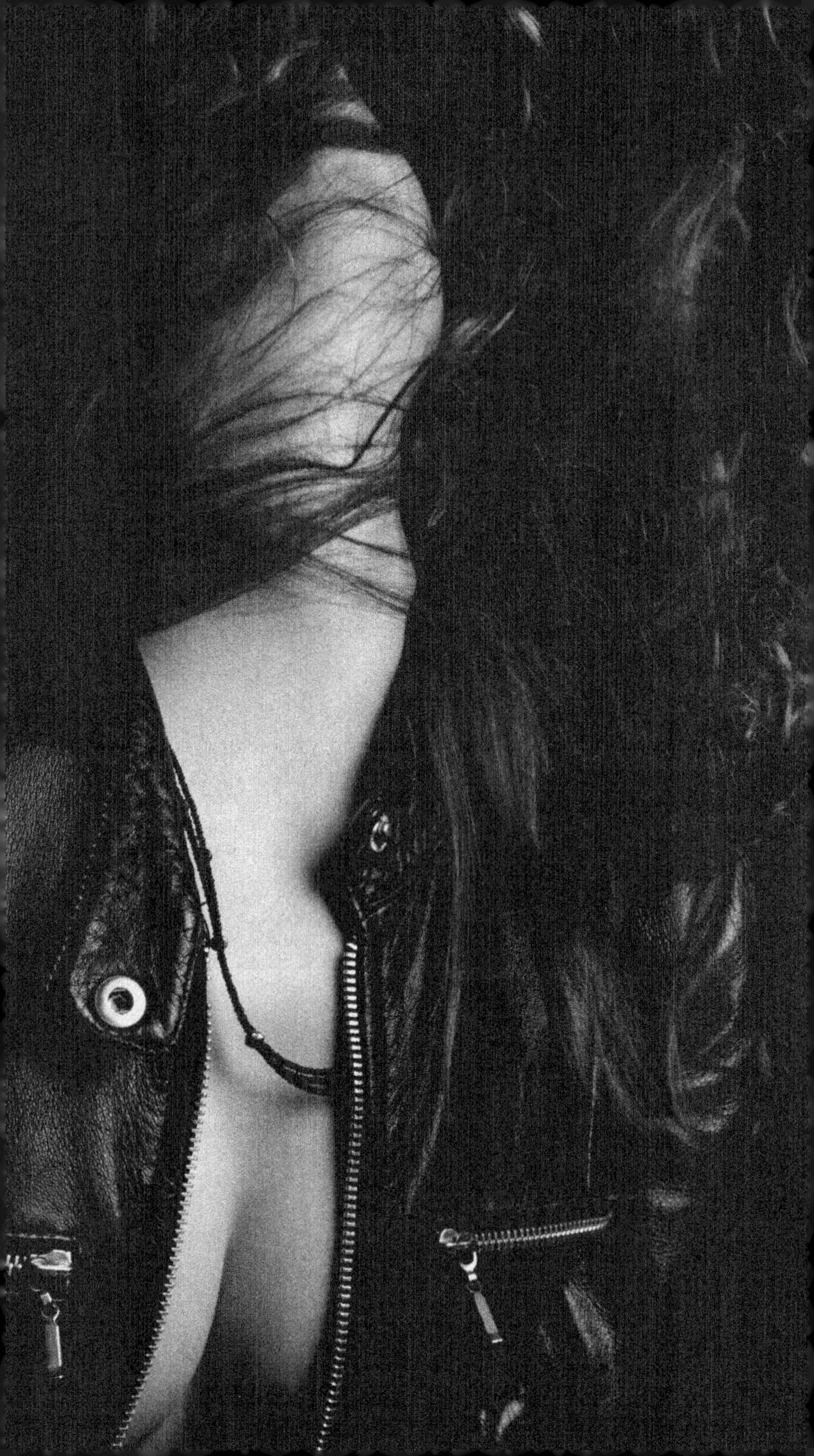

CHAPTER FIFTEEN

Matthias

She fucking joint locked me.

Discreetly, I shook out my wrist, wanting nothing more than to bend her over my knee and wipe that smirk off her face with a few well-placed spanks. The image of her bent over my lap with her pants around her knees as I laid into her bare ass had me adjusting my cock in my jeans before I slammed the door shut to the SUV and followed after her.

Blayd.

Kavanaugh hadn't been bluffing when he'd gloated that his boys had been teaching her self-defense. It wasn't a move that would have worked on me normally, but I was distracted, and she'd timed it perfectly.

I couldn't help the bit of pride that swelled in my chest.

"Keep to the shadows," I instructed the small team that had joined us just inside the gate. "Remember, shoot only when necessary. We don't want to alert any of Christian's men. The red armbands are Kavanaugh's men. Don't shoot them. And always watch your brother's back."

There was a murmur of understanding from my men. Vas handed Ava her earbud, and I grew jealous of the small smile she gave him. An actual smile. Not the shit she'd given me.

Lucky for my second in command, Mark had cleared the comm lines and announced it was time to make our move.

Vas took point, his Beretta 9mm at the chest-ready position as he led us through the maze of containers. Ava was sandwiched between us, her Smith and Wesson the perfect fit for her hands as she too held her gun at her chest.

Good girl, I couldn't help but think as I watched her like a hawk while sweeping my gaze around us. It was quiet. The sound of the ocean lapping at the cement retaining wall was easily heard above the muffled sound of our boots on crunching gravel.

Vas held up a closed fist, signaling us to stop where we were. The three of us waited in tense silence as he scanned his surroundings. With a quickness that only Vas could pull off, my *Sovietnik* holstered his gun before pulling out his karambit, a curved steel blade designed specifically for slicing and cutting.

Ava gasped slightly, her hand position faltering on her gun as she struggled to contain her surprise as Vas surged forward, wrapping his free hand around a stray guard's mouth before slicing open his neck.

The guard went down quietly. Vas supporting the dead weight to keep the noise of his fall from spreading. Turning her head to the side, Ava retched, a small choking sob burrowing up her throat following just behind.

"This is why you should have stayed in the car." I sighed, offering her a handkerchief. "You don't belong here, Ava. You're too fragile." Ava righted herself, her shoulders pushed back, eyes narrowed when she turned to me. With a small growl, she slapped the offered handkerchief from my hand and turned her back to me.

I shrugged, not giving any attention to her childlike behavior. She knew I was right, but that didn't make the pain in my chest disappear from seeing the flash of hurt in her eyes.

"Let's keep moving." Vas frowned at me in obvious disappointment. He looked like I'd just kicked his puppy, but he needed to learn, just like she did.

This was no place for her.

AVA

The nerve of that man.

The gall he had to say that I didn't belong.

Balls of fucking steel, that one. Who the hell did he think he was? I was already mortified enough, and the prick had to go and rub it in. Smear my face in it like some high school reject. I hadn't meant to vomit. In my defense, I'd never seen a man have his throat cut open like a filleted fish before either.

I'd seen Elias beat the ever-loving shit out of people, but I'd never seen anyone kill like that before. So violently. So easily. Vas hadn't even broken a sweat, and there was no remorse in his light eyes either. Just like Matthias, he was a killer. I knew that. I'd always known that. But seeing and knowing were two different things.

"Approaching containers," Vas whispered, the sound traveling through the comm lines in our ears that were activated by the vibrations in our jaws. So basically, whenever we spoke. Or coughed. Or in my case, vomited.

We rounded the corner, our group converging with Liam's. The containers loomed before us, their faded paint revealing the rusted, damaged metal below.

"Huh." I squinted at the first container and pulled out my flashlight for a better look. The small light was just enough to see what had caught my eye. I ran my finger down one of the latches, catching the small debris between my fingers and rubbing slightly. "Sand. That's weird."

"Why's that weird?" Vas asked curiously, leaning in closer for a better look. "This container could have traveled to hundreds of places, and this is what's left over."

I shook my head.

"Mark checked over the containers' shipping receiver." I held up my phone to Vas. I'd written down each individual country code this container had ever been to. "None of those regions have a sandy docking port. Those are all concrete ports."

"How do you know that?" Maksim asked from behind Matthias.

"I memorized the coded index where Elias sent his shipping containers," I informed them with a shrug. "There shouldn't be sand on this container."

"I'm missing the importance of the sand still."

I took a long breath. "There are only two international shipping ports that have sand where they land their containers. Ninety-five percent of countries require ports to be overhauled with cement because sand inside the machinery and containers can cause malfunctions over time. It would get into the small areas of the cranes and docking mechanism, causing system malfunctions and engineering and safety hazards.

"The only countries who have not enacted these safety

protocols due to their climate and economic problems are all in the Middle East."

I could practically see the lightbulbs going off in their heads.

"You're telling me that Ward Enterprises has been making arms and drug deals in the Middle East? How are they getting the containers past customs?"

"I don't know." I shrugged. "But there is no way Elias was doing this by himself. He didn't have the reach."

"Fuck," Liam cursed. "This goes deeper than we thought it did. Whoever was funding Elias is now funding Christian, and if they're moving into the Middle Eastern market, that funder has deeper pockets than we originally thought."

"Can you get the container open?" Matthias asked from behind me, his voice softer than it had been all evening. I nodded, approaching the small box that held the metal bars of the container locked tightly.

"Five-two-eight-four-three-seven-four-six-three," I whispered aloud as the small decoder in my hand wrestled with the numbers. "That can't be right."

But it was.

The lock beeped, and the sound of the container's locking mechanism disengaging was easily heard.

"What's not right?" Liam asked. The lines on his forehead puckered as he looked at me, concerned. "It worked."

"Those numbers," I rasped, stepping back as Maksim and Vas opened the double steel doors. "Those numbers spell my mother's name."

"*Yebena Mat'*," Maksim whispered in awe, interrupting Liam before he could respond. Maksim and Vas shined their lights on the container's contents, each giving a low whistle. "You're going to want to take a look at this."

Liam ushered me forward, his hand on the small of my

back in reassurance as we approached the inside of the barely lit container.

Not that I needed much light to see what was inside.

"Holy shit," I whispered, echoing Maksim's sentiment. "We got this all wrong."

CHAPTER SIXTEEN

Ava

Holy motherfucking balls, Batman.
 The container was full of cash.
 An entire pallet stacked with it.
Both containers.

There had to be well over a million dollars on each of those pallets.

"This is not what I had expected," Maksim breathed. We'd all gathered around one of the pallets, our flashlights running over the green American currency. "Is it real?"

"It's real, all right," Seamus whistled. "The serial numbers aren't sequential. The paper is used, not new. And some of them even have the security thread."

"Fuck me." Kiernan ran his hand along one of the bills. "This feels too real to be fake too."

"I can't believe he pulled this off." I shook my head in disgust, but there was a small amount of awe that twinged in the background. "There is no way he could have done this alone. Whoever Christian is working with would have had an operation like this already set up."

The container grew quiet, and all eyes were on me.

"You know what all this money is for?" Matthias blinked in disbelief. Of course he'd think I wouldn't know what was going on. To him, I was nothing more than a bird who had escaped her gilded cage. A tool to be looked at but never used.

"It's not really *for* anything," I told him. "This is why the container has sand on it but no code for it."

"How does a container without the proper receiving code enter a port it doesn't belong in?" Vas tilted his head to the side as he continued to stare at the mysterious pile of money.

"It doesn't." I smiled. "It's a ghost ship."

"You're telling me that whoever is behind running these containers is ghosting other ship's frequencies to gain access to Middle Eastern ports?" Liam asked, stroking his beard as he tried to put the pieces of the puzzle together.

"After 9/11, ports became severely restricted, even to shipping tycoons like Elias," I informed them. "The only way anyone is getting access to a port, say in Iraq, would be with prior authorization to move already scheduled goods. Like oil. Food. Medicine."

"None of which Elias normally ships," Matthias added. I nodded my head.

"Elias ships private goods and materials. His business was built on private acquisitions. He wouldn't be able to gain access to any of the ports needed to haul the cash," I continued. "This container was supposed to be carrying a private acquisition of Egyptian artifacts. That's what got their vessel into Africa."

"From there, whoever was running the ship would have spoofed another ship's signal to gain access to one of the Iraqi ports," Liam finished for me.

"Exactly," I nodded.

"I don't understand," Vas interrupted. "Why is getting cash from Iraq such a big deal?"

"Because it's stolen American money."

The group balked, their eyes widening, mouths slack as they stared back at the cash with a new sense of awe.

"You're going to have to explain that to us later, Red," Matthias growled as shouting filtered into the container from the outside. "We've got company."

"We're going to need a new storage plan," Liam sighed. "I don't have anywhere near enough room for this."

Matthias nodded. "I have a large underground safe beneath Dashkov Holding that should be sufficient enough to hold both pallets. You can leave a few of your men there to help guard it if you wish."

Liam nodded appreciatively.

"Let's get these pallets loaded onto the trucks," Liam hollered to his men. "Make it fast before someone starts getting suspicious."

A chorus of "yes, sir" could be heard, and within minutes, his men had a large box truck and a forklift in place, moving the money into the back.

"Fuck, I still can't believe how much money there is." Seamus smiled down at me as we watched Liam and Matthias's men secure the pallets.

"I can't believe whoever Christian is working for managed to pull it off." There was something gnawing at me. Something felt off, and I couldn't put my finger on it. We hadn't run into any of the port security or Christian's men. None. Except the one Vas had already taken out.

It was a small port, and the fact that no one had even stumbled upon us or that none of my biological father's men or even Matthias's had radioed in about movement didn't sit right. It was too quiet. Especially since there had just been a drop-off.

Fuck. The drop-off.

"Everyone get down!" Dima yelled over the comm system, the volume causing me to wince as my eardrum rattled.

Seamus and I dove behind the side of one of the containers, wedged between the two as gunfire erupted around us. I pulled out my gun, my breaths coming out in short, ragged pants as I tried to calm my racing heart.

Where was Matthias? And Liam?

From my position behind Seamus, who had his AR pointed toward the trucks loaded with the pallets, I couldn't see anything. But my job wasn't looking forward, it was watching his back. I turned my back to his, gun in the chest-ready position, my gaze on the back side entrance of where we stood.

A clatter of voices and the sound of slamming doors echoed around me, and I struggled to keep myself on point.

Shit.

A bullet whizzed past my head, embedding itself in the metal container just inches from where I was standing. A tremor ran up my body as I breathed in through my nose and out through my mouth, steadying my heartbeat. I could see a man's shadow lurking behind the container to the left of me. He was waiting to see how I'd respond.

But I wouldn't.

If I stayed silent and still, he'd get curious and peek around the corner.

There.

The man turned the corner slowly, gun raised, but he

wasn't fast enough, and neither was I. Before I could even think about pulling the trigger, the man's head exploded, blood and brain matter raining down along the rusted metal.

I looked up to see a smiling Nicolai, a large sniper rifle in his hand. He gave me a small salute before disappearing once again.

Well, fuck.

It wasn't like I hadn't killed someone before. I had, the one time, and part of me was relieved Nicolai was there, but I was equal parts disappointed. How would Matthias ever take me seriously if he didn't see what I had to offer?

"Take the truck and go," Matthias hollered from somewhere amid the chaos. The sound of a diesel engine roaring to life and the telltale squeal of tires on pavement were all I needed to hear to know the pallets were gone.

And hopefully safe.

My gaze landed on my fierce husband, but he wasn't looking at me. His eyes were on the approaching gang of men. Some of whom I recognized.

They were the ones I once called family.

Cousins who'd handed me chocolates and brought me Christmas gifts when Elias refused to buy me any. These were the men who'd been conscripted for no other reason than Elias's fear and anger. His greed for power.

And they were all about to die.

"Stop." I held up my hands, letting my gun hand go limp at my side as I raced out from behind Seamus, who made a grab at me. Gracefully, I dodged his hold and made my way toward the incoming mob. "Giano."

"Get out of the way, Ava," Giano hissed, his gun raised as he strode forward without missing a beat. "I don't want to shoot you, but I have orders to if you interfere."

"Who gave those orders?" I sneered. "Christian?"

Giano's jaw clenched, his grip tightening on his gun, but he'd stopped moving. They all had.

"Yes," he hissed through clenched teeth. "You know the rules about betraying the *Famiglia.*"

"Ava," Matthias warned as I outwardly laughed at how he was accusing me of betraying them. Me. The one who never belonged.

"You think this is a joke, Ava?"

Dante. His deep voice rumbled from behind Giano as he stepped from the crowd. He looked older, more worn than when I'd seen him last. "You would side with the Russians who killed your sister? The ones who put a bullet in her head?"

"We did no such thing, you fucking goombah," Vas snarled from behind me.

"Vasily," I hissed, reprimanding him with my tone for the use of the racial slur.

"No, don't correct the Russian cur, Ava," Dante sneered. "It just shows how little the dogs have grown."

A chaotic cacophony of angered voices rose up around me like a bad remake of West Side Story. Italian versus Russian, with a little Irish thrown in. Not really, though, since my biological father and his men were standing to the side, watching with keen interest as the two groups hurled insults at one another like hockey moms at a pee-wee game.

"Enough!" I screamed at the top of my lungs. I pulled the trigger of my gun once, twice, letting the bullets sink into one of the empty containers.

Seamus would later scold me for the improper discharge of my weapon, no doubt, but desperate times called for desperate measures.

"All of you are fucking idiots," I snarled as the group grew silent. "You all are so hellbent on getting at one another that none of you have bothered to stop and think about what the hell is actually going on."

"Red—" Matthias began, but I wasn't ready to be interrupted, no matter how good the use of my nickname made me feel.

"No," I snapped, turning to face the man I once called Uncle. "I've had enough of this shit. You want to know who killed Libby, Dante? Truly know?"

Dante nodded, visibly swallowing.

"Christian hired Marco Cane to kill her the day I was set to marry Matthias." I blinked back the tears threatening to spill over. I'd been so busy since I'd been rescued that I'd barely spared a thought for the loss of my sister. The only one who'd ever truly loved me besides Kenzi.

I wasn't even going to touch on how Christian had killed Elias. One step at a time.

"I'm not lying," I assured him calmly. "I have a paper trail that leads from Marco Cane back to Christian."

"Why would he kill her?" Dante asked, his voice nearly void of emotion. "Why kill his own sister?"

"Because she betrayed him," I whispered. "And if there was one thing Elias had taught him, it was that betrayal would never be tolerated. Look at the M.E. report, Dante. Open your eyes and see the truth, because if you don't, Christian and whoever he is working for will destroy not only us, but the *Famiglia* as well."

There wasn't a sound besides the mingling of our harsh breaths in the winter chill and the slight shuffle of bodies as we all took each other in. We weren't all that different. Each family was trying to survive and keep their empires running without spilling too much blood.

I could see the gears in Dante's head turning as his gaze

held mine, searching for the truth. That was all he would ever find.

"Walk away, Uncle." I smiled at him somberly. "We already have what we came for, and when you find the truth I've been telling you, come find me. I'll show you who your enemy really is."

Tension was strung tight between us for several more minutes before the rope of distrust slackened just enough to breathe.

"All those years Elias let you sit in on those meetings. I warned him you were wiser than you appeared." The edge of his lips turned up slightly. "Christian always called you *Little Lamb* because Elias would constantly refer to you as a lamb ready for slaughter."

I winced at the use of Christian's crude nickname. Dante didn't miss the small action, his eyes softening slightly.

"The thing is," he mused as he stroked his chin with his free hand. "You were never a lamb, my dear. You were always a wolf."

CHAPTER SEVENTEEN

Ava

"Are you finally going to explain what the hell Christian was doing with all that cash?" Dima sat down in the seat across from me, beer in his hand. After Dante and his men had left, we'd all gone back to Matthias's penthouse to unload the money into the large vault he had beneath the structure.

The entire room sat under the parking garage, almost completely cut off from the rest of the building. The only way to access it was either through the secret cargo entrance that was a few blocks down or the discreet set of stairs that were concealed beneath a grate in the floor of the garage.

My husband was the Russian version of Batman.

Just more of an asshole.

And sexier.

Fuck. Now I was imagining him in a bat suit doing naughty things to me.

Focus, Ava, focus.

He's a douchebag.

A liar.

A douchebag.

It was worth repeating twice.

"I'm trying to wrap my head around the fact that she said it was stolen *American* money." Seamus shook his head, his mind trying to wrap itself around the fact that we had millions of dollars sitting thirty or so levels below our feet. "I mean, come on, how would anyone steal that much American money?"

"And how did it get overseas?" Nikolai asked, setting a glass of bourbon in front of me. "There's what? Four or five million dollars down there? How did anyone transfer that overseas without being noticed?"

"Oh, it was noticed," I informed them, enjoying the toasty notes of the bourbon as its warmth slid down my throat. Damn, that was good. "At the beginning of the war in the Middle East, the US Government shipped billions of dollars overseas in the form of fives, tens, and twenties, all cash. It was sent to help with reconstruction. Schools. Homes. Businesses. And, of course, a decent bribe or two."

"Billions?" Dima perked up in his seat. "With a *b*?"

I nodded.

"How do you know all this?" Matthias asked curiously. "That's a lot of secretive information for someone locked in a gilded cage nearly her whole life."

I grinned over at my husband, who sat across from me at the table. It wasn't round like the one they had in the bunker, but rectangular and large enough to accommodate his men and most of Liam's.

"Even gilded cages have wi-fi," I told him. "Plus, Elias never kept much a secret from me. He talked openly, believing he had complete and utter control over me. His mistake, really. Something to be learned from."

Matthias's eyes flashed with something I didn't quite recognize, but I could see the anger behind the gray storm clouds at being compared to Elias. Kiernan coughed uncomfortably as the tension between us heated and crackled like a summer storm.

"Why cash though?" Leon tapped his chin thoughtfully. "Ward Enterprises under the control of Dashkov was a billion-dollar company. Why is the cash so important?"

"Because cash can't be tracked." I leaned back in my chair, whiskey tumbler in hand, my fingers dancing along the crystal as I silently tapped out the beat to "Renegade" by Styx. "Sure, money is money, but cash is its own ball game. These are untraceable small bills. Perfect for bribes, drugs, guns…" I looked over at Liam, who was completely at ease sitting in his chair, ankle on one knee as he, too, tapped on the glass of his beer bottle.

I'd wondered where I'd gotten that habit from.

Some things were just innate.

His emerald eyes met mine, sensing me staring at him. His brow furrowed as I studied him.

"Ground shipping companies," I finished rattling off as I drew my gaze away from my biological father. I wasn't about to ask him about that, not when he'd nearly blown the top of his head at the mention of Marianne somehow being complicit in my mother's kidnapping. How would he react if I called out the man who was supposed to be his father-in-law?

"Think of what else that money could buy." Vas slowly released a long breath. "Christian would have every politician in his pocket with money like that. The gaming commission.

The new mayor—if he's just as bad as the old one. He could've taken over more than half the underground and we would never have been the wiser for it."

Fuck. That was the general mood of the room as we all let that revelation sink in. If we hadn't intercepted this shipment, it would have meant the end for the Bratva and the Irish mob. They would have lost suppliers, runners, everything. People traded loyalties when there was cash involved.

"All right." Liam stood from the table, stretching. "The container might not have been what we thought it was, but that doesn't change the plan. We can still move forward with finding out who is funding Christian Ward, and the best way to do that is to schmooze the top players at the annual charity gala in two weeks. Meanwhile, we'll all keep gathering information. Keep our spies busy."

We all nodded and stood, clearing away our empty bottles and glasses. As I went to reach for my coat, Vas frowned down at me.

"Why don't you stay, Ava?" he asked. "This is your home, and honestly, we could use you around here."

Home.

This wasn't my home. It was another prison. Another cage. I wasn't naïve enough to believe that it had ever been a home for me.

"I don't think..." I began, my eyes searching out Matthias, who wasn't bothering to even look at me. I was expecting him to say no. To adamantly refuse, but he remained silent, his body turned toward Maksim, who was speaking to him in low tones.

"Good idea, Vasily." Liam smiled and clamped one of his large tattooed hands down on my shoulder. "I was thinking the same thing."

Now it was my turn to frown. I pulled my gaze from my

husband to focus on my biological father. He was smiling, his green eyes lit with mischief as he stared down at me.

"Do you not want me to come back?" I whispered so no one else would hear our conversation. "Did I do something wrong?"

Was this because of Marianne? Did he not want me around anymore because of what I'd said? Had I lost him that easily? Before we'd even gotten to know one another?

"We need a liaison," Liam whispered back. "You're the best choice. Plus, I think it's time you stop running. Don't you?"

Running? Who was running?

I wasn't.

Running implied a slowness I didn't possess. Fuck. I wasn't running from anything. I was bolting. Like the Flash or Superman. Speed of light. Not fucking running. Running was for pussies.

I wasn't a pussy. I was a strategist.

That's what I'd keep telling myself anyway.

"I'd make a horrible liaison," I told him truthfully. Liam shrugged.

"Guess we'll find out." He kissed the top of my head affectionately before walking away, giving time for Seamus and Kiernan to say their goodbyes.

"I'll talk to Vas about continuing your training while you're here," Kiernan told me. "Can't have you slacking. You still need a lot of work."

"Gee thanks," I grumbled as he hugged me. "I'll remember that next time you tell me to take it easy on you."

Kiernan laughed.

"Don't worry." Seamus winked at me. "You won't get rid of us so easily. We'll be around, big sis."

I let out a watery laugh and hugged him tightly. I didn't

feel like the big sister here. They'd looked out for me these past few weeks. We weren't very far apart in age, but I prided myself on being called a big sister. Especially after letting Libby down.

I'd be sure that never happened again.

The door shut behind Liam's men, and I was left standing alone with Matthias. Vas and the others had already made their excuses and were off doing who knows what. Shitty excuses, really. It wasn't a secret they were trying to get us alone.

"I'll sleep on one of the couches," I told him, breaking the tense silence. "Make it easier on both of us."

I didn't tell him the real reason I wanted to sleep in the living room was because the only open room was my old one. The one Libby had slept in and where her stuff had been left untouched. There'd be no going back in there. Not for me.

Too many memories.

Too much heartache.

I wouldn't let him see me cry over it. He'd think it was a weakness, and I couldn't afford to be weak in front of him.

"I've got business most nights." Matthias's low voice made my body thrum with electricity. *Knock it off, Ava.* "You can sleep in our bed. I won't be joining you."

Our bed. He still called it our bed. Not *his* bed.

"Okay," I murmured as I started toward the hallway that led to the master suite.

"Oh, and Ava." I turned back at the sound of my name. Matthias's face was drawn up in a scowl, eyes narrowed. "Don't expect to be staying too long."

Well, fuck.

So much for being home.

CHAPTER EIGHTEEN

Matthias

She was everywhere.
The scent of her jasmine perfume permeated every corner of the penthouse. Her clothes and belongings were strewn all over the bedroom we'd barely shared since she came back.

It was a trick. I knew it. Ava wasn't a particularly tidy person compared to my utilitarian lifestyle, but she hardly ever left clothes on the floor or her shoes by the door to trip me.

I'd let her sleep there on her own because there was little chance that I wouldn't give in to my base instincts and take her.

She was my wife still, and I respected that bond, even if I was already having Ben draw up the divorce papers. After that, it would be over and done. She'd be free to be whomever she wanted. Free to live her life without restraint.

I could hear her laughter from the living room most days as she sauntered about the penthouse talking to Mia or my men.

She was loud.

Obviously so.

The fucking minx was tempting me since I'd refused to speak to her since Vas suggested she stay. I'd raged at him for it, even though I'd shown her nothing but a calm disinterest. I hadn't wanted her back here. She may have been my wife, but she'd still betrayed me.

But for a good reason.

That was what my mind kept repeating like a broken record, but I wasn't ready to admit that. I didn't think I ever would be. My member throbbed as I heard her laughter filter down the hall from my office where she sat conversing with Vas over the plans we'd made for the upcoming gala. My mind kept conjuring up the unwanted picture of her bent naked over my desk.

Ass red from my punishing hand.

Or my belt.

Fuck, maybe even both.

My head was reeling. Mind buzzing.

I shouldn't want her still. Shouldn't need her. My brain was on board with that. But hell, my body wasn't getting that message.

"Get out, Ava," I growled as I stalked into my office, attempting in vain to will my rock-hard cock to soften. It wasn't working. "I need to speak to Vas."

The redheaded vixen glared at me, her emerald eyes darkening as she brushed passed me muttering "asshole" under her breath as she shoulder checked me on the way out.

I let that go.

"You shouldn't be so brusque to your wife." Vas's tone dripped with disappointment, and it made me feel guilty. Somewhat.

"And you should mind your own business," I warned him as I sat down in my chair. "Plus, she won't be my wife much longer."

My *Sovietnik* groaned.

"Tell me you didn't."

"Ben will have the papers here by the gala," I told him, grabbing a small bottle of whiskey from inside my desk. It was a rare year, aged in an antique coffee barrel whose sides had been charred to the point of perfection, drawing out the old oils of the coffee beans that had once been transported.

Perfection.

"You're a fucking idiot."

I shrugged, not caring in the least what he thought.

That's what told I myself anyway.

"So, what did you need to discuss with me so urgently?" Vas asked, rearranging himself in his chair.

I huffed a small laugh.

"Nothing, I just didn't want her in here with me."

Vas groaned but didn't make a move to leave.

"You really are an asshole, *sir*." He drew out the *sir* like an insult.

"*You* shouldn't have invited her to stay," I snarled.

"I was trying to help your stubborn ass," Vas insisted angrily. "You have your head shoved so far up your ass..."

"Remember who you are talking to, Vasily," I warned him. "We may be brothers, but I am still your *Pahkan*."

"*Prosti, brat*," he apologized contritely. "You're right."

We sat there in silence as I poured each of us a small glass of my classically aged whiskey. Leaning back in my chair, I closed my eyes as I savored the bitter, charred notes of my drink, letting the flavors roll and take over my senses.

Had it come to this? That my men would go against me because of a woman? My woman. I'd known they'd grown attached to her. Come to love her like brothers should, but I never thought my own *Sovietnik* would chastise me.

I couldn't let her relationship with them interfere with business. My business. Ava wasn't just my weak link. She was theirs as well.

"I found her outside the door last night." Vas broke the silence. He took a sip of his whiskey and sighed.

"Again?" I asked, my forehead creasing in concern.

"Third night this week, and she's only been here four," Vas confirmed. "Never seems to be at the same time, and just like the other two nights, she's completely out of it. I think she's sleepwalking."

I shook my head. "Ava has no history of sleepwalking."

"No." Vas nodded. "She doesn't. But guilt and trauma change sleeping patterns. She still refuses to go into Libby's room. Won't even talk about it."

"I don't see you going into Libby's room either," I pointed out.

"I've been waiting for Ava." Vas shrugged. "Libby was her sister. She deserves to be the first to go in. The first to see everything like it once was."

I nodded my head, taking another sip of whiskey. He was right, of course.

"I tried talking about it, but she's refusing to," Vas continued, crestfallen. "She won't discuss anything to do with Libby. Didn't even want to see the urn we placed her ashes in or talk about spreading them like Libby wanted."

There was another point of contention between us. His authorization to bombard the Romanos and Wards at the funeral site. It wasn't something I would have authorized, and he knew that. He'd taken the opportunity to bribe the funeral home director and had him place someone else's body inside the casket while he took Libby's and had it cremated.

Libby Ward had wanted to be cremated and spread on a cliff that overlooked the ocean. True freedom—that was what she'd told Ava once—was found on the wind, not in the ground. Vas had been furious to find that they were burying the woman he'd come to care for next to her vile father. I didn't approve of his method, but I understood why he did what he did.

Didn't mean I had to like it.

"I'll talk to her about it."

Vas quirked a skeptical eyebrow at me, raising his hands in a gesture of peace when I growled at him. Just because I was ignoring Ava didn't mean I wouldn't talk to her when the moment called for it, and having Ava constantly sleepwalking in the middle of the night meant this talk was warranted.

Downing the rest of my drink in one gulp, I stood from my chair and went in search of my wife. I expected to find her in the kitchen with Mia, which was where I found her most days since she'd been here, but when I walked into the kitchen, she was nowhere to be found.

Mia, my housekeeper, was busy humming an old Russian tune as she puttered around the large chef's kitchen preparing dinner.

"Oh, Matthias." She brought her hand up to her chest. "You startled me."

I gave her a small apologetic smile. "Prosti, Mia," I told her. "I was looking for Ava."

Mia wiped her hands on the kitchen towel slung on her shoulder and smiled up at me.

"She went down to the gun range to practice her marksmanship."

I frowned. "By herself?"

Mia balked at my tone. "I'm sorry, sir," she started. "I didn't think you'd mind. I was told she could come and go as she pleased."

"No, you're right, Mia." I held up my hand to keep her from rambling on. "She isn't a prisoner. I'm just surprised she didn't ask someone to go with her." Mia was still frowning, but she nodded her head before turning back to her work.

Sighing, I ran a hand through my hair.

Mia loved Ava like a daughter, and I wasn't delusional enough to believe that my housekeeper, who'd known me longer than most, wasn't cross about how things were playing out. She was just too professional and polite to say anything.

Unlike Vasily.

I made my way down to the range. It sat just above the parking garage, the space nearly soundproof. There were ten lanes in total, laid out side by side. Pistol only, but we did allow the occasional P90s or ARs. Just not high-powered rifles or shotguns. Those had a specific range out at the compound.

Ava stood in one of the last stalls, her ears protected by a set of hot pink earmuffs, eyes covered with a pair of safety goggles that were also lined in hot pink. I had to chuckle at that. Ava hated pink; it was what Elias would force her to wear to make her more feminine. One of the twins must have picked them up for her. She probably didn't have the heart to tell them she didn't like it.

She didn't hear me approach or sense me standing behind her. Ava was too immersed in what she was doing. Each time, before she fired, she'd drag the gun back into the chest position, her elbows tight to the side before taking a deep breath, extending her arms, and firing off a round.

Then she'd do it again.

It was a good tactic, if she was aiming to perfect her stance, but the frustration rolling off her had nothing to do with getting in and out of the proper shooting position, but with her aim. I beamed as I looked down the range at the paper target she'd been shooting at.

MATTHIAS was scribbled in big block lettering at the top with the eyes crossed out.

Damn, my woman was vicious.

No, not my woman. Not for much longer anyway.

Some of her marks hit, but most of her shots were hitting the side of the paper, and I knew why. She turned abruptly when I tapped her on the shoulder, pride swelling in my chest as I watched her set the gun on the table, barrel pointing down range. Plenty of my own men who'd had years of bad safety training couldn't remember to do that simple task.

We may be Bratva, but we weren't stupid. Gun safety saved lives. This wasn't some bad Miami Vice movie.

"You're not hitting your mark because you're anticipating the recoil," I told her after she removed her earmuffs. Anticipating the recoil of a weapon was one of the most common mistakes. A gun with more mass tended to manifest lower recoil kinetic energy and, generally, result in a lessened perception of recoil. Ava's Smith and Wesson was still lower on the mass index than other handguns of the same caliber. It was meant to be lightweight and compact for concealed carry.

By anticipating the recoil, she was pushing forward on the butt of the gun before it had a chance to fully fire, causing her marks to land higher and a bit to the side of their intended target.

"I know," she huffed. "It's not as easy as it looks."

I smiled down at her and winked. "I know."

Ava snorted derisively.

I peered over into the next stall and grabbed a spare pair of earmuffs and glasses.

"Put on your ear protection," I told her, dumbstruck when she did as I said without arguing. "Get into position." I sidled up behind her as she put herself back into her shooting stance.

Bringing my hands to her waist, I moved in closer so her back was touching my chest.

"You keep releasing your breath as you fire," I instructed. "I want you to hold your breath as you pull the trigger and release it as you let the trigger go. You anticipate the recoil by pushing the butt of the gun forward. Instead, I want you to let it naturally come back into your hand when you fire."

Ava nodded, taking a deep breath as she readied herself. I stepped back to observe. She did just as I instructed. Another deep breath in, she held it as she slowly pulled the trigger, her body relaxed. She didn't flinch this time, her breath coming out slowly as she inched her finger off the trigger.

Dead center mass.

"Good girl," I told her with a small smile. "Again."

AVA

I wasn't sure how long we were down there, but it felt like hours. Matthias watched and instructed, improving on what Seamus had already taught me, helping me hone my skills. He said it was about building muscle memory. The ability to perform the action without thinking.

"Why'd you really come down here?" I asked as I put my gun back in its case to be taken back upstairs and cleaned. "I don't think it was to give me shooting tips."

Matthias sighed as he ran a hand down his ragged face.

He hadn't been shaving, and his beard was getting thicker. I liked it, imagining what that full beard would feel like scraping against the sensitive skin of my inner thighs.

"Careful, Ava," he warned, his voice gravelly as he took in my blown pupils and darkened eyes. "Your emotions are written all over your face, and unless you want me to fuck you up against this wall, you'll wipe it off your face."

"Oops." I shrugged nonchalantly and waited for him to answer my question.

"You need to go into Libby's room, Ava."

And I was done.

"I'm not having this conversation, Matthias," I hissed as I made a move to grab my gun case and hightail it the hell out of here. This was not something I wanted to discuss. I wouldn't be going into Libby's room to pack up the meager belongings she had brought with her from the house. I wouldn't be digging through old memories to have them tainted by my failure.

It wasn't going to fucking happen.

"Last night was the third time he's found you sleepwalking, standing outside her bedroom door like a fucking ghost." Matthias growled, grabbing the gun case from my hand and throwing it down on the stall table. He backed me up against the far wall, crowding my space. His face darkened, clouds rolling over his light eyes like a summer storm. He could probably see into my soul with how deep his focus was.

"Why do you even care?" I snarled, baring my teeth at him. "I won't be here long, remember? You want her shit gone? Do it yourself."

"That's not what this is about, Red, and you know it."

I barked a laugh.

"Isn't it?" I asked, my hysteria rising. "You're the one who thinks I betrayed you. And maybe I did, Matthias, but never maliciously. I did what I did to protect Mark. That was all. I had no idea what was on that drive, I swear."

"You did betray me, Ava," he whispered angrily, his hand going to my throat. "There is no maybe. You gave him information that very few people knew about. Information I trusted you with."

"Fuck you, Matthias," I screamed, spit flying from my mouth, but I didn't move to push him away. "I never told him anything about you."

"Then how did he get my dead brother's name, Avaleigh?" he roared at me, face turning an ugly shade of red as his gripped tightened around my neck, making it harder to breathe. "The last thing he whispered in my ear before he locked me up was my brother's name. A name I told you in confidence. A name that only Vasily and Tomas knew."

"I never gave him anything," I gasped, clawing at his hand now that it was starting to cut off my air supply. "He never asked me one thing about you. Even if he did, I wouldn't have given him anything."

"You lie!"

"You're the liar, Matthias," I choked. "You're lying to yourself, and you know it."

"And what am I lying about, hm?" He cocked his head to the side, his grip refusing to loosen.

"You want to believe I betrayed you, because otherwise you'd have to face the fact that I am more than just a pawn to you," I struggled to get the words out. A wave of dizziness washed over me as I began to feel lightheaded. Matthias must have noticed the change because he loosened his grip. "You don't want to admit that you have feelings for me."

Matthias threw back his head and laughed. I fought back the tears, my eyes and heart stinging as he openly rejected what I knew to be the truth.

"You're a fool, Ava."

"And you're nothing but a coward, Matthias Dashkov," I hissed at him, baring my teeth once again, ready to fight. Instead, I chose a different tactic. I rolled my hips up. He was standing so close that the simple action caused me to brush against the growing erection in his jeans. "You're using what I did as an excuse to put distance between us, and I've had it."

"I am not a coward," he roared in my face, his body pushing into mine, his pelvis rocking into mine, causing a frisson of delicious electricity to skate up my spine. My pussy was embarrassingly wet already, and I hated it. Hated that he had this control over my body, but from the feel of his rock-hard cock against my legging clad pussy, he wasn't in control of his either.

"You're the one who betrayed me." Another rock of his pelvis into mine, another groan of desire leaving my lips. "For what? What did that FBI agent promise you? Freedom? Look how that turned out. Right back where it all started. You just didn't have a scapegoat this time. You were the one running, Ava. Admit it. First from our agreement, then to that FBI agent, and now to Kavanaugh. Don't preach to me about being a coward. That's the pot calling the kettle, baby."

"Fuck you, Matthias." Anger bubbled to the surface like molten lava threatening to spew. "I didn't run to Kavanaugh. You refused to have me back. I wanted to come back. I wanted to be with you. You're the one who keeps pushing me away. All I ever wanted was you, and all I want now is to be your partner. Not just your wife. Not just your sex toy to be taken off the shelf when you need a quick fuck. I've never been anything other than a pawn to you, and I'm sick of it. I'm sick of loving someone who doesn't love me back."

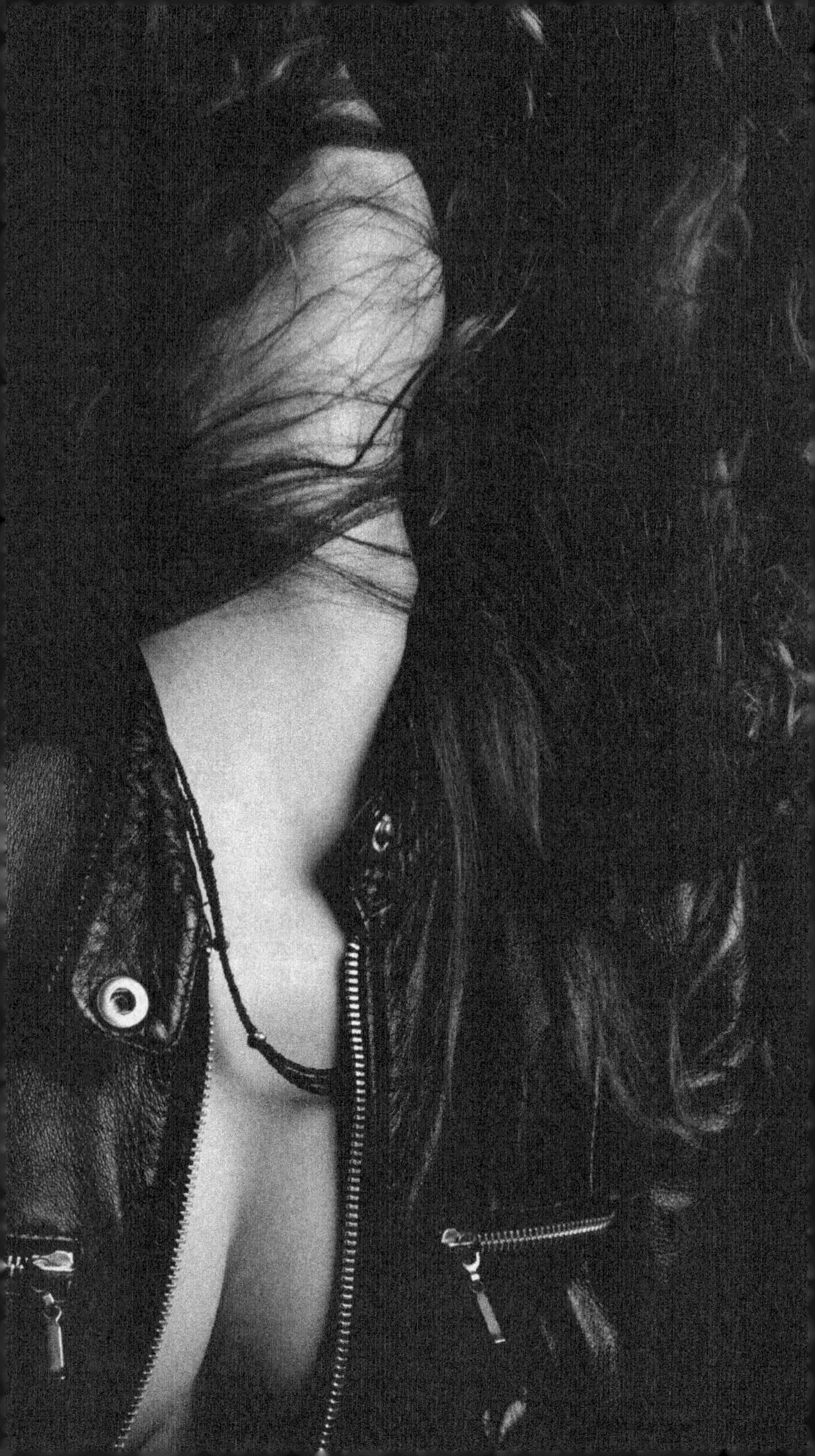

CHAPTER NINETEEN

Matthias

My body froze against hers.

She loved me.

Fuck. That was a revelation.

Ava loved me.

My chest tightened at her words, heart racing even faster, cock hardening painfully as I processed her words.

How could beauty love a beast?

I snorted internally. She may love me, but I could never love her. Even if I did, she betrayed my trust, and that was something I could never forgive.

"What do you want me to say, Red?" I sneered at her. "That I love you? That I need you? That I can't live without you?" I taunted. "Because we both know those would be nothing more than pretty lies wrapped in ugly packaging."

Shaking my head, I let out a frustrated sigh. The tears in her eyes glistened like the light of a grand chandelier. I knew it wasn't what she wanted to hear, but it was necessary.

Loving a woman was a weakness, but loving Ava?

It would be my downfall.

"The only person you're lying to is yourself, Matthias," she stuttered, taking in a wobbly breath. "I may not be able to read people the way you can, but I can read you like an open book, and you are nothing short of pathetic.

"Did I ever once ask you to love me? Or tell me that you need me? Or ask you to throw yourself on a sword if I left? No. I asked you to treat me like a partner. I asked you to stop lying and hiding secrets from me. I've lived the last eighteen years without love, and I'll sure as hell survive the next however many years without it. I'm not some needy little schoolgirl. What we had before this all went to shit was fine with me. I liked what we had. It was nice and safe and warm."

She paused to take a breath, the corner of her mouth turning up into a wicked smirk as she resumed grinding her body against mine. Her hands came up under my shirt, nails digging into the skin of my chest.

Blyad.

"Now," she whispered wantonly. "Are you going to just stand there and whine, or are you going to fuck me up against this wall like you promised?"

My chest rumbled at her obvious challenge.

Fine. She wanted to get fucked?

Then she'd get fucked.

"You want me to fuck you, Ava?" I leaned in and ran my nose across her shoulder and up her throat to her ear. "Want me to make you come?"

Ava moaned when I licked the sensitive skin of her neck, right behind her ear.

"Fuck, you taste so damn good," I murmured in her ear. Running my hands down her backside, I squeezed her ass cheeks and lifted her. Ava's legs wrapped around my waist tightly. Her small hand came up behind my neck, her fingers slipping into hair. She jerked me forward, her mouth slamming into mine in a fevered kiss.

I groaned into her mouth as she rolled her hips into mine, forcing me to slip my arm around her to help her maintain her balance. Ava was sin personified. The holy grail of woman. I wasn't a fool. There was no mistaking that my wife was every man's wet dream.

"Please." She pulled away from the kiss, her lust-filled voice low and strained. Her mouth went to my neck, nipping and biting lightly as I spun on my heel and through the range door that led into a small recreational room. Slamming the door shut behind us, I dropped Ava to her feet.

She looked up at me, her pupils dilated, eyes widened slightly as she took in my nearly feral state. My chest was rising and falling rapidly at the thought of what I had planned.

Her throat bobbed anxiously as I approached her, my eyes tracking every minute movement she made with predatory sweeps. My hands reached out to snatch her by the waist, turning her until her back was against my chest.

My hands swept over her clothed form, pinching and grabbing at the soft skin hidden underneath. Without saying a word, I bent her over the arm of the couch, one hand curling into her soft ginger locks.

With a flick of my fingers, I had her pants unbuttoned. A few seconds later, they were between her knees, along with her panties. Next came my jeans; the jingle of my belt buckle caused Ava's thighs to clench, and I couldn't help the low chuckle that escaped me.

You won't be getting that, little girl.
Not anymore.

My hand clenched tighter in Ava's hair, a low whimper leaving her lips when I refused to let her look at me. This wasn't about us. This was just about sex, and watching her come would crush my resolve. It always had. Ava was breathtaking when she came.

Ava mewled, shoving her ass back into me as I ran my fingers up her seam. Christ. She was already soaked. I danced my fingertips around her clit before shoving two of my fingers into her pussy. She moaned wantonly as I fucked her with my fingers, ramming them in and out of her, curling them just enough to hit that sweet spot.

Then, without warning, I lined myself up with her, and in one smooth thrust, I buried myself to the hilt.

Ava yelped at the sudden intrusion and when she tried to turn her head to look at me again, I held firm, slapping her on the outside of her thigh as a small reprimand.

"You don't get to look at me, Ava," I hissed as I gripped her ass tightly, swiveling my hips, forcing her to take more of me while stretching her and making sure she'd feel me for days.

Whimpering, she closed her eyes, her body tensing as I pulled out until just the tip of my cock was still inside her.

"You want to be fucked, Ava?" I asked her. She didn't respond, so I slammed back into her, causing her to scream, before it melted into a delicious moan.

"Answer me!"

"Yes!" Ava screamed as she tried to move her hips, but I would let her.

"Stay still, Ava," I growled, once again removing my cock until the tip was barely in her. "You're not in control here. I am. Now, tell me you want me to fuck you."

The redheaded vixen below me released a frustrated growl but remained silent.

"Tell me, Red." I slapped the opposite thigh. "Or I'm going to leave you wanting."

"Please, Matthias," she snarled. "Fuck me."

"Good girl."

Then I slammed back into her, relishing yet another one of her sweet moans of pleasure that was tinged with glorious pain. I greedily worked my body against hers, my grip tightening on her ass, and a low groan leaving my parted lips when she tightened her inner muscles around my cock.

Snarling at the control she was managing to exert over me, I wasted no time in pushing her farther into the arm of the sofa until she was nearly bent in half over it.

"Matthias." Her pain-tinged pleas fell on deaf ears as I continued to ruthlessly pound into her soft body, knowing full well that this position was deeper than before. "It hurts, please..."

"So did your betrayal." I viciously pulled her hair back, forcing her to arch her back, her hips coming up slightly more.

"Gah!" she howled as I pried her ass cheeks apart and dug my finger into her small hole, twisting it back and forth.

"Do you like that, my little traitor?" I sneered in her ear. "You wanted me to fuck you. You're getting what you wanted, no?"

Ava went quiet. Only the sounds of her harsh breathing and moans filling the space around us as I let my control slip, pounding into her like a rutting animal. I pounded into her faster and harder, relishing her small cries of pain as I tortured her ass and gripped her hair.

She wanted to be fucked; I'd fuck her. I'd always been controlled with her. More vanilla than I liked it, but I'd planned on introducing her to my darker, more primal needs in time.

Now, I didn't have to.

She'd get it all and feel the like whore she once accused me of treating her as.

"I..." Ava didn't get the rest of her sentence out before the walls of her pussy clenched rhythmically against my cock. The next thing she was doing was screaming my name.

"Fuck," I swore as my balls tightened. "So fucking tight."

I wasn't going to last much longer. With one more roared expletive, I pulled out of her tight, warm heat and released myself on her lower back. My free hand came up to rub at my shaft, making sure every last drop of cum had found its way onto her fair skin.

Releasing her hair, I straightened myself before pulling up my pants. I took in her disheveled state. Her breathing was labored as she remained bent over the couch, chest heaving, body coated in a fine sheen of sweat.

She was stunning.

Without another glance, I turned and strode from the room, leaving her behind.

Ava wanted to be fucked.

So I'd fucked her. That was all she would get from me.

CHAPTER TWENTY

Ava

The harsh, unrelenting pounding of the scalding water beat down on my back as I scrubbed at my skin. The hot water did nothing to soothe the ache in my chest Matthias had created.

Fucking bastard.

Asshole.

I'd complained once about him treating me like a whore. Now I honestly knew how it felt.

Fucked and dismissed.

He wanted to play it that way? Fine with me. I had no problem playing his game, and I'd be sure to play it better. The best way to win a game was to know the rules; that way you knew how to break them.

JO MCCALL

Matthias had shown his cards, and now I knew exactly how to play him, just like he played me.

This wasn't a game he was going to win.

"You need to relax, Ava," Leon instructed as he led me around the large space he'd cleared in the formal dining room. The suave Italian was trying his best to turn my two left feet into dancing feet. Which was like trying to turn an ugly duckling into a swan.

It only happened in fairy tales.

I was under no impression that I was Cinderella. In fact, I was more likely to be one of her flat-footed stepsisters. Leon winced as my heeled shoe stepped on his black leather Louboutin Greggo for the fifth time.

"At this point, we might have to surgically remove those shoes with how swollen his toes will be." Vas cracked up from the sidelines where he was playing DJ.

This was utterly humiliating, and both Dima and Vas were getting far more entertainment from my pain than they should have been.

Leon swore under his breath in Italian as he signaled for Vas to cut the music.

"How do you not know how to waltz?" he asked me. "Didn't Elias take you to parties?"

I snorted. "Yeah, but I was never allowed to dance. I was an ornament, nothing more. Do you honestly think he'd allow for me to have a modicum of fun and entertainment?" I scoffed. "That would take away from *his* entertainment, which was making me as uncomfortable as possible."

Leon sighed, running a hand through his perfect dark Italian locks.

"The gala is only a week away, and you need to learn to blend in, Ava," Dima spoke up from the sidelines.

"Matthias hates to dance anyway, so I should be fine," I pointed out. Something was off. The three of them exchanged uncomfortable glances, their gazes avoiding mine. I didn't need Matthias's fancy body language knowledge to know they were hiding something. "What aren't you telling me?"

Vas coughed, his mouth twisting in distaste.

"You aren't going as Matthias's date." His tone was hard and almost akin to disgust. This decision was apparently one he hadn't agreed with. From the looks on all three of their faces, none of them agreed with their boss.

"So what?" I asked, fearing I already knew the answer. "We're going stag?"

Dima shook his head, arms crossed against his chest.

"You'll be going as my date," Leon huffed. "Matthias has..."

"His own date," I finished for the Italian. Of course he had his own date. Besides his inner circle and Liam's main men, no one knew we were married. Matthias, it would seem, wanted to keep it that way.

"Okay." I took a long, slow breath as I gathered myself together. We had a job to do, and I wouldn't let this affect me. I'd play his game, for now, but it wouldn't be long before all bets were off. I needed more of those delicious orgasms he gave me, and I'd get as many as I could. "Let's do this."

"Remember," Leon reminded me as we took our stance. "Let me lead."

Fuck, my feet hurt like hell. Who liked wearing heels and dancing around like that all night? It was ridiculous. I sat at one end of the tub, letting the salted water lap at my bruised and sore feet.

Leon was a taskmaster, and I'd refused to give up. It had nothing to do with representing Leon at the gala. I could give two shits about what some stodgy paper pushers thought of my waltz. I wanted to show up Matthias. The man who refused to publicly acknowledge we were even married. Instead, the asshole decided to attend the function with one of Vivian's hookers.

Wonder-fuckin-ful.

There was a moment, while I was staring out the window of the high-rise, watching as the city below came to life under the light of the moon. Streetlamps flickered on. Neon signs lit up the darkened alleyways. Men and women left the safety of their homes, dressed in their best clothes, hair done up, ready to hit the city's clubs for a night of fun and debauchery.

Something I'd never experienced.

I'd already said Matthias was playing a game with me.

Now it was my turn to play one right back.

And maybe, just maybe, I'd get to live a little for once in my life.

After all, *girls just wanna have fun*.

THE SATIN red dress clung to my every curve like a second skin, its ruched sides leaving my upper thighs nearly bare, showcasing the brand-new needlework etched into the right side.

I was every man's wet dream.

My vibrant ginger hair was tucked beneath a long blond wig, my face painted with the utmost care in shades of neutrals that didn't detract from the red matte lipstick that graced my full plump lips.

The wig itched slightly, but it was the only way I could go out without worrying about one of Christian's goons recognizing me. Hell, I'd barely recognized myself, especially with the new artwork painting my normally bare skin.

It was just past ten o'clock on Saturday night. I'd made an excuse to Vasily and Leon last night after I'd soaked my burning feet into a prune-like state, giving them a vague excuse about why I was spending the night at McDonough's instead of at the penthouse.

There was no lie to what I told them. I had uttered that what I needed was space, and that was true; I did. The staunch atmosphere of the penthouse was beginning to suffocate me. The boys were rarely there, and Matthias's ability to pretend I didn't exist had reached an all-time high.

What I hadn't told them about were the few pit stops I would be making along the way, and my plans for the next night. Seamus and Kiernan had been more than excited to show me the tattoo shop they owned.

It was managed by a middle-aged man named Ioan, who was an all-star in the ink community. He stood a bit taller than the twins, with muscles that rivaled Maksim's. His hair was a Galway black, eyes as blue as the ocean, and his smile could melt the panties off any lady. Hell, there was a line of women eyeing him up in the waiting room, ready to shoot their shot with him by bravely getting tattooed.

More than a few of them had given me the stink eye as the Irish gentleman happily led me past his other waiting walk-ins to his booth in the back, talking animatedly about ideas for my own ink.

The thrum of the needle against my skin was heaven. Each time he drew the needle across my thigh as he etched his artwork onto my body, my body felt alive. It wasn't the same tingle of electricity that skated up my body when Matthias caused me pain that mingled dangerously with my pleasure.

No. This was something different altogether. A new form of freedom that had never existed before. Matthias once said my body belonged to him, and in a way, it did. It always would, but it was also mine. Libby, Kenzi, and I had always dreamed of getting matching tattoos, and once he was done with the piece on my thigh, I had him do three small ones behind my right ear.

Three small birds in flight.

The design was nothing extravagant, but Ioan sensed there was meaning behind the tattoo.

"Ready to see it?" he'd asked as he handed me a mirror. "Let's start with your leg."

Slowly, he helped me stand while Seamus brought over a full-length mirror. I gasped at the imagery in front of me. Ioan had completely freehanded the complex design, and I was taken aback at such an accurate representation.

"You were never a lamb, my dear. You were always a wolf."

When the tattooist had asked what he could use as inspiration, I'd given him the words Dante had left me with.

Now, I was looking at a juxtaposed design of a female with curly locks, melded together with a snarling wolf. The entire piece was black and white, except the eyes of the woman and the wolf were a stark emerald green. Just like mine.

It was absolutely stunning, and I'd told him so. But it was the three simple birds behind my ear that had me tearing up. Maybe one day I'd find Kenzi, and she'd get them too. A tribute to our lost sister.

The bass of *Club Clover* sounded even from across the street, the line stretching for blocks as people waited in anticipation of finally being let into one of Seattle's most exclusive venues. Also owned by the Kavanaughs.

"You look fucking stunning, sis," Seamus crowed as he moved in beside me. Kiernan flanked my other side. They were no slouches themselves. Their normally unruly red hair was combed back, and they'd replaced their normal everyday wear of jeans and T-shirts with black trousers and matching jade green button-down shirts.

Panties were going to spontaneously combust tonight.

I could already see a few of the women in line eyeing them up like they were nothing more than sizzling pieces of meat to be bitten into and spit back out.

The boys led me forward, past the red velvet rope and into the smoky atmosphere of the club. When I'd told them I'd never been to a club before and I wanted to give it a try, they were more than happy to drag me out with them—with a few added stipulations, of course.

The wig was a must and something I wasn't going to argue about. I'd always wanted to be blond like my sisters. I had to always stay within one of their sights and was under no circumstances allowed to leave without them.

I hadn't planned on most of those things anyway, so I had just shrugged and agreed.

"Oh my gosh!" Someone grabbed my arm, yanking me away from the twins and into a warm hug. "I'm so excited to meet you."

Pulling free from the grasp, I was prepared to fight. Until the twins came up beside my supposed attacker with broad smiles on their matching faces.

"Jesus, Margaret," Seamus chuckled. "Ye almost got yourself clocked by your cousin without even being introduced."

"Cousin?" My mouth parted slightly as I stared at the woman before me. She was gorgeous. A curvy ginger bombshell with pale Robin's egg eyes and a freckled face. She wore a pair of tight-fitting black leggings and a green tank top. Her heels, like mine, gave her a bit of height, but she still stood a good inch or two shorter than me.

"Shit," she cursed, flushing slightly as she twisted her fingers together nervously. "I'm sorry. I just got really excited."

I couldn't help but laugh at her enthusiasm. It was contagious, as was her broad smile.

"You just took me off guard." I smiled warmly at her. "Thing One and Thing Two didn't tell me about you."

Margaret rolled her eyes as she elbowed the twins in the sides.

"That's these boys for you," she laughed. "None of the Kavanaugh brothers have any manners."

"I beg your pardon?" Seamus brought his hand up to his chest and pretended to look shocked. "I have amazing manners. Thank you very much. My mother raised me well."

Margaret snorted. "Yeah, in a pen, like a pig."

It was Kiernan's turn to laugh, his usual stony exterior melting slightly.

"Come on." Margaret grabbed my hand and tugged me along behind her through the maze of people toward the back of the club. "Let's sit and get a drink. The boys told me you've never been to a club before." I shook my head. She had to nearly yell at me to be heard over the roar of the music, and if she didn't have a firm grip on my hand, I would have lost her in the din and haze of the club.

The minute we sat down on the plush green velvet of one of the back corner booths, a waitress wearing a short black miniskirt and a green crop top came up to take our order.

"A blackberry mojito for me and a..." Margaret looked at me a bit skeptically, probably wondering if I'd ever ordered a drink before. She didn't know I'd spent the better part of a year working at a dive bar.

"Jameson on the rocks, please."

The waitress nodded as she wrote down our order and took off.

"Girl, that is some hard shit right there." Margaret laughed. "I'd thought you'd order something like a margarita or a white claw."

"I worked in a dive bar for a while," I told her, thanking the waitress when she came back a minute later with our drinks. Damn, she was fast. Margaret must have seen something in my face because she chuckled before taking a sip of her drink.

"Seamus and Kiernan own the club," she giggled. "Whenever they're here, one of the waitresses is taken off floor duty to only serve their booth. No having to wait or anything."

That made more sense.

"This place is amazing," I told her as I looked around. It was the truth. The blend of music, lights, and the smoky ambiance all melded together to create an almost ethereal experience. Our booth was just on the edge of the dance floor but still tucked back far enough to provide a modicum of privacy.

The hints of green and cherry wood that were spread throughout the club paid tribute to their Irish heritage without being overwhelming. There weren't any Irish flags or colors outside of the green. No high-top bar stools or pool tables. This place was more elevated and swankier, a tribute to the new generation of Irish taking over.

It was very much the style of the twins.

A song came on I didn't recognize, but Margaret did, her face glowing as she clapped her hands together excitedly.

"Come on!" She ushered me out of the booth, dragging me behind her onto the dance floor. "I love this song."

Margaret raised her hands above her head and swayed her hips to the beat of the music. Her eyes closed as she got lost in the beat. Looking around, I saw the twins grinding against a couple of college-age girls who already looked to be far past drunk.

Not sure what exactly I was supposed to do, I mirrored Margaret's movements until my body seemed to find its own rhythm among the beat.

One song became two, which became three, and soon I found myself tiring. The man beside me had been trying to grind his body against mine for the last few songs, and I was done with it. The twins were too busy making out with their drunken conquests, so I settled on seeing if Margaret would join me back at the booth.

"I need a drink," I yelled and mimed that I was thirsty. We'd been at the club for almost two hours, and the first round of Jameson had already worn off. A thin sheen of sweat covered my forehead and the back of my neck, and I was dying of thirst.

Margaret nodded, pushing past me so she could lead me back toward the booth. I followed behind her, attempting to keep up with her quick pace.

The knife came out of nowhere, and if I hadn't been so intently focused on my surroundings so I wouldn't lose sight of my newly acquired cousin, I might have missed it.

I leaped back as the blade came slicing down at me.

"Jimmy?" I swallowed back the lump in my throat as I stared at the man before me. Jimmy Burlosconi worked for Dante as an enforcer, but something in the back of my brain told me this wasn't Romano sanctioned.

I hoped.

"Don't take this personally, princess," Jimmy sneered. "But a job's a job, and I ain't passin' up the bounty on your head."

Bounty?

Someone put out a bounty on me?

Who?

My suspicion that Jimmy wasn't working for Dante was right. He wouldn't need to put out a bounty on my head to get Jimmy to do the job. Jimmy worked for him, which means someone else out there wanted me dead.

"Fuck you," I snarled at Jimmy, dodging another blow. Someone screamed *"knife,"* and the crowd on the dance floor parted easily.

Jimmy snarled as he lunged forward. I braced for the impact, ready to knock the knife from his hands, but I was too slow.

"Fucking pox bottle," Kiernan growled as he slammed his fist into Jimmy's face. The hitman's blade clattered to the ground as he hit the floor.

"Who do you think ye are coming into our club and attacking our sister?" Seamus snarled, his foot landing in Jimmy's stomach. "Get him up."

Two of the club's bouncers hauled Jimmy to his feet and hauled him off the dance floor without another word.

"Are you okay?" Seamus turned to me, his eyes scanning me for injuries. I nodded.

"He didn't get me," I assured my brother. "Those lessons with narkey-hole over there paid off."

Seamus burst out laughing at my use of the Irish insult he had taught me to use. Kiernan didn't look nearly as amused at me calling him out on being moody all the time.

"Fuck ye teach her that for?" Kier shook his head at his

brother. "Father's gonna be fucking furious if he finds out yer teachin' her that shite."

His twin simply shrugged and grinned before he bent down to grab Jimmy's forgotten knife.

"Thank you, ladies and gentlemen," he hollered to the surrounding crowd. At some point, the music had been killed and the lights turned on. "The show is over. Free drinks on the house for the next half hour."

Shouts and cries of excitement rose up around us as the lights dimmed, and the steady thrum of music started up again.

"Oh my god!" Margaret rushed to hug me when I reached our booth, the twins following closely behind. "Are you okay?"

"I'm fine," I assured her before turning back to the twins. Something was bothering me about Jimmy, and it wasn't the fact that he'd tried to knife me. "How the hell did Jimmy know I was here? And better yet, how did he know what I was wearing?"

"Fuck if we know," Kiernan growled. "But trust me, sis, we're gonna fucking find out. You good?"

I nodded my head as I took my seat next to Margaret, taking a long sip of the Jameson she'd ordered for me. Dammit. How the hell did he know I was at the club? There were only a few people who knew I'd be here with the twins. Even fewer who knew what I'd be wearing, and they were all part of Liam's crew.

Shit.

There was no way it was Liam. He didn't need to put a bounty on my head to kill me. He'd had plenty of opportunity to do it himself.

Unless he wanted it to look like someone else had done it. I'd like to think that Matthias would avenge me if I was murdered. Liam wouldn't risk a war killing me himself without an alibi. But what was his motive?

As the eldest Kavanaugh, I was technically the first in line to inherit the Kavanaugh fortune and the underground, but I'd already told Liam and the twins that I didn't want that. Sure, I could stake my claim, but why would I? I didn't want anything to do with that world if I could help it. I'd told Liam I was more than happy to help with the legal side of the business when everything was said and done, but I wouldn't take away from what the twins had worked so hard for.

That wasn't fair to them.

Something had shifted in Liam after I'd told him that, which was right before I accused his wife of being a dirty, rotten, cheating liar.

Not my finest moment.

"Um, Ava?" Margaret tentatively called my name. She sounded nervous and on edge. I shook myself from my thoughts and looked over at her. Her face had turned slightly pale, eyes widened as she stared transfixed at something behind me.

"I think he's here for you," she whispered without blinking. She looked like a fox caught in a trap.

A chill skated down my spine; the tiny hairs on the back of my neck pricking up, sensing that I was being watched. I didn't need to turn around to know who she was referring to. There was only one person who could make someone look like they pissed their pants.

I swore I could hear his heavy footsteps approaching, even over the blaring sound of the music. My body thrummed like a live wire, knowing I was being watched.

No. Hunted.

But the question was, who was the prey?

Because it certainly wasn't me.

The heat of his body pressed up against my shoulder, but still I refused to look at him. Instead, I gulped down the rest of my drink before my blood-red lips pulled into a dark smirk.

"Nice of you to join us," I let the words roll off my tongue as sensually as I could manage, "husband."

"You're in a lot of trouble, my little traitor."

CHAPTER TWENTY-ONE

Matthias

"What brings you here?" Ava turned in her seat to look up at me, her emerald eyes shining brilliantly in the dancing lights.

"One of my men saw you here, rang me as a courtesy." It wasn't a lie, exactly. One of my men had called me after witnessing what had gone down on the dance floor. My gaze roamed her body, and from my cursory once-over, she appeared unharmed.

I don't know what I was thinking. Rushing down here like that, but I couldn't get the image of her being stabbed from my mind, her bloody body laid out on the wooden floor beneath us. Luckily, that hadn't been the case, but the imagery was hard to shake.

And so was the pain that constricted my chest.

I was meant to be pushing her away, and instead, here I was, in one of Kavanaugh's night clubs because I refused to accept what my own men had told me. That she was alive and unharmed. I'd refused to accept it until I saw her with my own two eyes.

And now I had.

"Look," she sighed, taking in a long breath before letting it out slowly, "I'm here to have fun. Don't ruin it, please."

"Why would I ruin it?" Ava thought I'd come here to drag her back to the penthouse. She didn't know I knew about the knife incident. She simply believed I was here to bring her back and lock her away.

That had never been my intention.

Not that the thought of locking her away in my bedroom, tied to my bed, didn't have merit, but it was honestly unfeasible. Especially now with Kavanaugh in the picture.

"Why not?" she asked, her head tilting slightly, her fake blond hair cascading down one shoulder like a waterfall. "You've been ruining everything else."

"Let me show you how much I won't be ruining your night." I grinned at her as I pulled her from her seat and lead her toward the side of the dance floor that was darkened by shadows. A small area the lights just barely reached. It was the perfect spot for privacy.

It didn't escape my notice how many men had their gazes on her lithe figure as she swirled and rocked her hips against my pelvis in time to the beat. Their lustful gazes on her body caused my jaw to clench, teeth grinding as I struggled to keep from ripping their throats out.

I slipped my hands over her hips, a small gasp leaving her painted red lips when I pushed her ass harder against my straining cock. My head dipped down along her neck, and I

SHATTRED REMNANTS

breathed in her perfect sent. Jasmine. She always smelled like fresh Jasmine.

Ava's hands came up to tangle in my hair as I nipped, kissed, and licked down her jaw, her neck, and onto her shoulder while my hands roamed her body. Plucking and massaging at her breasts until she was a panting mess in my hands. I'd slipped us farther into the shadows where no one could see us.

I'd never been much for public sex, but the heightened awareness of being caught playing with her on the dance floor in her father's club made my cock alarmingly hard.

A growl idled in my throat as I grabbed her chin in a harsh grip, turning her face to the side and up.

Our lips met with a fury that rivaled the greatest hurricanes. It wasn't slow or languid but hurried and passionate, like we were afraid this would be the last kiss. My tongue penetrated her lips, plundering her mouth without mercy, taking complete control. Ava had no choice but to take it, her ass rocking against my growing erection.

Fuck.

What was this woman doing to me?

AVA

Moaning into his kiss, I swiveled my ass against the hard-on he had growing in his trousers. Matthias could dismiss me all he wanted, but I knew the effect I had on him. One hand pinched and caressed at my breast while another slipped up the hem of my dress from the back, his fingers lazily creating a path toward my pussy.

I'd been wet since we'd stepped onto the dance floor.

Leaning back into his chest, I was already panting, anxious for his touch.

Matthias's fingers skated over my mound before parting my lower lips and gently brushing against that little button of pleasure. I bit back a moan, my hands digging into his forearms as his touch sent waves of electricity through my body, my empty pussy clenching with need.

"Matthias…" His name was a breathy plea on my lips.

"What do you want, Krasnyy?" His voice darkened, an edge to his tone as he struggled to remain in control.

"Please…"

"Use your words, Red." I didn't have to see his face to know he was smirking.

Asshat.

"I want your fingers inside me." Luckily, it was dark, and he wouldn't see the stain of red that was no doubt tinting my face the color of a ripe tomato.

Without preamble, his fingers surged straight inside me, my pussy welcoming them into its hot, wet embrace.

Matthias groaned. "You're so fucking wet for me," he breathed into my ear, nipping at the lobe harshly, causing a moan to slip from my parted lips. "Careful, Red. Someone might hear you and then come investigate. I would hate to have to end this night on a bloody note if someone saw you this way."

I nodded, unable to get any words out. I leaned my head back against his shoulder and rocked my hips into his touch. Matthias continued his assault on my throbbing pussy, hooking his fingers in just the right spot that I was seeing stars, my hips bucking into his fingers unapologetically, like a cowboy riding a wild stallion.

"Oh god." I choked back another moan as my body shuddered, the coil in my belly tightening as his pace became more frenetic.

"Come for me, my little traitor." He pinched one of my nipples—hard—while he bit down on my neck, and I had no choice but to follow his command.

Over the hill I tumbled, my entire body nearly convulsing as my inner walls clenched violently around the digits he had buried deep inside me. My legs shook, and I felt Matthias's grip on me tighten fractionally to keep me up. His fingers slipped from inside me, and I whimpered at the loss.

"Taste yourself," he whispered and held his fingers up to my lips. I opened my mouth, my tongue darting out hesitantly to lick at the tip of his finger coated with my juices before I sucked them into my mouth.

I'd never been one of those women who was turned on by the heroine sucking her own cum from a man's fingers. Now, as I licked and sucked at Matthias's, I could definitely see the appeal.

It wasn't about the taste, which was slightly musky and sweet, but how his eyes darkened at the sight of me sucking his digits like I would suck his cock. It was also the growl that lifted from his throat. The way his pupils dilated as he took me in with a deep hunger that left me breathless.

"So why did you really come down here?" I asked as I straightened my dress. Matthias chuckled, his grip now on my waist as he leaned against the wall of the dance floor. My legs still felt like jelly, and I wasn't inclined to move. Not when he felt so warm against me. "I doubt it was simply because one of your men said he saw me partying it up."

Matthias let out a frustrated sigh, letting his head fall back against the wall with a soft thud.

"He saw what happened with you and Jimmy."

"And what?" I stepped from his hold, turning myself to face him, hands on my hips as I glared at him. "Were you worried that if I died, you wouldn't be able to use me in your plan?"

Matthias's eyes narrowed as he glared down at me, his posture stiffening.

"Oh, wait," I scoffed. "I'm no longer useful that way, am I? So why bother coming down, Matthias? Did you suddenly grow a conscience or something and start giving a fuck? You've made it perfectly clear how you feel about me, even if we do fuck."

"Just because I distanced myself doesn't mean I don't care, Ava," he told me, his face softening slightly at my agitated state. "I just don't trust you."

"Because you never gave me the chance to tell you my side of the story." I pointed my finger at his chest. "You just assumed I betrayed you. Assumed I'd been playing you the whole time. Well, newsflash, asshole, I hadn't been. I never once told anyone anything about what you told me. That's including your brother's name. Hell, I never even told Libby, and I told her fucking everything."

"It's not that simple, and you—"

"Save me your fucking bullshit," I spat at him. "You want to know what I think? I think you married me on a whim to get the upper hand on Elias, and now that he's dead, you don't need me anymore. You got your use out of me and a couple of good fucks, and instead of owning up to it like a man, you hide behind your thoughts of betrayal. I thought that maybe, maybe, I could get you to see my side. To let me tell my story, but the thing is, you don't want to hear it because it won't make one lick of difference, will it?"

"Ava..."

"No." I choked back a sob, the tears flowing freely. God, I had to stop crying. "I'm done, Matthias. I thought I wanted to play your game, but I don't. I'm done, and once the gala is over, I'll be gone and out of your life forever. Just like you wanted."

There was no looking back now, and I doubted things would ever be the same. There were two ways this would end, and I knew one thing for sure. One of those outcomes had the potential to destroy me in worse ways than anything Christian ever had.

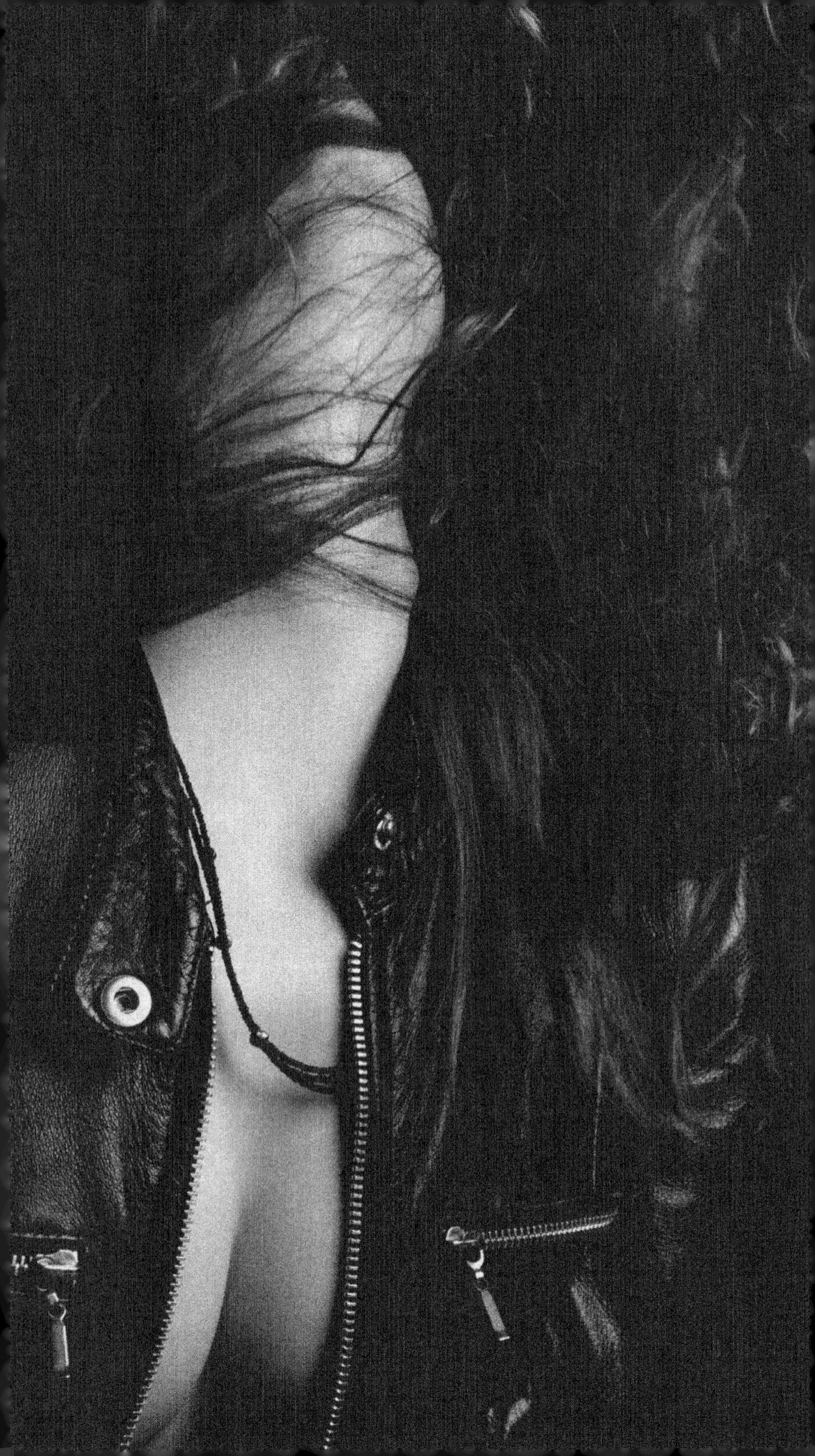

CHAPTER TWENTY-TWO

Ava

I lay on Matthias's bed, staring at the ceiling.

The sound of my breathing was the only thing to be heard throughout the vast space other than the familiar, comfortable clicks of the pocket watch he'd left on his dresser. He never went anywhere without it, which told me he'd been in a hurry to get to the club after he'd received the call about the assault.

I'd been back at the penthouse for almost an hour, my stomach churning as my mind raced a million miles an hour. He hadn't come back yet, or if he had, he hadn't come back here to me, which told me what I needed to know.

I was nothing but a mere pawn on his chessboard, not the queen I'd always thought I'd be. Our marriage was nothing more than a farce, a tactic he'd never had the chance to utilize because the enemy's king had already been wiped from the board.

Now it was time for a new game, a new adversary, and I didn't belong anymore. He'd find another pawn. Another distraction. Another tactic to take down the enemy.

I bolted up with a start as the door to the room swung open, bouncing against the wall harshly. Matthias stalked into the room, looking worn and disheveled.

"What do you want?" I snapped at him, glaring angrily.

"You wanted to tell me your side of the story," he muttered gruffly, but his voice was soft. "So, I'm here to listen."

I sucked in a deep breath; a sob lodged in the back of my throat as tears sprung to my eyes. He sat down at the end of the bed and stared at me, waiting patiently. The smell of whiskey and smoke wafted around him. The whiskey was his comfort, and the smoking was a habit he hadn't quite kicked when he was stressed.

Knowing that he'd been sweating over coming in here made me feel slightly better.

"Are you sure you want to hear it?" I asked, tilting my head to get a better view of him. He'd changed into a pair of gray sweats and a white T-shirt from the stash of clothes he'd been keeping in a duffel bag in the living room.

"There's a difference between want and need, Ava." He fixed me with a hard look. "I may not want to hear it, but I need to. You were right when you said I was using it as a reason to push you away."

His eyes were dark, haunted, and I could see the pain etched into them like a chisel on stone. Rough, chiseled, and covered in cracks. I was no stranger to how much vulnerability Matthias showed when he placed his trust in someone; it was so rare. The man had more than two hundred men under his command, but the only people he ever trusted were the men of his inner circle—and me.

I'd betrayed that trust, even if it hadn't been willingly. Even though it hadn't been deliberately. But the air needed to be cleared. There was one thing that needed to be addressed, and that was the issue of his brother.

A name I'd never uttered outside this bedroom to anyone.

So, I told him my story. From the moment Jonathon Archer walked into my apartment and threatened to throw me in prison for Elias to kill to the moment Seamus and Kiernan had saved me. I left nothing out because there was nothing for me to hide.

When I finished, I expected him to leave. To shout. Anything. Instead, he turned to me, tugging my body toward his before slowly and methodically removing my pajamas piece by piece. Then he laid me back against the pillows.

"What are you...?"

He silenced me with a stern look while his large, tattooed hands roamed my naked body. It'd been a couple of weeks since I'd been rescued from the *stables*, and although my superficial wounds had mostly healed, there were many that still hadn't.

His touch mapped out the scars like a road map, memorizing each burn of the cattle prod, each scarred line from the knife, the still healing graze of the bullet I'd taken for Kiernan. Not that he'd appreciated it. Touches turned to kisses as Matthias turned me every which way, inspecting, caressing, committing each wound to memory.

I had no doubt that he was tallying each one to personally inflict them back on Christian.

Matthias's tongue darted out to swivel inside my belly button. The erotic gesture caused me to giggle. His head dipped lower, his nose running through the soft curls of my mound. I drew in a deep breath as he parted my thighs. I felt a rush of wet heat sweep through me at the primal action.

"Always so wet for me, Krasnyy," he growled, the vibration sending a jolt straight to my cunt. My pulse raced, chest heaving as he swept his tongue over my center, causing me to whimper.

"Only you," I gasped as he flicked his tongue over my clit. I moaned loudly, my back arching off the soft duvet as I tried to push my hips closer to his mouth.

"That's right, Red." He smirked against my pussy lips. "Only me."

"Matthias," I whimpered his name as he began to lap at me in earnest, a string of embarrassing sounds leaving me, but I didn't care. He'd sunk two of his thick digits into my wet heat, sliding his fingers in and out a few times before curling them in just the right spot that had my hips bucking off the bed.

"Easy now." Matthias's arm pressed down on my hips, keeping me in place as he assaulted me with his tongue, his teeth, and his fingers like there was no tomorrow. Just when I thought I'd reach the end, when the coil in my lower stomach couldn't tighten anymore and I'd fly over the edge—he stopped.

"No," I whined when the heat of his body left me wanting and aching for more.

"Don't worry, Red." He smirked as he removed every stitch of clothing that separated his skin from mine. "I won't leave you wanting."

He crawled up my body, leaving hot, electric open-mouthed kisses in his wake until his cock was in my face.

"Open wide, baby girl."

I didn't need any further encouragement. Opening my mouth, I held his gaze in a thrall as he clenched his ass, jutting his hips forward until the head of his dick was at my lips. Still holding eye contact, I licked a drop of precum from his tip and then sucked him in my mouth to take him as far as I could. The flat of my tongue ran along the underside of his shaft as he began a slow, rhythmic pace of fucking my mouth.

"Fuck, Ava." He groaned as I dug my nails into the muscles of his ass, being sure to leave marks. The thin thread of control he had snapped, and he leaned forward, bracing himself against the wooden headboard before he began rutting like a wild animal.

All I could do was grip his ass cheeks harder, setting a harsh, unrelenting rhythm as he fucked my mouth for his own pleasure. Drool dripped out the sides of my mouth as I gagged, struggling to breathe around his girthy length.

My pussy clenched with need, long, muted moans echoing in my throat, sending pleasurable vibrations up his cock as he pounded into me.

"*Blyad*," he cursed in Russian as he pulled out of my mouth, flipping me over until I was on all fours.

"Fuck," I groaned as he pulled my hips back harshly, impaling me on his rock-hard cock in one movement.

"I missed this feeling," he growled as he pounded into me from behind like a dog in heat. The walls of my pussy clenched around him when his hand struck my right cheek. I clawed at the bedsheets, the sounds leaving my throat like those of a wild animal, a bitch in heat. If he hadn't been sending me into an orgasmic bliss, I might've been humiliated.

Hands tangled in my hair, he hauled me up until my back hit his chest, pumping even harder. I cried out, the angle of this position causing him to hit even deeper. One hand came up to pinch at my nipple, rolling it between his thumb and forefinger harshly. Teeth nipped at my neck, and the hand that had been in my hair rubbed at my clit furiously.

"Come for me, Krasnyy," he rumbled in my ear. "Come all over your husband's cock."

I did just what he'd asked. A string of incoherent words ripping from my mouth as my orgasm washed over me like a tidal wave.

"Matthias!" I threw my head back against his shoulder as I screamed his name, my inner walls clenching tightly around him, squeezing until he, too, was crashing over the edge.

He collapsed forward, taking me with him, his dick still inside me. We were both covered in sweat, panting and out of breath. Matthias gently pulled out, the squelch of wetness bringing a hue of red to my cheeks. I'd been expecting him to leave again, like he had before, but he surprised me.

Matthias was always surprising me.

Getting up from the bed, he entered the bathroom. I could hear the water running, and my eyes closed for a moment, relishing in the soothing sound. His footsteps on the wooden floor echoed quietly as he climbed back onto the bed.

I didn't protest when he opened my thighs to clean between my legs. The first few times Matthias and I'd had sex, he'd foregone any kind of aftercare unless it involved one of his many instruments. The simple gesture of a wet cloth made my heart swell.

He threw the rag into the laundry basket and climbed back into bed, pulling the covers over both of us. Dragging my body into his, he wrapped his arm around my middle and buried his nose in the crook of my neck.

I knew I shouldn't let this small gesture affect me. This could have been another game, but as the warmth of his body seeped into mine and the sound of his breathing evened out, I realized that if it was another game, it was something for future Ava to deal with.

Right now, I wanted to bask in the comfort he was willingly providing. Even if it would later cripple my heart.

***

It amazed me how fast the next week flew by.

The days were spent with me practicing my dancing with Leon, and now Matthias, who had decided to partake in teaching my two left feet to work. The pair of them dressed me in heels and dragged me across the living room floor like a sack of flour. There was nothing but praises and laughter at how far I'd come, but I knew the honest truth.

I sucked at it.

Once dance lessons were over, I was then passed off to Vas, who took over where Seamus had left off on my knife lessons. The man was much more fun to learn from, especially since nothing he taught me came with a history lesson.

He built on the fundamentals I'd already been taught as he moved from one step to another, and by the end of the week, I'd started to finally hit moving targets.

The feeling of accomplishment that coursed through my veins was like nothing I'd ever experienced before. No one had believed in me before, not like my brothers or Vas did. I'd always felt under accomplished and stunted due to my lack of knowledge and know-how. Sure, I had a degree, but that degree had been achieved online, and although I'd aced almost every class, I'd graduated without any real-world experience.

Plus, teaching wasn't something that was useful in Matthias's and my father's world. They didn't need someone to give the enemy a history lesson; they needed someone who had their back and who could think under pressure.

Vas had assured me that what I brought to the table was the most useful information they'd had on Ward in years, but what would happen when we'd torn apart his empire and I no longer had the information they needed?

I didn't have dirt on anyone else. Just them. So what use would I be?

Not that I had much time to ponder that, because the moment I stepped out of Vas's knife-wielding badass club, Matthias was on me.

So far, we'd christened the kitchen...again...the living room, the hallway, the elevator, the pool...it was an ever-growing list.

The man had become insatiable, and I wondered at the sudden change. Had Jimmy's attempt on my life rattled him enough that he'd forgiven me? Or had it been the fact that he'd seen what Christian had done to me? I tried not to be suspicious of the sudden one-eighty he was pulling, but the part of me that knew things were too good to be true couldn't help but linger in the back of my mind.

I shoved those thoughts away as I stared at the brilliant white of the bedroom door before me.

Her room.

Jesus, I couldn't believe I was going to do this. I didn't want to, but for once, the penthouse was completely empty. Even Mia was out for the day. Matthias and his men were up in their formal offices, securing everything we needed for the gala tonight.

Meanwhile, I was trying to face my demons.

Seeing as how I'd been standing outside her door for the past hour, it wasn't going well. I felt like David facing Goliath, except the door in front of me seemed much more daunting than a biblical giant.

It felt more like Hydra from the *Legend of Hercules*. Each time I convinced myself to open her door, another piece of guilt or doubt shoved itself forward, preventing me from grasping the handle.

I'd tried to call Kenzi.

No answer.

I was starting to worry. She never went this long without trying to contact us. It was the reason I was standing here, heart racing, body shaking, hands trembling on the golden doorknob of regret. If anyone knew what had been going on with Kenzi, it was Libby. The two shared everything.

Taking a long, slow breath, I turned the knob and swung the door open.

The scent of her gentle perfume washed over me, the tears burning at the back of my eyes. I'd gotten her and Kenzi that perfume one year for Christmas. Dante had generously lent his credit card to me, telling me to buy them whatever I wanted.

The unique and enchanting design was what had caught my attention. I hadn't been looking for perfume, but one of the ads from the site I had been surfing caught my attention. It was a limited-edition bottle created by Viktor & Rolph, one of the top perfume designers in the world. The dark rose quartz bottle was contained in a luxuriously crafted thorn case, hand numbered in rose gold. Varied flowers soldered to the top elegantly surrounded the bottle's lid.

There were a total of only fifteen of these bottles in existence, and we each had one. I'd been immediately attracted to the olfactory notes of rose, orchid, and jasmine. I'd had Dante personally contact the business to have each of the scents mildly modified so that one particular scent stood out with each individual bottle.

For Libby, it was orchid. Gentle, elegant, and sweet but easily wilted if it wasn't looked after properly. Exactly like my sweet sister.

Kenzi's bottle held stronger notes of the centifolia rose, a complex hybrid that was often referred to as the *cabbage rose* for how the flower resembled a cabbage head. The scent was sweet, but the rose bush itself was strong and resilient. A perfect homage to my stubborn sister.

Then there was my bottle—jasmine. The scent that Matthias confessed drove him crazy. Jasmine was a diverse plant with subtle notes. It was deceptive, with its pretty white petals and fruity scent. Jasmine grew differently depending on its region and harvest. Some forms of jasmine were deciduous, while others were an evergreen. It could be a shrub or even a climbing vine. But the most important thing was that, just like the cabbage rose, it often refused to die. Some countries even considered it an invasive species.

Each individual perfume scent represented us as an individual, but the uniformity of the bottle represented us as a united front. Sisters who always had each other's backs.

Except I hadn't.

I'd let Christian take Libby from our lives. I'd been powerless to stop him, and I never wanted to feel like that again.

I held back the flow of tears, closing the door behind me with a gentle click before taking a deep breath and walking farther into the room. Everything was exactly as she'd left it. Her clothes were strewn over one of the chairs near the closet, laptop closed on the edge of her bed next to a bag of Cheetos. Kendra never allowed the twins to eat junk food, and Vas had been more than happy to introduce her to his favorite snacks.

Vas.

Jesus. I'd been so caught up in ignoring my own grief and pain that I hadn't even thought of his. Hadn't thought about how it must hurt him not entering her room and being able to smell her perfume one last time. He'd waited for me. He'd known I'd needed this.

Libby loved Vas in her own special way. We might not have gone to an all-girls school, but that didn't mean we weren't kept segregated whenever possible. Every boy knew who Elias was and what would happen if he tried to make a move on one of his daughters.

Steadying my breathing, I tipped up the edge of the mattress at the head of the bed, my hand searching underneath.

Bingo.

I grasped on to the small object and pulled, yanking it free from its hiding spot. Not that it was much of one. Libby had been hiding her diary in the exact same spot since she learned how to keep one.

With trembling hands, I opened it to the first page. Inside was a small picture of the three of us she'd taken with one of the instant print cameras she gotten for her birthday. Libby loved photography; it was something she'd always wanted to pursue but knew she'd never have the chance.

Women were a bargaining chip to people like Elias. A commodity to be traded for the betterment of the family.

FIRST ENTRY

Ava is gone. Between Maleah and me, we'd come up with a solid plan for getting her out from beneath our father's thumb. Kenzi is still overseas at school, but like she promised, she's been in contact with me nearly every day. It's lonely here without them. The house is emptier, and the feelings of sadness swirl around me constantly as I face the darkness alone. Something is wrong here. Father has lost his mind since Ava left, and I'm not naive enough to believe it has anything to do with her safety.

They don't think I know.
They don't think I listen.

But I hear everything within these walls. There are no secrets in these halls. For years, I've listened and learned. Much like Ava has. She doesn't talk about what she hears, and I know it's because she thinks she's keeping us safe. Protected. Afraid that our father's wrath will turn on us.
But I know something she doesn't know.
A secret few know.
Not even Uncle Dante.

CHAPTER TWENTY-THREE

Ava

I stare at the page, reading it again and again as I reaffirmed what a selfish asshole I was. Neil was right. I hadn't been thinking of anyone else but myself. I'd been blind to my sister all along, thinking she was nestled safely in the dark. I'd been wrong, and I left her alone without anyone to turn to or rely on. Without anyone to share her secrets with.

Did her secret have to do with me not being Elias's daughter? Had she always known we weren't blood related? Not that it wasn't too hard to see now that I looked back on it. I didn't resemble Elias in the slightest. Nothing about me could be found in him. It was just another thing I'd let myself be blinded to, and I wasn't even sure why. *Not even Uncle Dante*.

Dante knew I wasn't Elias's daughter. Did Libby think he didn't know? I read on.

SECOND ENTRY

There's a man in the house. One that reminds me of Ava. His Irish accent is thick, ginger hair even brighter than my sisters. There is something wrong with his eyes though. They're not the bright vivid green Ava had, but a dulled jade, like there is some kind of haze over them.

The man was yelling at my father. Screaming at him for how his obsession with a woman was going to cost them everything. He threatened him. Told him to get his house in order, to get rid of the mess he made.

"I sent the woman to take care of your obsession years ago," the man snarled at my father. "And you come back with her spawn?"

"She doesn't know anything," my father assured the man. He laughed, a deep, horrendous cackle that made my skin crawl.

Through the crack in my father's office door, I saw the man reach out and grab him by the throat, striking his knee with a short cane. At this vantage point, I was able to see him more clearly. Jesus, he looked so much like Ava it was unbearable. Was this someone she was related to?

When I asked Father who he was after the man had stormed from our house, he refused to answer. Snapped at me to mind my own business. Reminded me of my place. But I wouldn't forget him. The man with the silver cross cane.

SIXTY-SEVENTH ENTRY

The man was infuriating. A dog with a bone. He followed me around like a lost puppy, barely letting me out of his sight, even to use the restroom. It was like he thought I might try to escape. I wouldn't. Not with Ava here. This place was much safer than my home, especially now that my father was wanted for weapon smuggling, drug smuggling, and human trafficking.

That last part was hard to stomach.

I didn't have high regards for my father, but selling women? Children? Part of me wanted to believe that was a line he would never have crossed. Apparently, he'd been doing it for years. I've been digging into my father's company more and more. None of Dashkov's men, including the Hound, have restricted my access to the internet.

They don't believe I'm any kind of a threat.

To them at least.

My father and brother were a whole different story.

I'd managed to snag a few of my father's black books from his office, and I didn't like what I found.

Ava's going to need these soon, so I'll keep them tucked away in a safe spot for now. I'm not ready to show her. Not ready to face what he's truly done to her. I've only managed to decode a quarter of the book, keeping the answers in my head, because if anyone found out...there would be war.

SIXTY-SEVENTH ENTRY

All this time, I thought she was safe.
She wasn't. And worse, Kenzi lied to me. She lied.
How could she keep something so important from me?
So vital?
And now she's spewing this bullshit about doing what was right for the family.
Did they brainwash her?
Kenzi hated my father and mother for how they treated her.
Less than what she deserved, in my opinion. All because she couldn't bear children.
Father sold her off, but I can't figure out where or to whom.
There wasn't a person's name, but an organization.
"The Chameleon Agency"
Kenzi, what has father done to you?

SEVENTY-FIFTH ENTRY

Today should be a day of celebration, but there is a heaviness in the air I don't understand.
I know they're not really getting married, because technically they already are, but I still wish she was be happier.
I want to tell her everything, but I know now isn't the time. I've been bursting to share my secrets, and not just the ones that hover darkly above our heads.
Vas kissed me last night, and not just on the lips.
Well, not just the ones on my face.
My body had never felt more alive as he caused wave after wave of pure and utter bliss to rush over me. I'd never been kissed before, let alone done anything like that...and he hadn't wanted anything in return, even though I had easily seen him straining through the sexy sweatpants he constantly wore.
I still hate him.
Sort of.
A little.
Well, darn...

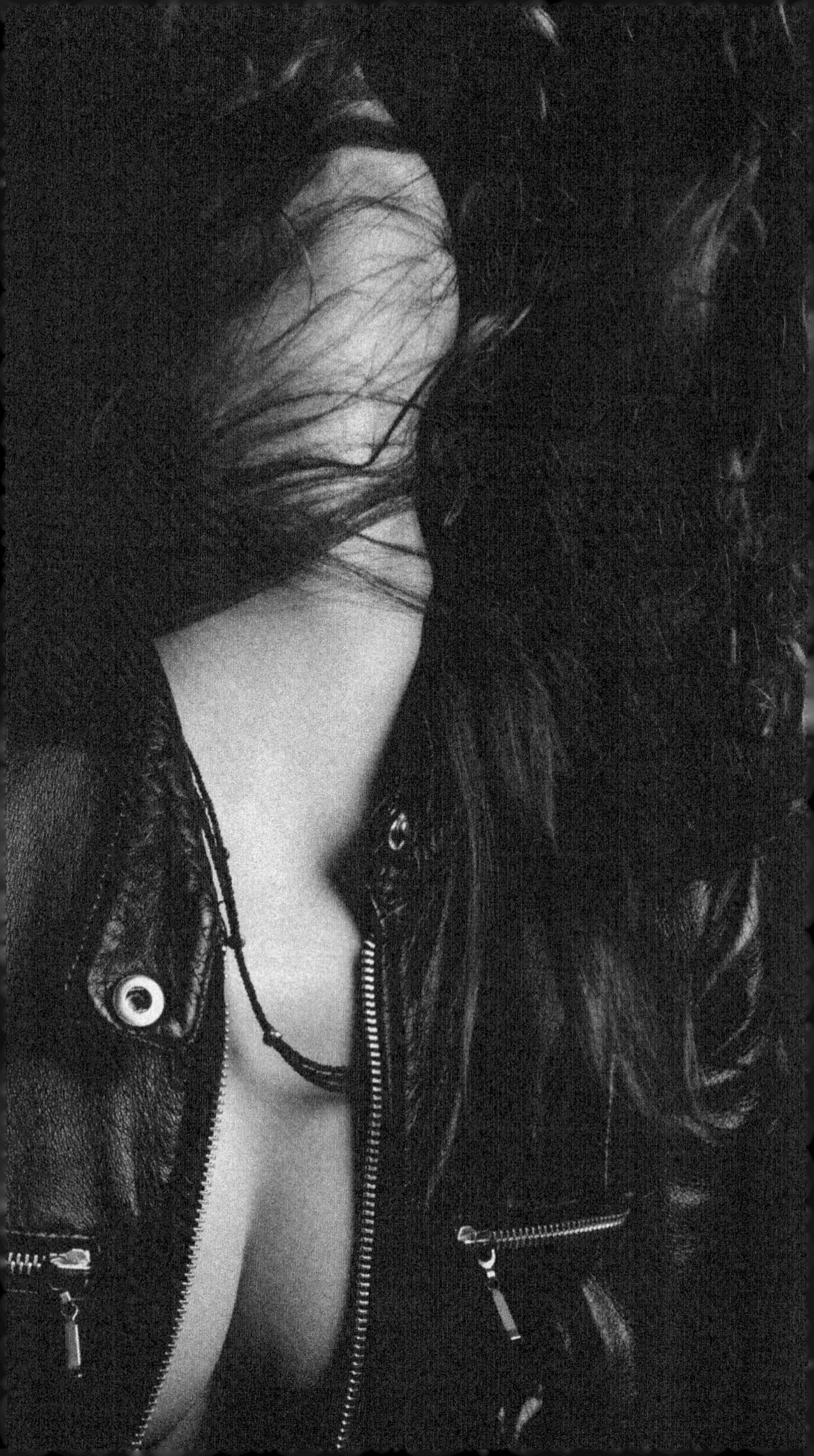

CHAPTER TWENTY-FOUR

Ava

If I hadn't been ugly crying before, I was now. For seventy-five entries, she poured her heart and soul into every word she wrote. She paid attention when no one, including me, thought she had a clue.

I gave a watery laugh at how easily she'd become a viper in the grass. Anyone who looked at her would have thought her to be an airheaded heiress. Looks were deceiving.

Once I'd finished grieving, my tears drying on my cheeks, I swept back over the entries, dog earing several pages that stood out. I thumbed through the blank pages, searching in case I missed anything, when my eyes caught sight of several rows of dark scribbles.

131892
1937

1-3-6
14-3-1
19-1-7-2(3)

19747 6 2095 230091

Demeter   091322

CHAPTER TWENTY-FIVE

Ava

It was a code.

But what did it mean?

Sighing, I tucked the journal underneath my arm as I stood from the bed and made my way toward the door, grabbing her bottle of perfume along the way. I stopped, taking a deep breath as I took one last long look around the room.

I missed her, but I would never, ever go a day without remembering her. And I'd make sure Christian paid for what he did. I'd find Kenzi, wherever she was, and make sure she was safe. That was my promise, because my sister's death would not be in vain.

THE SOFT CLICK of the door signaled an end. Tomorrow, after the gala, I'd be sure to tell Vas what her journal read about him, but right now I needed space as I continued to decipher what I'd read.

Who was the man meeting with Elias?

Libby's entry stated he looked like me. The man with the cross cane. What did that even mean? Did he have a cane with a cross on it? What did the cross look like? What did he mean he sent a woman to deal with Elias's obsession?

The only obsession I'd ever known him to have had been my mother. I'd always thought her death was the result of a home burglary gone wrong. The man who'd killed her had confessed, but now that I was in this world and had seen firsthand the kind of power Elias had held, I wondered if that had all been a setup.

Now that I thought back on it, I'd never been given up to social services. The detective on the case who'd found me in the small closet hiding place had given me directly to Elias.

The fucker had been on his payroll.

And what was The Chameleon Agency?

Did they have something to do with Kenzi's disappearance?

And the numbers. I thought I knew how to decode them but—

"I'm so sorry, Mrs. Dashkov."

I'd been buried so deep in my head that I hadn't been paying attention to where I was going and had run right into Ben, Matthias's lawyer, as he came striding out of his boss's office.

"No, that was on me." I gave him a small smile, hoping he didn't notice my blotchy, tear-stained cheeks. "I wasn't paying attention to where I was going."

"I'd understand that you would have a lot on your mind," he assured me somberly.

"Matthias isn't here," I told him. "He said he wouldn't be back until right before the gala."

"Ah, yes." Ben nodded, his eyes full of pity as he looked down at me. "He'd told me that he wanted me to drop off the paperwork for you two to sign."

"The paperwork—"

"I know this is a trying time, Mrs. Dashkov," he said as he reached into his coat pocket. "Coming out of this won't be easy, and honestly, we all think he's making the wrong decision." He handed me his business card. "Just know, if you ever need anything once this is all over, don't hesitate to call."

He walked away before I had a chance to even consider what he was saying. A heavy ball of dread dropped into my stomach as I turned Ben's card over in my hand.

I'd understand that you would have a lot on your mind.

At first, I thought he been referring to the gala tonight, but the mention of paperwork had my stomach twisting with unease, the ball of dread inflating by the second. I stepped into the office, eyeing the manila envelope Ben had placed on his desk with a heavy dose of anxiety.

Jesus, this was not what I needed.

Not now.

I gulped back the lump stuck in my throat, fresh tears welling in my eyes as I slowly unwound the twine holding the envelope closed.

It was something I should have expected, but the last week had been going so well. I never thought this was an option.

Hell, even if the last week hadn't gone well, I never thought this was something he would do. It was a low, dirty blow, and he knew it.

Maybe he hadn't told Ben he'd changed his mind.

Maybe, just maybe, this was all a misunderstanding.

But as I slipped the papers back into the envelope and placed them back on the desk, I'd begun to doubt everything we'd done since the night I'd told him everything.

He could have been playing me this whole time. Pretending. Getting his money's worth. After all, he had lost 5.5 million dollars because of Elias. He'd taken me as collateral, and he'd been doing nothing but collecting for it since the night he took my virginity. And now—now he was making sure to get a few last dips in before he shut me out completely.

I'd tried to play his game by throwing the truth in his face. By telling him I couldn't do it anymore, and that I was leaving. On the dance floor of Clover, I'd made my move. and when he came to me to hear me out, I thought I'd finally moved a few steps ahead.

When he'd fucked me that night, I knew I was winning, and when he'd kissed me goodbye this morning, I thought I'd finally won.

But the papers in his office stamped in bold red ink that read *DIVORCE*, told me I was the one who'd been played.

CHAPTER TWENTY-SIX

Ava

I sat quietly in front of the vanity as Mia's niece, Leanna, primped and prodded me to near perfection. She'd sugared every inch of my body, tweezed my brows, oiled me, moisturized me, and who the hell knows what else she'd done that I didn't know about.

I kind of enjoyed it.

The last time I'd been pampered like this was the day of my sham of a wedding, and even then, it had been nowhere this extensive. It had also just been Libby and me.

My mind was still trying to decipher the handful of journal entries I didn't understand. What secret did she know that Dante didn't? It couldn't have been about Elias not being my father because Dante had been well aware of my parentage. What was it that she thought she knew?

Then there was the mysterious "man with the silver cross cane," who looked like me. Was he a relative? I knew it wasn't Liam. She'd described the man as older.

And Liam didn't use a cane.

So, who was it? Was the obsession he was referring to meant to be my mother? If so, "taking care" of her no doubt meant he'd sent someone to kill her. But why? And why had the Portland police labeled it as a robbery gone wrong and not a murder?

There were too many unanswered questions. Too many possible scenarios and not enough evidence. Unfortunately, it was something I'd have to really dig into until after the gala.

That didn't mean I hadn't started, though.

"North Precinct, how can I direct your call?" The woman's voice was nasally, bored, and I could hear the faint chomping of gum through the telephone. Wonderful, already off to a great start.

"I'm looking for the detective in charge of a certain case," I asked her. "How do I go about finding him?"

I could practically feel the woman behind the phone rolling her eyes.

"Well," she sighed impatiently. "Do you have the case number?"

Damn. I hadn't thought of that.

"No, but I have the address of the incident and the victim's name, date of birth, and social," I informed her. "Can you make do with that?"

"No guarantees, but I can try," she huffed. "What's the victim's name and date of birth?"

"Katherine Moore, born February 17, 1978," I told her.

"Okay, give me one second." The line went silent, but I

could hear the faint sound of nails clicking against hardwood in the background.

"Says here the case is closed." She came back on the line. "And that detective isn't in a good way."

"What do you mean?"

"Died a few years ago," she sneered in disgust. "Suicide after IA found out he was a dirty cop. Paid off by the Italians. Why you so interested anyway, kid? This case if over thirteen years old."

"She was my mother," I whispered.

"Ah," the woman sighed. "Look, here's what I can do for you. The case is closed, so everything is open record, but that shit can take months to request. If you can verify some information for me, I'll get the case documents in the mail to you. Also, looks like she has some stuff in storage; old evidence and some shit. I'll send those along too."

"I'd appreciate that." "

"Listen, kid," the woman warned softly. "Detective Jonny Morelli was not only a shitty cop, but a shitty person. Whatever you're looking for, be careful, because some very powerful people seemed to have had their hands on this case."

"Thanks." I put a smile in my voice. "I will."

"Good, now," she clacked her nails, "where am I sending everything?"

I HADN'T BEEN ALLOWED to keep anything from my old life when Elias took me in. Not even a stuffed animal. He'd made me leave everything behind. I wasn't sure what the precinct could have, but it was worth having her send it to me.

"You look amazing." Mia halted my wandering mind as she entered my room with a vivid smile while holding a small tray with a cup of heavenly coffee sitting on it.

"Thank god." I stood from the small chair Leanna had me sitting in to meet her aunt. The smell of coffee filtered through the room. I inhaled the robust, aromatic liquid before taking a long, slow sip, letting the bitterness wash over my tongue.

"I figured you might need some." Mia laughed lightly, setting the empty tray down on the small nightstand next to the bed. "Leanna has been in here for hours with you, and I doubted that she'd think about your abundant need for caffeine."

Leanna huffed as she began stowing away the items she'd brought with her. "There were more important things to worry about than coffee, Auntie." Leanna's English heritage had her pronouncing the word auntie with a long 'ah' sound, making the word elegant and posh. She only had a mild accent, but the use of the English long *A* sound was something that had been drilled into her brain, no doubt.

"I'm amazed you got Ava to sit still so long without it," Mia commented warmly. "Now, are you almost done? Everyone will be meeting in the foyer soon."

"I'm done," Leanna smirked. "Wouldn't have taken so long if this one," she jerked her thumb at me, "wasn't such a big baby."

I scowled at the younger girl. "No one warned me about how fucking awful it would hurt to yank the hair out of my legs."

"You nearly took my head off." Leanna giggled.

True enough. The strawberry blond aesthetician gave me no warning when she ripped the hairs from my legs with the sugar mixture she used. It hurt like hell, and I'd been so stunned that I'd nearly kicked her straight in the face.

Twice.

Getting the Brazilian done had been far less painful than my lower legs. That shit burned.

"Come on now." Mia hurried me to drink my coffee as she waltzed into the closet. "Let's get you in your dress so you won't be late."

Groaning, I set down my now empty cup of coffee, looking at it longingly, wishing it would magically refill on its own.

It didn't.

With Mia's help, I managed to get the long, silken dress on without much trouble. It was soft and golden against my skin.

"There now." Mia led me to a full-length mirror inside the bathroom that was tucked in one of the small closets. "Don't you look a sight."

The woman in the mirror looked nothing like me. Well, she did, but I felt barely recognizable. Leanna had swept my long unruly locks into a side braid, twisting the ends up into the braid itself on the side. Long, thin pieces of hair framed my nearly naked face. I'd told her I wanted simple. Nothing extravagant or too bold.

Neutral and simple, those were the two things I liked the most, and she'd done a spectacular job. My face was gently dusted with a bit of bronzer and blush to highlight the contours. She'd applied a smoky, neutral look to my eyes, blending out the harsh black lines of the eyeliner to give it a softer, gentler effect that complemented my nude lipstick.

A pair of emerald crystal leaf earrings dangled from my ears to match the radiant shade of my silken dress.

It was a breathtaking piece of work. The dress. The V of the top was wide, settling past the edge of my collarbone, and dipped to just before the end of my sternum. The sleeves cuffed at my wrists, the fabric of the arms slit in just the right manner that allowed the fabric to shift open, exposing the creamy expanse of my skin.

The top was separated by a silk piece of fabric that acted as a belt, tying up in the back, allowing the skirt to pleat at the top. The long skirt had a slit straight up my thigh that allowed a glimpse of my silver Louboutin heels.

Now this is what a *queen* looked like.

Everyone was waiting for me as I strode into the foyer.

My breath caught in my throat at the sight of Matthias in a black tuxedo, his hair slicked back, stormy eyes shining. Damn, he made that thing look delicious. His gaze held mine. There was hunger there; I saw it as his eyes dipped from mine to wander over the curves of my body. The ones he'd said he loved.

Leon waited patiently next to him, his back to me as he whispered to Matthias, who looked like he wasn't paying any attention to what one of his top brigadiers was saying to him. Looks, though, were deceiving. Matthias saw everything. Heard everything. It's what had kept him alive for so long. He'd grown up having to decipher everyone's body movements and expressions to sus out their intentions.

Paranoia was a thing when you had assassins after you all your life.

"You look stunning," Matthias murmured to me when I stopped in front of him and Leon. The Italian was frowning at his *Pahkan* but nodded his head in affirmation.

"Yes, very beautiful, Ava," Leon commented.

"What's wrong?" I asked Leon, a frown of my own forming.

"Nothing." Matthias's body tensed. "We were just discussing what vehicles we will be taking. It would be more prudent if we traveled separately. That way it will be harder to target all of us at once."

"Okay," I agreed hesitantly. "You and I can take the SUV with Vas. Keep things as normal as possible."

"We aren't going together, Ava," Matthias's face hardened. In my heels, I was nearly as tall as he was. Still a few inches short, my head coming up to his eyes instead of just under his chin, but it gave me an advantage.

"I don't understand. We've been doing well. I thought that you'd want to go with your *wife*."

Matthias pinched the bridge of his nose.

"We can't go together." He sighed, exasperated. "No one knows you're my wife."

"Kind of the point in going together," I pushed. This wasn't something I was going to let go of. "There is no reason we can't make it known now."

"We just can't," he argued. His eyes darkened, and he was growing aggravated. His brows were furrowed, jaw clenched tightly. "I'm not going to argue about this. This isn't the time to be making our relationship status known. There are other more important things to take care of now, and telling people we're married is not at the top of my list."

Silence descended over the three of us as the doors to the elevator glided open to reveal a tall, leggy raven-haired woman wearing a scandalous red dress. She reminded me of Jessica Rabbit if she'd had dark hair. Big tits, small stomach, and all legs.

"Sorry I'm late, Matty," she apologized, her voice a breathy sigh. "Traffic was terrible."

Matty? Who the fuck was this chick? She didn't look like one of Vivian's girls.

"No trouble." Matthias smiled down at her. "We were just talking about transportation."

"Oh, perfect." The woman beamed up at him, showcasing pearly white teeth, before her attention turned to me. "Oh, hello, you must be Leon's date. Ava, right? I'm Serena."

She held out her hand for me to shake. I took it gently, resisting the urge to strong-arm her.

"Nice to meet you." I gave her a small, closed smile.

"Matthias told me he had a woman staying here, and I just couldn't believe it," she said, not unkindly. "How do you two know each other?"

"She's a liaison from the Kavanaughs," Matthias grunted. "Temporary house guest." Serena nodded her head, eyeing me before turning her attention back to Matthias.

"Well, shall we?" she asked, motioning toward the elevator. Matthias nodded, offering her his arm before strolling away without even a glance back at me.

"Ava..." Leon whispered my name tentatively, like he was afraid I'd spook and take off. "You ready?"

Swallowing back the despair welling up inside me, I shook my head.

"I realized I forgot something," I told him. "Leanna will kill me if I don't bring it."

Leon nodded, simply urging me to hurry since we were already late.

I made a beeline down the hall toward Matthias's room, making a sharp left into his office while Leon had his back turned.

The manila envelope was still sitting on his desk—exactly where I had left it. Picking it up, I dumped the contents out before grabbing one of his red calligraphy pens and signing my name on the dotted line.

If Matthias refused to acknowledge me as his wife at the gala, to his date...then he wouldn't have a wife. I'd thought the papers had been a mistake, and he'd just forgotten to tell Ben he didn't need them anymore.

Now I saw it for what it really was.

If he didn't tell anyone we were married, there was no shame after our divorce. No need to explain.

I wasn't going to be playing any more of his games.

Matthias and I were done.

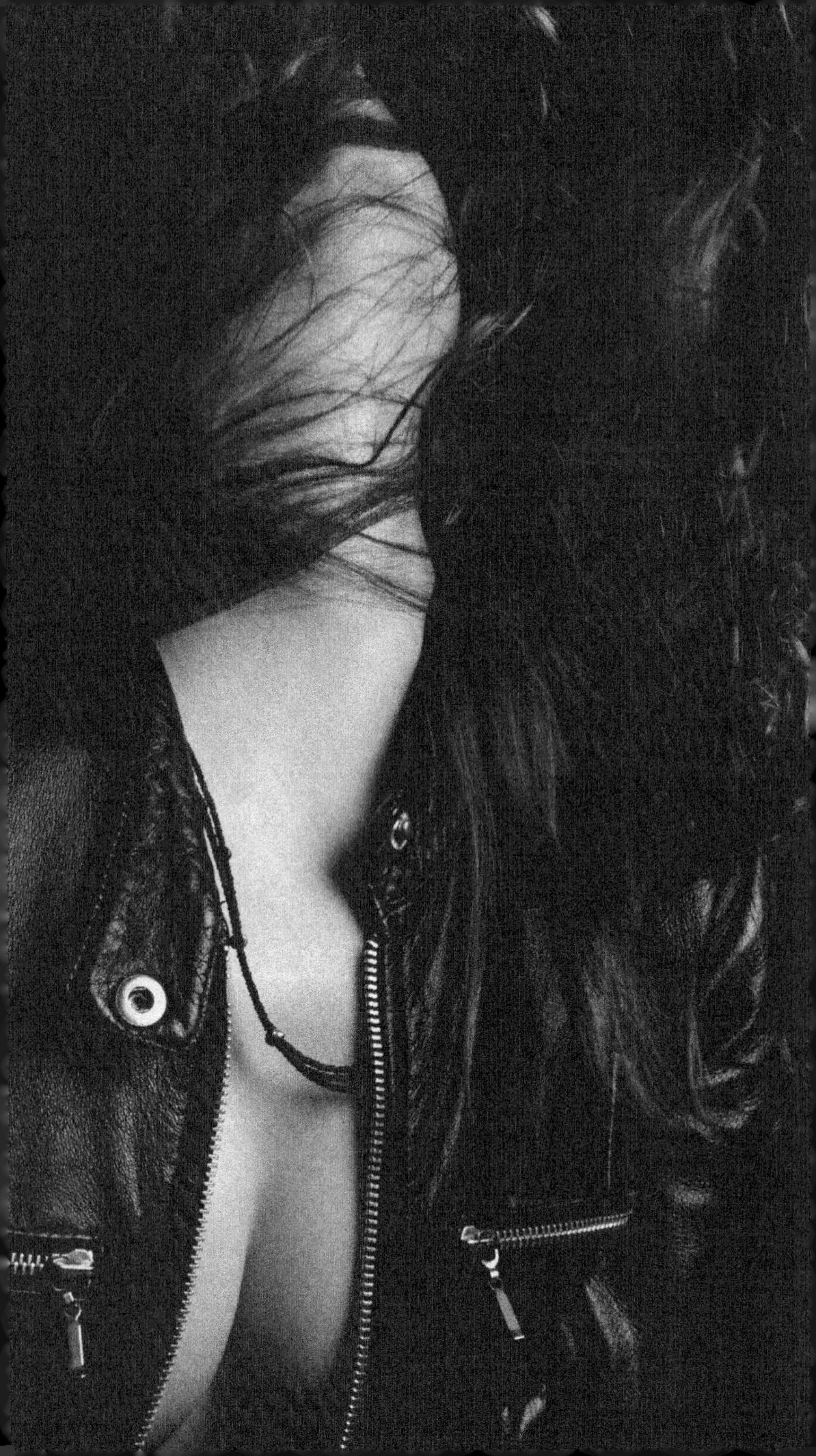

CHAPTER TWENTY-SEVEN

Ava

The drive was quiet.

Maksim drove, his hands white knuckled against the steering wheel while Leon fiddled with his phone next to me. I'd told him he could sit up front. I knew he often got car sick sitting in the back, but he'd told me it would look odd if we weren't both getting out of the back seat when we arrived at the gala.

Like a couple.

Meanwhile, the man I was actually coupled with was sitting in the back seat next to Jessica Rabbit's sister. Not that it mattered. Soon there wouldn't be anything between us, and he'd be nothing but a faraway memory fading into the distance.

Maksim pulled the car up to valet, handing the young

pimply faced boy the keys, then he came around to open the door for us. Leon slid out first, straightening his jacket before holding out his hand for me.

Gracefully, I slipped from inside the car and stared in awe at the red-carpet entrance to the building. Reporters lined the roped off edges, snapping pictures, calling out names to get the attention of their latest victims. They all wanted a story, one that would get them front-page headlines of the latest tabloid or gossip magazine.

My gaze caught Matthias smiling, his arm wrapped tightly around Serena's nipped in waist as they posed together for one of the reporters. She clung to his arm, staring up into his face with stars in her eyes. She caught me staring and shot me a wink.

Bitch.

Matthias's gaze caught mine, and his smile faltered for a second, no doubt catching the sadness lingering in my eyes, before it was gone.

"Come on," Leon whispered in my ear. "Don't pay attention to them. It's just a show."

"Some show," I muttered as we joined the line of wealthy patrons seeking entrance to the grand gala.

"Remember," Leon kept his voice low as he smiled at the crowd of onlookers, "look for anyone you recognize as having done deals with Elias. This is where the big money plays, and there's a good chance one of the people here is funding Christian."

I nodded as we handed over our tickets, entering the fancy lobby of the swanky downtown hotel. The ceiling was curved, dotted with recessed lights on either side of the large skylight windows that lined it. The room had a purple hue to it; the light casting a gentle glow off the purple painted walls and carpet woven with gold geometric octagons.

The ballroom was cast in darker tones—aged wood and walls painted in a deep mauve. A large strip of balcony overlooked the massive space from either side, and against the far wall, set in the center, was a recessed stage with a string quartet playing an elegant, haunting tune.

Waitstaff circled the room carrying silver trays of champaign and hors d'oeuvres of varying tastes. Leon grabbed two glasses of the champagne; Armand de Brignac, a brut rosé. The seductive notes of soft spice, red currants, and sweet almonds swept across my tongue, causing my palate to come alive.

Everything was too grand and over the top. Almost fake. Like a show or a play. I guessed that was what everyone was kind of doing, putting on a play. I let my eyes linger on Matthias as he flashed a smile to an elderly couple with Serena hanging on his arm; he knew exactly how to play to the audience.

The pain in my chest grew, my heart growing cold and bitter as I continued to watch the two of them flit around the room. That was never going to be us. Besides the Clover, he'd never once showed an interest in me while we were in public. Not before he called me a traitor and certainly not after.

He'd used me, and now he was through with me.

If we didn't need this mission to go well, I would have already walked out and left. If it had just been about Matthias, I wouldn't have looked back, but it wasn't. It was about Libby and Kenzi. It was about my mother, because whoever this mystery benefactor was, he had something to do with her kidnapping.

"Ye know, if you watch them any harder, they might spontaneously combust," Seamus chuckled on my right. I'd been so caught up in my abject misery, I hadn't heard him approach.

"Maybe that's my plan." I shrugged a shoulder. "Where

have you been? Liam said you'd be out of range for a few days."

"Had a few things to clean up," Seamus muttered. "Nothing we couldn't handle."

"This have to do with Jimmy's knife attack?"

"Something like that." He emptied his glass of champagne. "Fuck, this is why Kier and I opened a nightclub. This place is gawdier than Narcissus's ass."

I wasn't sure what I found funnier. The fact that he sounded like a petulant child or that he'd properly referenced a mythological person's ass. Whichever it was, I couldn't help but laugh at the absurdity of his statement. A few heads turned my way, brows crunched in distaste, but I paid them no mind.

"It wasn't that funny," Seamus scolded, but he was smiling too.

"After the day I've had, it sure was."

"Well, let's see if we can make it better." Liam came to stand to one side of me, holding out a champagne glass. I took it with thanks. "Come with me."

Taking Liam's offered arm, he led me around the room, my eyes sweeping over a sea of faces, most of whom I didn't recognize. We didn't stop to talk to anyone; he just kept moving until we circled back to where we had started.

"We'll make another round in a moment and start up some easy conversation," he told me.

"And what are you going to introduce me as?" I asked curiously, a bitter note seeping through, unintended. It wasn't his fault that Matthias didn't want anyone to know I was his wife, but now I wondered if Liam would want to introduce me as his daughter.

Maybe something was wrong with me.

"My daughter, of course." The lines on his forehead

creased as he looked down at me, puzzled. "What else would I introduce you as?"

"Oh, I don't know. I wasn't sure if you wanted people to know..." I let the statement hang, trying to act aloof, like I didn't care if he claimed me or not.

"Of course, I want people to know, Avaleigh."

I cringed at the use of my full name. Liam pursed his lips, turning me to face him, my hands clutched tightly in his.

"Do you know why your mother named you Avaleigh?"

I shook my head, my gaze on the floor as redness crawled up my neck in embarrassment for letting the simple use of my name affect me so much.

"I know your name has been used to belittle you over the years," he explained, his finger coming up beneath my chin, forcing my head up. The green of his eyes didn't show the pity I'd been expecting, merely fatherly concern. "But I want you to understand why I choose to use it. I can't believe your mother never told you."

"My mother didn't tell me anything about her past," I huffed. "My whole life was a lie that she'd created, and even though I know it was to protect me, I feel that if she'd confided in me, I would have been better prepared."

"You were just a child," Liam said softly. "No parent wants to lay such a heavy burden on their child so young."

I shrugged a shoulder. "No child wants to lose a parent so early, but that's the way of the world sometimes."

Liam nodded thoughtfully.

"Well, let me give you a little something she couldn't," he told me with a warm smile. "Your name is made up of two different names of the people we loved the most. Your great-grandmothers. Ava was your mother's grandmother, and Leigha was mine. The two of them were inseparable growing up in Ireland, and even when they were married, they were still joined at the hip.

"Their families traveled to America together to start anew," Liam continued. "A fresh start. Your mother and I were practically raised by them."

"Really?" Nan seemed so maternal and caring. She didn't seem like the type of mother who would leave her children for someone else to raise.

"Don't get me wrong." He sighed. "Our parents loved us and were by no means neglectful. But they were building a shipping empire alongside our grandfathers. It often kept them out of town or out late at night. They kept us out of the public eye. Boston at that time was a no-man's-land. Gangs were fighting for territory, and drug trafficking was slowly spreading across the east coast. Everyone wanted a piece of it.

"It nearly killed your mother when they died." Liam spoke softly. "The two of them were more like mother and daughter. After their funeral, we made a promise to each other that our first daughter would bear their names. The same way our first sons would bear our late great-grandfathers' names."

Seamus and Kiernan.

"But you named your daughter Saoirse," I pointed out.

Liam chuckled. "It didn't seem right naming her Avaleigh," he admitted. "Marianne never had that connection with them. They died a few years before we met her."

Something about that made me warm inside.

"I'm sorry," I whispered.

"It's all right, lass." He smiled bleakly. "I wished you could have met them."

"Me too."

"Now, enough of this." He straightened himself and drew

me to his side. "Let's go manipulate the fuck out of these rich, snobby bastards."

"Language, old man." I laughed at him, and he snorted in amusement.

"You are definitely my daughter."

"Did you recognize anyone?" Liam asked on our second round. More people had begun to filter in throughout the night, and the quiet conversations from before had picked up.

"A few of them." I confirmed. Subtly, I motioned with my champagne glass toward a portly man who laughed egregiously at something one of his men had said. I'd seen him drinking his weight in whiskey throughout the beginning of the night, and now he was red faced, his toupee slightly shifted. The young girl on his arm looked more alarmed by the second as one of his hands roamed her backside.

"His name is Acastus Chloros," I sneered. "He was one of Elias's biggest purchasers of underage girls."

Liam growled. "Like the one on his arm?"

I snorted derisively. "I doubt she's underage if he brought her here, but she probably was when he bought her."

Liam cursed under his breath.

"But he's not connected or wealthy enough to pull any strings." I rubbed at my eyes tiredly with one hand.

For the next hour, I pointed out the people I recognized one by one, detailing their sins to my father. None of them could pull off a cash grab like the one we'd intercepted, but that didn't mean they didn't have their own personal sins to atone for. Liam was determined to bring down the sex trade in Seattle.

We'd just passed a small craps table that had been set up for entertainment when a delicate laugh sounded in my ears.

My entire body tensed at the familiar lilting sound, my feet frozen to the wooden floor as I searched for its origin.

I found it.

The laugh belonged to a woman in an elegant pink chiffon dress. Her back was turned, but there was no mistaking the wild curls of ginger hair that hung loosely down her back. The woman laughed again. Gentle and musical.

"Ava," Liam whispered urgently, trying to grab my attention, but it was too late.

"Mom?" I called, loud enough the woman would hear me, but not enough to grab the attention of everyone surrounding her.

The redheaded woman turned; her brows creased. Any hope I'd had in my chest deflated the minute I saw the woman's face.

She wasn't my mother.

Of course she wasn't, I chided myself. *Mother is dead.*

She looked exactly like her though. The same lithe frame and curly hair. The same delicate laugh that I'd remember anywhere. I hadn't called out my mother's name, but the woman had still turned when I called out *Mom*. Why?

When her gaze fell on me, her eyebrows shot up, eyes widening, mouth slightly parted as she took me in.

"Katherine?" My mother's name was a choked sob on her lips. The man next to her jerked around at her exclamation. I recognized them. "Oh my god."

This was my mother's mother.

Sheila McDonough, and next to her stood the man with the silver cross cane.

CHAPTER TWENTY-EIGHT

Ava

He was a tall, imposing man with slightly curved shoulders. The grip on his cane was tight, his knuckles turning white, face paling when he saw me.

This man knew who I was.

"Sheila." Liam stepped between the two of us as she came barreling at me, tears spilling down her cheeks. She would have easily bowled me over. I couldn't move, my body frozen in surprise and fear. "This isn't Katherine."

I sent the woman to take care of your obsession years ago...

The man with the silver cross cane.

This was the man who'd sent someone to kill my mother?

Her own father?

That didn't make any sense.

"You look so much like her." Katherine's soft-spoken voice broke through my haze. I looked up into soft green eyes that were wet and shining with unshed tears. "So much like Katherine."

I swallowed hard, a sob burning in my chest, but I was acutely aware of the man lingering just behind her. Watching our every move. Listening to our every word.

"I'm Avaleigh." My voice trembled slightly, lower lip wobbling. I hadn't realized how hopeful I'd been when I'd heard her laugh. *Her* laugh. "I'm her daughter."

The woman, Sheila, smiled warmly as she brought a hand up to my cheek, her thumb wiping the lone tear that escaped from my eye. "She used to always say if she had a girl, she'd name her Avaleigh after her great-grandmother and Liam's."

I sniffed. "He told me."

Her gaze narrowed, shifting to Liam.

"You couldn't have warned us?" she hissed at my father. "How long has she been with you? Why didn't you call us? We would've come down sooner. How did you find her?"

"Sheila." The man behind her reprimanded. The woman flinched slightly, barely a micro expression. I looked at my father to see if he'd seen it, but his relaxed demeanor told me he hadn't. "Now is not the time."

"Oh." Sheila deflated mildly. "Of…of course not, dear."

"Hello, Avaleigh," the man introduced himself. "I'm Seamus McDonough. Your grandfather."

"It's nice to meet you." I tried my best to smile brightly, reaching out and shaking his offered hand. My teeth clenched at the strong grip he had on my hand, pressing my fingers together painfully.

"Same to you." He let go and put his arm around Sheila. "Liam, you have my number. We'll be in town another few days. Reach out, and we'll have lunch."

Liam nodded.

"Of course, Seamus," he confirmed. "I didn't even realize you'd be in town. I would have arranged something sooner."

"Some of my shipments ran into some trouble," Seamus McDonough sneered.

"You've never had problems at the shipping ports before," Liam pointed out, befuddled. "Let me know if there is anything I can do to help. The Kavanaughs are always here for the McDonough clan."

Seamus snorted. "It's nothing we can't get sorted out ourselves, boy." He dismissed my father with a short flutter of his hand. "Just a few rats taking a part of the cheese that doesn't belong to them."

"The offer still stands."

Seamus's lips thinned. "Understood. Let's go, Sheila."

Sheila bit her lower lip; conflict splashed across her face. "But—"

"Now, Sheila," Seamus barked. Sheila let out a heavy sigh before casting me a bleak smile and following her husband.

"Something isn't right about him," I told Liam when they'd moved out of earshot. "Did you see the way she reacted to him? She was afraid."

"Seamus can be a hard man, but he's never laid a hand on his wife," Liam assured me.

"I think you're wrong," I protested. "She acted like he was going to hit her at any moment. Trust me, I know the signs."

"You can't keep going around making these accusations, Avaleigh." Liam's voice darkened, an edge seeping into his tone. The same one he'd had when I'd mentioned Marianne.

"And you can't keep assuming that everything I put forward is bullshit because you think you know someone better, *Father*," I growled at him. "I'm not accusing anyone of anything. I'm stating an observation based on years of experience. Sometimes a fresh set of eyes can provide clearer details that someone else might have missed."

"You've done nothing but state your *opinion* since I rescued you," he snarled in my face, his body shaking, hands clenched at his sides. "Do you think you can throw your opinion around like that when you don't know anything about our world? Or the people? Those are your grandparents. That is your grandfather you are accusing of domestic violence. A man I've known nearly my entire life, who helped raise me when my own father died, who has always had my back. And you expect me to, what? Just drop everything because you think you see something that might or might not be there?"

"No," I hissed, the adrenaline hitting me before I had a chance to push it back. "I want you to listen and observe. I want you to take a step back and try to see it from my perspective. I didn't ask you to go around accusing him. I didn't ask you to go beat the shit out of him. I asked you to consider my side.

"I thought I could share what I've seen, what I've learned, but you are just like everyone else." There was no stopping me now. I was on a roll. "You don't want to listen to what I have to say unless it's convenient for you. Unless it fits your narrative. You don't want to believe that my mother was kidnapped because then you have to question everything you've known about her. It's easier to write her off as the bad guy than believe you've let a snake into your bed.

"You don't want to hear about Seamus because then you'd have to reevaluate how you were raised, and I get that it's hard, but it was hard for me to come to you. And if this is how it's going to be, if this is what it's going to be like being your daughter, constantly questioned and never believed—then I don't want to be your daughter."

Turning away from him, I took a moment to gather myself, taking a few slow, deep breaths.

"By the way," I turned back to face him, "my *grandfather* is one of the men who did business with Elias. Think on that for a bit."

THE NIGHT WAS A COMPLETE WASH.

I'd managed to successfully avoid both Liam and Matthias for the rest of the gala. I doubted either one of them noticed my absence, and if they had, they'd chosen not to pursue me. No one here could have funded such a large coup, or if they could, they didn't have the proper resources or contacts to pull it off.

A man on stage was animatedly gesturing around him, thanking any number of patrons who donated to the silent auction charity the gala was being held for. A whole bunch of hot air, if you ask me. I was still running the numbers through my head, the ones on the nearly hidden page in Libby's journal.

They'd been bothering me all night.

It was like my brain had been processing everything, but my mind wasn't seeing it clearly.

"You need to fix this, Matthias," Leon's voiced hissed. I'd been standing behind a large pillar near one of the hallways that led toward the kitchens. It was quiet and out of the way and a place the snobby high-class posh assholes wouldn't approach me. Too near the working-class citizens.

"There's nothing to fix," Matthias growled. "It's over after tonight. Once the gala is done, we're through. I only needed her for the information. Nothing else."

"Her family is powerful." Leon's tone was bitter. "You

shouldn't have gotten her involved with all of this. You should have just left well enough alone, but we all know how you like to punch the fucking bear, *brat*."

"Careful with your tone, *brat*." Matthias sneered.

Jesus, they were talking about me.

"All I'm saying is that if you don't fix this, she's going to go running back to them."

"Good," Matthias chuckled darkly. "Let her."

My heart shattered in my chest, my mind spinning. It really was over; he admitted to it. Admitted he'd just been using me. Needing a spot of fresh air to sort through the emotional kettlebell that had just been lugged at me, I headed toward the employee door at the back.

It hurt more than I thought it would, his confession to Leon, but there was no denying that I'd fallen for him. I definitely didn't regret signing those papers. Now all I had to do was find a way to move forward without him. Without anyone, if that's what it took.

I still wasn't sure where Liam and I stood.

Not after my big blowup. It was necessary though. Probably could've been slightly more tactful about it, but there was no hopping in that time machine. He needed to understand how I felt and that I wouldn't tolerate being treated like a commodity. That my voice was just as important as Seamus's or Kiernan's. That what I said had merit.

Sometimes you live in a haze for so long that you forget it's there. He needed someone to push him and show him the demons lurking among the shadows.

"What are you doing out here?"

Speak of the devil.

"Getting some air," I told him like it was the most obvious thing in the world. "Why else would I be out here?"

"I was worried when I couldn't find you," Liam scolded angrily. "I thought maybe something happened to you."

"Why do you care?" I snapped, folding my arms against my chest as I stared him down. My heels, and the five or six glasses of champagne I'd had, making me bold.

"You're my daughter," he told me, confusion etched in the lines on his face. "Why wouldn't I care?"

"You didn't seem to care about what I had to say," I bit out. Liam stared at me, his brow furrowed, sadness lining his aging eyes. He felt bad. Seeing the remorse so openly displayed, I softened my voice. "I get it. You barely know me. I barely know you, but I need you to trust me or at least listen to what I have to say without automatically dismissing my observations and opinions. I'm done being everyone's pawn. An instrument to be played with and then put away again when it's no longer useful. That's all I've ever been. No one has ever listened. No one has ever cared what I had to say.

"Elias was the man I thought to be my father for the last twelve years, and even though finding out that wasn't the case lifted the heavy weight from inside me, it doesn't mean that the damage he caused isn't still there. Do you understand?"

Liam swallowed hard, a stray tear escaping as he clenched his eyes tightly closed and took a shaky breath.

"I'm sorry, Avaleigh," he apologized, his voice filled with sorrow and pain. "You were right. I wasn't listening, and for that I'm sorry. I shouldn't have gotten upset; I should have listened. You have this uncanny ability to see connections where no one else does, and as much as I don't want to believe Seamus McDonough has anything to do with this, I think you might be right. Please, forgive me. I promise, as your father, to do better in the future."

With a small sob, I launched myself into his arms. He

grunted in surprise when my body hit his but immediately wrapped me in his warm embrace.

"It's okay." My father petted my head, running his calloused palm in a soothing manner. "Everything is going to be okay."

Something inside me warmed as he whispered reassurances in my ear. Elias had never comforted me before. He'd never offered any type of assurance. No one had, not even my sisters. They had been six when the abuse started. They didn't understand what was going on. I'd been left to learn how to self-soothe, but now, in my father's embrace, I felt nothing but peace for the first time in years.

"Everything's going to be okay, lass," he whispered again. "I promise."

Why did I think his words had a deeper meaning to them that I didn't understand?

CHAPTER TWENTY-NINE

Ava

Once the Niagara Falls of tears had ceased and I'd cleaned up in the ladies' room, Liam escorted me back into the ballroom, where Seamus, my brother, waited. He gave me a small wink and a wide smile.

"I heard they're putting up this super rare book for the auction." Seamus grinned at me excitedly. "It's one of J. R. R. Tolkien's first editions, leather bound."

That caught my attention. I'd told him of my love for Tolkien's books. My mother and I used to read them out loud to one another at night before bed.

"Oh, I love Tolkien." I glanced up at the stage, waiting for them to announce the next item.

"Katherine did too," Liam told me. "She always had a copy of The Hobbit in her purse wherever we went. Used to drive me crazy when she'd pull it out of nowhere. Even did it on one of our movie dates."

"Did you take her to see an action movie?" I questioned curiously.

Liam grumbling under his breath told me exactly what I needed to know. My mother hated action movies of all kinds. Even ones with romance in them.

"Serves you right then."

"Who says no to Bruce Willis?"

"I do." Liam and Seamus gasped, feigning offense, but I just shrugged a shoulder. "Just saying."

"Blasphemy," Seamus muttered, disappointed. "You'll have to be disowned."

I giggled, covering my hand with my mouth so the sound wouldn't travel far.

"Now, ladies and gentlemen, for our next item, we have a rare treat for you." The auctioneer beamed down at the crowd. "A rare leather bound first edition of J. R. R. Tolkien's *The Hobbit*, first printed in 1937, which includes the original artwork by the author himself."

Now the item definitely had my attention. There were only six of those left in circulation in good enough condition to sell, and one of them had belonged to Libby. The book was the only thing I'd been able to take with me when Elias came for me. One night, while I'd been crying myself to sleep, Libby had crawled into my bed and told me to read her my favorite story. So I introduced her to the world of Bilbo and the Ring of Power.

Just like I had the first time my mother read it to me, Libby fell in love, and I gifted her the books several years later for her sixteenth birthday.

"This book was generously donated by Kendra Ward, and all proceeds will go to the Society Against Sex Trafficking."

The auction announced excitedly. Jesus, if he only knew that her husband and son practically funded the sex ring in Washington, he probably wouldn't be as enthused. "The bidding will start at twelve thousand dollars."

"Fucking bitch," I snarled under my breath. "That belonged to my mother."

"How did Kendra Ward get it?" Seamus wondered.

"I gave it to Libby for her birthday," I told him. "We used to put secret messages in the pages when Elias kept us apart. We used the book as—that's it!"

"Ava?" Liam looked over at me. "What's wrong?"

"We need that book."

Liam frowned. "I know it belonged to Katherine, but I can't be spending that much money on a book for sentimental reasons, lass. I'm sorry."

"No, you don't understand." I took a deep breath to steady myself. "I read my sister's journal when I found it, and she stated that after the raid on Elias's house, she managed to take and hide two of his little black books. The ones that hold all his blackmail information and accounts. Anyone and everyone on his payroll is in those books. Including his benefactor."

"What does this have to do with the book?" Seamus questioned.

"One of the pages in her journal had a bunch of numbers I've been trying to decipher, and the first set of numbers was one, three, one, eight, nine, and two," I told them. "January third, eighteen ninety-two. The year Tolkien was born. Under that was nineteen thirty-seven, the year *The Hobbit* was first published."

"Still not following, lass," Liam admitted. "Why the book?"

"We used to write coded messages to one another using

the book as the decryption key." Jesus, I can't believe I didn't put this together sooner. "Beneath those numbers are a string of numbers that correspond to the page number, paragraph, and word in *The Hobbit*."

Seamus shrugged. "So we go pick up a cheaper copy at Barnes and Noble."

"It doesn't work that way," I stressed. "The page numbers won't be the same and the message won't be right."

"You think the coded message is you sister telling you where the books are?" Liam asked dubiously.

"I know it is."

"All right then, lass." He smiled. "Let's go buy an enormously expensive book."

TEN MINUTES LATER, I stood near the side of the stage with the book in my hand. It was heavy and comforting to hold it once again.

Don't worry, Libby. I'll finish what you started.

"Someone want to explain to me why you broke our low profile to bid on a damn fucking book?" Matthias roared, stalking up to us, his footsteps heavy against the floor. "We were supposed to be keeping a low profile, not flaunting our wealth."

"I wouldn't have bid on it if it wasn't necessary, Dashkov," my father assured him calmly. "It wasn't planned, but Ava found something, and we require the book to decode it."

"And you didn't bother to inform us about it so we could be better prepared?"

"Last time I checked, I don't answer to you."

"No, but we are supposed to be working together."

"Didn't look like you were working all that hard when you

had Serena Belsky's tongue shoved down your throat," Seamus muttered angrily before his eyes went wide, a hand clamping against his mouth.

"It's not what it looked like," Matthias growled, his eyes turning to me, but I kept my face blank. At least I hoped I did.

"You could have at least waited until the divorce papers were filed before you went sticking your tongue where it doesn't belong." I shrugged my shoulders. "I'd say you should've been a bit more discreet, but no one knows we're married, so..."

"Ava." Matthias's voice was soft, nearly pleading.

"Don't worry. You can suck on her tongue all you want," I told him. "I signed the papers Ben left. So don't worry about me. Now, if you'll—"

A heavy body hit mine, knocking me to the ground as glass shattered and screams tore through the room.

"Everyone, get down!"

No. Not again. Please, not again.

"Ava!" Someone screamed my name. "Ava!"

My heart was beating so fast I thought it might burst straight through my ribcage. An icy chill ran through my veins, blood thumping through my body like ice. I stared at the face next to mine; his eyes were closed, the foggy storm hidden from my view. His face was pale, breathing shallow.

Why was he so pale?

"Matthias?" I croaked. "Matthias?"

I lifted my hand to nudge his shoulder, but he didn't react.

"Matthias?" I tried again. A cold sweat broke out all over my body, my vision blurring as tears clouded my eyes when I looked down at the wetness covering one side of my body and his. "Somebody call 9-1-1."

Hands grabbed me underneath my arms, hauling me up.

My back hit a warm chest, of smell of citrus and cloves overwhelming my senses, calming me. My father.

"Matt." Vas came running from the other side of the stage, a large red bag slung over his shoulder. He crouched next to his leader, his friend, his brother. I'd never seen him so frantic before, but I could tell that despite his panic, he was still in control. "Matthias, can you hear me?"

Nothing.

A sob escaped my throat.

He couldn't die.

Please.

Something caught my eye; the rustling of the curtains. A head peeked out from behind them, blond hair falling in soft waves down one shoulder, crystalline blue eyes dancing with mirth as she stared at the carnage before her. Then she was suddenly gone, as if it had all just been a figment of my imagination.

Kenzi?

No, it couldn't be. I would have spotted her when Liam and I worked the crowd. But there was no mistaking those eyes, that fair skin.

It had to have been Kenzi.

But why?

Sirens filled the air, drawing my attention back to the matter at hand.

Matthias.

Another sob racked my trembling body as I watched the paramedics load him on the gurney.

"Matthias," I sobbed, reaching out to touch him as they passed, but my father held me back.

"Shh," he cooed in my ear, holding me tighter to him. "Let them do their job."

"I want to go with him," I pleaded, my sobs turning into cries of hysteria. "Please, I have to..."

"They aren't going to let you go, little one," he whispered. "He needs immediate attention."

"But..."

"Shh," he cooed again before the gentle baritone of his voice began to vibrate through me.

"Hó bha ín, Hó bha ín.
Hó bha ín, mo ghrá.
Hó bha ín, mo leana,
Agus codail, go lá."

IT WAS HIM. He'd been the one singing to me after I'd been shot. The deep, soothing voice that had kept me pushing forward while I was stuck in my fever dreams.

My father held me tight against him while I sobbed. The blood-covered book was clutched tight to my chest as I watched the paramedics leave with the pieces of my shattered heart in their hands.

Somewhere a phone rang, a furious voice hurled insults, then the phone was shoved in my face.

"It's for you," Vas snarled, but he wasn't directing it at me.

I hiccupped, staring at the small device in his hand for a moment before taking it.

Lifting it to my ear, I whispered, "Hello?"

"So close, big sister," Kenzi's voice filtered through the line, bitter and brimming with resentment. "I wasn't aiming for him, but I'll take what I can get."

"Kenzi, what are you doing?"

"Taking revenge," she hissed. "You all killed her, and now I'll kill you, one by one."

"Whatever Christian told you isn't true, Kenzi," I pleaded with her, begging her to listen to me. "He's the one—"

"Don't lie to me, Avaleigh." Her voice was cold, a bone-deep chill.

"Please, you have to listen—"

"I wonder what other surprises lie in store?" she cackled. "I'd get a move on if I were you. Unless you want to miss the main event. I heard it's quite explosive, and I like to make sure my targets are completely roasted."

The line went dead.

"Matthias!" I took off at a run, slipping from my Louboutin heels as I clutched the book in one hand and the skirt of my dress in the other. Dodging through the crowd, I could hear everyone behind me calling my name, but I wasn't stopping. She'd been aiming for me. The bullet had been meant for me. The ambulance would have been transporting me.

"Wait!" I called, but it was too late. The ambulance had already pulled away from the curb and was merging into traffic. The lights whirred and the siren sounded once before—

A heavy explosion filled the air, the blast wave knocking me off my feet. I hit the ground hard, my head bouncing off the concrete. The world around me was muted, like the sounds were all underwater. Hands grabbed at me, but I didn't move.

I couldn't. I was frozen, unaware of anything but the sight of the burning wreckage before me where the pieces of my heart had just died.

NOTE FROM JO

Are you all sharpening your knives and getting your pitchforks ready? Should I be hunkering down in a shelter somewhere in case you come for me.

I feel like you must be.

Thank you to all my amazing alpha readers who stuck with me through the slow process of writing this book. I honestly never thought I'd get it done in time.

To my beautiful kickass beta readers. I promised to never give you chapter sections to read again and that's exactly what I did. Your input into this book was amazing and invaluable.

A huge thank you to Beth at VB Proofreads for being so amazing and lenient. I appreciate you so much.

Kay, thank you so much for always giving me encouragement and being willing to talk things out.

Jenna L. My hype girl, thank you for loving this book so much and always keeping me on track.

And a huge thank you to Zoe Blake, who will probably never see this, for always having an open line to answer my never ending questions and for keeping me inspired to write

NOTE FROM JO

this series. I wouldn't have even started if it weren't for you and a sexy Russian named Gregor.

And thank you to everyone who has read my book and shown their love for Matthias and Ava's story. You will never know how much it means to me to see my writing out there and loved by you all.

Till the next book.

Stay Savvy,
　Jo McCall

ALSO BY JO MCCALL

SHATTERED WORLD

Shattered Pieces

Shattered Remnants

Shattered Empire - Coming soon

IRISH RULES SERIES

Irish Whiskey Rules

Irish Chaos Rules - Coming Soon

Irish Street Rules - Coming Soon

CAGED HEARTS SERIES

Savage Thievery - September 2022

Savage Ultimatum - Coming Soon

NAUGHTY NANNY TEMPTATIONS

(Part of a Shared World Series)

The Nanny's Dark Desires - May 2022

TWISTED FAIRY-TALE

(Part of a Shared World Series)

Claimed by Them - February 2023

STALK ME

@jomccallauthor

BookBub
Amazon Profile
Goodreads
Wicked Romance Book Box

Printed in Great Britain
by Amazon